"Tom—" As if sensing his resolution, Merritt moved slightly, blocking his way to the door. She glided forward, wrapping her arms loosely around his shoulders. His hand laced through the thickness of her hair against her neck. He had meant to hold her back; he ended up holding her close.

"I don't know if my wanting you is right or wrong," she whispered softly. "Tonight I don't care. I just need to be held. Please don't deny me that. I've had so much taken from me, Tom, so much. Don't let me lose this, too." To her horror a lone tear began to slide down her cheek.

The show of emotion affected him as no seduction could ever have. He drew her closer, wanting nothing more than to protect and cherish her as she deserved to be, if only for that one moment....

To Grandma Myrna
and Pap

For showing me how meaningful
the commitment between
two people can be, and that love endures,
not just day to day, but forever.

———————◆———————

CATHY GILLEN THACKER
is also the author
of this title in
Love Affair

TOUCH OF FIRE

Promise Me Today

CATHY GILLEN THACKER

A Love Affair from

HARLEQUIN

London · Toronto · New York · Sydney

First published in Great Britain in 1985 by
Harlequin, 15–16 Brook's Mews, London W1A 1DR

© Cathy Gillen Thacker 1984

ISBN 0 373 16075 5

18-0885

Printed and bound in Great Britain by
Richard Clay (The Chaucer Press) Ltd,
Bungay, Suffolk

Chapter One

Twenty-seven-year-old Merritt Reed surveyed her sixth-grade class over the heaping bowl of hot buttered popcorn on her desk. "Whose turn was it to bring the record album?"

"Mine!" Brian Anderson strode to the front of the class, the album tucked discreetly into the crook of his football-jerseyed arm.

"It is educational, isn't it?" Merritt cautioned, recalling the new school board's last dictum on music permissible for school use. Beside her, drafted class helper Kristin Stratton was pouring Hawaiian Punch into paper cups.

"Oh, yeah," Brian promised broadly above the conspiratorial titter of his classmates. "It's real educational, Ms. Reed. I made doubly sure of that."

Merritt rolled her eyes heavenward as she continued ladling out popcorn. Dark coffee-colored hair fell casually to her shoulders, emphasizing the faintly classic lines of her face, playing up the healthy glow of lustrous cared-for skin. "I can hardly wait to hear it," she murmured under her breath. Ten to one, their "background music" had little to do with improving their collective intellect. Still, it would be interesting to see how far their class clown thought he could go and still maintain a vested interest in the rules. "How is hearing this record going to improve our minds, Brian?" she questioned routinely, fixing him with a challenging stare. "What are we going to learn from it?"

The class continued to giggle surreptitiously as Brian fiddled with the stereo. "Uh, well, you might say it's kind of a *historical* song, Ms. Reed. In fact, the whole album's historical."

"Maybe I'd better shut the door," Merritt decided at the last minute. Heaven knew they didn't need to disturb any of the other students on the Cincinnati, Ohio, elementary school's second floor. Her group of gifted students had been labeled prime troublemakers more than once. A title, Merritt had to admit, they'd done their best to earn.

She was just reaching for the doorknob when the needle hit the groove. The thundering beat of rock music followed. "See?" Brian crowed triumphantly. "It's a golden oldie."

"And so much more," Merritt agreed as the throbbing bass rattled through her teeth. No doubt she'd end up explaining this little indiscretion to the superintendent of schools, too.

The sound of a male throat clearing directed Merritt's gaze upward, across the darkened concrete hallway. Lounging insouciantly against a row of gunmetal-gray lockers was a man who looked just three or four years older than herself. Merritt took in wavy light brown hair, full-bodied, clean, and layered to medium length. His eyes were green, framed by sand-colored lashes and equally light brows. The cheekbones were high, the jaw square and clean shaven, face etched with life. He was perhaps two or three inches taller than she, dressed casually in heather-brown tweed blazer, bone-colored oxford cloth shirt, and well-fitting brown corduroy slacks. He had the build of an athlete, the taut trim lines of a runner. Noticing Merritt's intense, lightning swift scrutiny, the visitor grinned. He stepped nearer, his lips parting slightly. The provocative scent of his after-shave mingling with the distinct scent of his skin sent another thrill coursing down Merritt's spine.

"Ms. Reed?" The timbre of his voice was low, inherently seductive.

"Yes," Merritt began, trying without success to still the rapid pounding of her heart against her ribs. And then the lyrics of the promised record overtook the entire second floor. Merritt grimaced, feeling acutely responsible as "We don't need no education..." barreled deafeningly through the hall.

"If that doesn't bring the PTA down on me from a national level, I don't know what will," Merritt muttered, chagrined. Swiftly she pivoted, and signaled Brian to turn down the volume. He did at once, but not before reaction swept the floor. Disgruntled adults poked their heads out of every door. Blushing slightly, Merritt indicated she had the situation well under control. Inside her classroom, the pulsating beat of hard rock continued to roar. The stranger grinned. "One second." Merritt ducked back into the class and decisively flicked the volume knob down low. "Historical, hmm?" she prodded Brian as the music adjusted to an acceptable purr.

"You gotta admit it's ancient," he parried equably. "I was just a kid when that was copyrighted!"

"We'll discuss this later." Merritt frowned, not nearly as upset with her sixth-graders as she wanted them to initially think. She turned to the frolicking class. "Keep it down, comrades," she advised. Moving back into the hall, she shut the door behind her, leaning slightly against the portal for strength. Now it was the visitor's turn to evaluate. Personally and physically Merritt had the distinct sensation she passed muster. Her ability to control her students was another matter indeed.

"It takes courage to turn your back on that, even for an instant," he observed, not bothering to mask the slight lilt of above-it-all amusement coloring his low tone.

Merritt bristled at the slight look of censure in his provoking gaze, but she managed to keep her voice calm. "When it comes to sixth-graders, believe me, I have a limitless supply. And they run equally with the energy, I'm afraid. As for their party today, they've earned it. And contrary to the views of most of the other teachers on this floor, I think it's healthy for them to let off a little steam every now and then. It helps prevent the rush of 'fixed' lockers, cherry-bombed toilets, and 'accidentally' set off fire alarms."

"To whose inconvenience?" the man murmured, still holding her defiant blue gaze with his own.

Merritt forced a smile, trying to remain cool despite his baiting manner. No doubt this was one of the same personas non gratas who were responsible for the books currently being yanked off their reading lists, the banned music. He probably didn't approve of the most rudimentary sex education, either. Never mind the questions her students routinely and curiously asked! "What can I do for you, Mr.—?" Her tone was brittle with disdain.

"Hennessey. Tom Hennessey." The man's handshake was warmer, more decisive than Merritt expected. "I'm Johnny Porter's uncle. My sister Ellen had a conference scheduled with you this afternoon. She was called out of town on business unexpectedly. I said I'd stand in for her. She'll try and reschedule later."

Merritt was unable to hide her dismay. "Any idea when?" It was the second appointment Johnny's mother had broken. Efforts to reach her on the phone had been just as futile. Ellen Porter was either out of town, in conference, or out on a customer-related call. "Johnny and I both need her fullest cooperation in this matter if he is to survive the school year with anything resembling decent grades."

At the implied criticism of his sister, the man's sinewy frame tautened. Hands moving to loosely circle lean hips, he glanced away impatiently, then back to Merritt. To her undermining, the throbbing beat of pulsating rock could be clearly heard through the closed classroom door. "No," he said tightly. "I don't know when Ellen will be able to work in a visit to the school. But as I said, it will be soon. And as I also indicated, I'm here to act in her stead."

"That's all well and good, Mr. Hennessey. But we're going to need more than that from Mrs. Porter. Johnny is in jeopardy of being dropped from the gifted program altogether, the decision to be made in a matter of another six weeks if his grades do not in fact come up. You'll have to forgive my bluntness, but he doesn't have time to wait for Mrs. Porter's professional and personal convenience. And frankly," Merritt added a bit more peevishly than was due because of his ever deepening glare, "neither do I."

"I can see how hard you're all working," Tom Hennessey drawled sarcastically. As he spoke a stray piece of popcorn rolled beneath the door and halted between their feet. His eyebrows rose another fraction. "Particularly since no one in that 'gifted' group needs any education if I'm to go by the blaring lyrics of their current 'theme' song."

Merritt had asked for that one by good-naturedly allowing Brian's record to continue to play. Raking a hand restively through the silken blunt-cut hair brushing her shoulders, she fought for calm and hazarded a glance toward the classroom behind her. Slowly, but stealthily, the music's volume was again increasing. To her chagrin Hennessey noticed, too. He grinned, and acted as if her professional competency had just been even more thoroughly disproved.

"I'm afraid the rest of the discussion will have to wait until after classes are dismissed, Mr. Hennessey.

Because of the confidential nature of the discussion, I'd also prefer Johnny not to be present.''

Judging by the grim set of his chiseled lips, Tom Hennessey's first instinct was simply to walk. For Johnny's sake, evidently, he fought it. "How long?" While he waited for an answer he looked her up and down in a coolly appraising manner that both infuriated and enthralled.

"Fifteen minutes." Merritt fought the warmth his study had perpetuated. Darn him, for making her aware she was a woman, and he all virile male.

"All right." Tom sighed heavily, relenting with obvious chagrin. "But let's wrap this up as soon as possible." He added at her glare, "I've got to get back to work, too."

As soon as possible, Merritt fumed inwardly. *A child is in trouble and all Tom Hennessey can think about is getting back to work. His own parents can't take the time to even show up.* "There's a teachers' lounge to your left, Mr. Hennessey. Please feel free to help yourself to a Coke in the refrigerator." She swallowed, conciliatorily offering the next for Johnny Porter's sake only. "It'll be my treat."

"Thanks," Tom said, seeing through the insincerity of her motives. "But I never let a woman pay my way." And on that note he pivoted and walked toward the lounge.

Chauvinist! Merritt thought, strolling back into her classroom. The rest of the party passed in a rowdy blur. The only other person in a more reflective, somber mood was Johnny Porter. While others were passing notes, giggling wildly, and sailing paper airplanes back and forth, he sat quietly, munching on popcorn, occasionally saying something to Kristin or Brian, for the most part not participating in the end of the six-week exam glee. Because of his unprecedented failure in school? Merritt wondered. The intuitive knowledge he'd flunked his exams as he'd flunked everything else thus far? Or was there something else bothering Johnny, something no one had informed her about?

Merritt was still cleaning up popcorn off the linoleum floor when Tom Hennessey strolled in minutes later. School had been dismissed for the day. The second floor was quiet except for an occasional rustling of papers, dragging of furniture, or slamming of doors as one by one all the other teachers departed. "Did you see Johnny?" She had to get the conversation back on a civil, impersonal level if she were to help John, and that was, as always, her first priority.

Tom nodded, pulling the classroom door shut behind him for privacy. His gaze drifted languidly over her blue denim skirt, blue and white pinstriped shirt, the coordinating powder blue sweater she had draped in a casual knot about her neck, her shapely calves, and comfortably heeled leather loafers. "I walked him to his bus. John wasn't too happy Ellen had been called out of town again, but those are the breaks." Merritt's gaze lifted to impersonal green. "Ellen has a tough schedule at the moment. It can't be helped. Johnny knows that."

Merritt wondered. "Who takes over on the home front?" she asked casually. Would Johnny be going home to an empty house?

"He'll stay at a neighbor's until Ellen can get home. Overnight, if necessary, and Ted—John's father—is out of town, too. They've worked out a deal."

Merritt resisted the urge to say "How convenient." She had seen enough neglected children to know Johnny wasn't beginning to get the kind of parental guidance and attention he needed. Nor did he have any brothers or sisters to turn to for moral support or hedge against familial loneliness.

"Here, let me help you with that." Before she could protest, Tom knelt to help her scoop popcorn into the trash. Their hands touched accidentally, the warmth of his flesh sending a tiny rivulet of sensation radiating the length of Merritt's arm. Their eyes met. She fought the drift of awareness settling over her like a deep soft cloud, the temptations he seemed to be so willingly proferring.

"What about Johnny's father?" Merritt queried, moving to set aside both wastebasket and broom as soon as the chore was finished. According to school records, Ted Porter was an attorney with a prominent local firm. "I'm aware he's been working on a case in the state capital, has been for the past month or so."

"Ellen has the major responsibility for the boy," Tom Hennessey interjected grimly.

"So Ted Porter's secretary said," Merritt agreed. "Tell me, does anyone in that family have time for Johnny and his recent troubles in school?"

Tom was silent for a moment, staring down at her through half-shuttered eyes. His jaw tautened resolutely. He moved back against the chalkboard, leaning negligently against the white-scrawled green backdrop. "I'm here now. And we don't seem to be doing much talking about John or his problems—just your rage at Ellen's inconsideration and inability to show up."

That stung. It was also more accurate than Merritt would have cared to admit. "I'm sorry." Her shoulders slumped slightly as red crept into her face. She walked back to her desk, reaching inside resolutely for her grade book and notes. "It's been a rough day, with the party. Not a good time for the conference to begin with."

"But the only time Ellen had open," Tom interjected with a commiserating sigh. "And once the appointment was made, then broken again, it didn't do much for your mood."

"Right." Merritt glanced down at the popcorn maker and punch still cluttering her desk. Maybe they could start over. "Care for some punch? A bag of popcorn? There seems to be plenty left."

"No, thanks. The Coke was sufficient." He grinned again. "And I decided to let you pay after all. There's an IOU with your name scribbled on it in the change dish next to the fridge."

Merritt's mouth twisted in wry acknowledgment as they both took a seat, he on the other side of her desk. "John's failing nearly every subject. Were you aware of that?"

Tom shook his head negatively. Merritt thumbed through her grade book until she found the appropriate pages. "I sent a note home with Johnny after the first three weeks, because his work was so far below what we know him to be capable of doing. According to Mrs. Porter—Ellen—she never received the note, which isn't surprising. Johnny knows he's doing badly and of course is not too proud of the fact."

"Is he trying?" Tom cut in, getting right to the heart of the matter.

Merritt took a deep breath. "I would have to say not."

Tom frowned. Hands shoved into his pockets, he strolled the room restively. The rigid set of his jaw said that if he talked to John it would be a very one-sided discussion.

All Merritt's reservations came tumbling back. "Frankly, Mr. Hennessey, a marine sergeant-style pep talk was not what I wanted from Johnny's family. I'm more interested in the reason for Johnny's failure, his lack of interest in everything going on around him."

Hennessey carried on a silent debate. The desire to confide in Merritt lost. "Maybe John just needs to apply himself." Tom stuck with the macho approach.

"He needs to snap out of his apathetic mood," Merritt concurred, waiting.

"If you're looking for *True Family Confessions,* you're asking the wrong person," Tom informed with a measure of deadly quiet. This was precisely why Merritt had wanted so desperately to meet with Ellen or Ted Porter in the first place. Only they had the key to Johnny's current unhappiness.

"I see." Merritt stood. "Please have your sister get in touch with me, Mr. Hennessey. It's important."

The man nodded, intent gaze still riveted on her slender form. "I'll see what I can do, Ms. Reed. And thank you." He paused, taking her hand in his firm warm grasp. "Both for your time and your concern."

It was another two weeks before Ellen Porter called. They couldn't meet at school during regular working hours because of the harried businesswoman's schedule, so they agreed to meet at a Hyde Park restaurant for dinner. Merritt donned a pair of charcoal-gray wool trousers and a soft white Emerald Isle turtleneck sweater. She pulled her freshly shampooed hair back with jeweled barrettes, fastening the shining length at the crown. Wispy bangs curled free to brush at her forehead.

The restaurant was located in an unprepossessing white building just three blocks from Merritt's home. The interior was darkly paneled, with a low sculptured ceiling, and plush wine-colored carpeting. Candles glowed softly on every table; soft piped-in music filled the air.

"Something smells terrific," Merritt remarked to the gregarious proprietor as he seated her at a red-checkered table near the rear of the crowded dining room. Tall, freckled, and redheaded, the slightly anorectic Gianni was the least authentic tradition in the history of the popular neighborhood tavern. A transplanted New Yorker, he'd adapted the Italian name for reasons that were strictly public relations. Merritt could have sworn he was part Irish. He swore he was half Scotch, and the rest a melting-pot mix.

"Veal Parmesan," Gianni said, grinning, stooping forward to encompass her with his tall spindly frame. "We've missed you, Reed. Where have you been?"

Merritt returned the hug. After Eric's death, she'd gone there often to sit and talk, stir idly at a meal she hardly tasted and could never remember later. As time had passed she'd become adjusted to being alone. New interests had surfaced, including her quest for a master's degree in education, something she had finally achieved over the summer term. "I've been busy, Gianni, with the kids at school."

"I'll bet." He didn't look the least bit envious. Still not dating yet, hmm?"

Merritt blushed. "Give me a break. No Dear Abby tonight, okay?" Abruptly she became aware of someone hovering at her elbow. She turned, confronting Tom Hennessey. Her disappointment at not seeing John's mother was relayed in her dramatically exhaled breath. She frowned, guessing frustratedly, "Not another conference down the drain!"

Tom flashed her a polite, indulgent smile, their gazes locking for an exceptionally long moment before he reached around and pulled up a chair. Sinking into it unceremoniously, he removed a breadstick from the basket in the center of the table. "Ellen was afraid you'd react badly and just give up on her and leave when she didn't show up at the appointed hour." He sighed exasperatedly, as if regretting his part in the untenable situation. "I volunteered to make sure you stayed until she did arrive."

"And you said you had no man in your life," Gianni scoffed, handing them both large scrolled black menus. After a brief outrageous wink he scurried off toward the reception area, where more patrons waited to be seated.

Tom watched Gianni depart, then turned back to Merritt, his brows arched in obvious question. Merritt sighed heavily. "Forget it. He's matchmaking. He's been married for five years now and still acts like a newlywed, hence he wants everyone else paired up and singled off, too. And since Debbie became pregnant it's even worse."

Tom glanced at the young, obviously pregnant woman standing next to Gianni. A white chef's apron covered the bloom of her petite figure. "When is she due?" he asked with sensitivity.

"The first of February, I think."

A silence stretched between them. Unable to think of a subject on which to converse unargumentatively, Merritt fidgeted restlessly in her seat, wondering how to get out of another conference with Tom. She wanted to help John. She didn't want to do it through Tom. Unfortunately, she didn't see any way out of it.

He had dressed in a blue Harris Tweed jacket, snug-fitting jeans, Tattersall shirt, and tie. He was freshly shaven and outrageously handsome—a fact she had no doubt he knew. It showed in every confident move he made.

Tom paused, his mouth thinning alarmingly as he misread her discomfiture. "Contrary to the way it looks, Ms. Reed, my sister cares deeply about her son."

Merritt's jaw hardened stubbornly at his censuring tone. "Then why isn't she here?"

"She is," he shot back smoothly, gesturing toward the entrance. "She just walked in."

Merritt was spared further discussion as a slender blonde in a well-tailored business suit strode hurriedly into the restaurant. As the harried woman neared their table Merritt noticed the shadows of fatigue circling the woman's eyes, the way her hand shook slightly as introductions were made and handshakes exchanged. "I'm sorry I'm late," Ellen Porter apologized, settling her heavy briefcase on the seat of an empty chair. "One of the banks we do business with had trouble with their computers, or so they thought. It turned out to be the inexpertise of one of their new operators, a college-hire working his way through school." She laughed nervously, smoothing her hair. "I cleared it up in no time, but I couldn't get away until someone was there to cover for me or the problem was solved, because those transactions had to be run tonight, regardless." She turned a grateful glance toward her brother. "Which is why I asked Tom to come in my stead. Thanks for filling in until I could get here." She gave his hand an affectionate squeeze.

Tom nodded, his eyes dark with concern for his sister's fatigue and ragged state. "Well, if that's all you need me for..." Palms on the table, he started to rise. Merritt stared at her water glass, feeling nothing but relief. From her point of view, the attractive man would have served as nothing but a distraction.

"Oh, please stay," Ellen pleaded before Merritt could concur the conference would be best conducted in private. Again, she noticed how Ellen's hand shook as she fastened it around her brother's arm. "You haven't had dinner yet, have you?" Quiet desperation laced her tone.

Tom shook his head. He regarded his sister with contemplative silence. "Well, then, it's settled," Ellen decided jovially. "We'll all eat. And the tab's on me. I insist. Penance for being late."

Gianni returned to take their orders and chat genially with both Ellen and Tom. After he'd departed, Merritt explained the results of Johnny's test scores in terms of basic skills, achievement, and ability, his grades previous to his sixth year in elementary school, and the staff's feeling he was quite capable of again making straight A's if only he would apply himself. "Frankly,

I'm more concerned with Johnny's attitude," Merritt continued after their dinner of veal Parmesan had been delivered to the table. She pushed her salad aside and buttered a crusty roll.

Tom cut into the veal. "Maybe he's just going through a stage," he offered pragmatically.

"His interest could pick up again on a whim," Merritt agreed, though her cool tone indicated it a most unlikely prospect. "And maybe he will outgrow his current moodiness. He's always been popular with the other students, and I'm happy to report that is still a constant despite his aloofness. However, if his grades don't come up, he will be dropped from the gifted program."

Tom glanced over at his sister protectively, then turned back to Merritt with a casual lift of his hands. "Would that be so terrible?"

"In my opinion, yes," Merritt delineated firmly. "Gifted children need special education if they're to meet even a small part of their overall potential."

Tom leaned back in his chair, listening intently, as was his sister. "How does the program differ?"

"Academically, they're given much more to do. They're encouraged to think creatively, question everything. We move at a very fast rate, and try to provide for the systematic development of the learning process. We have creative thinking games, complex and creative problem solving sessions in which the sky is the limit as far as ideas go. Additionally, we teach the children how to identify problems, gather research independently, assemble the data, and communicate the results. If John did not have this additional stimulation, one of two things would happen. He would become extremely bored and vent his frustrations by becoming a class-A troublemaker, or he would simply do much, much less than he was capable of doing. Either way, it would be a tragedy because John has so much to give."

Ellen nodded. "Well, we don't want him using his energies mischievously, that's certain."

Merritt grinned. "Johnny's always been an innovative prankster, thinking ahead to proposed results." The food strike he and Brian Anderson had organized the year before had paralyzed the school cafeteria for weeks until the head dietician found out what was behind the sudden surge in home-brought sack lunches. "But lately, not only does he fail to instigate any of the commotion, he fails to enjoy it, too. In fact, I haven't seen him smile about much of anything all year, which is why I'm worried."

All three were silent. "As far as I can tell there's no problem with any of the other children at school," Merritt said quietly. "Both his vision and hearing check out. Could there be any other reason he might be depressed? A death in the family? Loss of someone close? A favorite pet, perhaps?" She was fishing. Inadvertently, she hit a chord.

Tom and Ellen exchanged a glance. He seemed to be telling his sister she didn't have to confide anything in Merritt if she didn't wish. The petite blonde took a deep breath and plunged on regardless. "Ted and I separated at the beginning of last summer. Didn't John tell you?"

Merritt shook her head.

Ellen glanced up at the ceiling, blinking back tears. "Well, it's no wonder. Ted came back several times, largely for Johnny's sake, only to leave again. Currently he's in the state capital trying a case—or so he says. I think it's more of an excuse to be near his mistress."

That much of a confidence Merritt hadn't wanted. Just the fact that Ellen and Ted were separated would have been enough to explain Johnny's preoccupation. "I'm sorry," Merritt said inadequately at last. Tom sent her a quelling glance. Obviously, he blamed her for upsetting his sister.

Ellen nodded in response to Merritt's sympathy. Her hands were trembling slightly. She slid them into her lap, out of view, looking as if she were going to burst into tears at any moment. Surreptitiously Tom signaled for a round of after-dinner drinks.

Merritt was about to ask that she be excluded when she saw the commanding look on his face. To not participate at that point would only add to his sister's unease. Merritt felt she had done enough toward upsetting Ellen for one night, however inadvertently. "How about some Irish coffee, Gianni?" she suggested lightly, picking up on Tom's cue. "We'll call it international night," she teased, realizing after the fact it wasn't a combination he would have suggested. She, either, if she'd been less rattled. But with Tom watching her every move, it was hard to order coherently, much less call to mind any appropriate after-dinner drink.

Gianni rolled his eyes as he wrote down the order. "School teachers." He grimaced with a shake of his head, striding off to fill the order for all three.

Merritt glanced up to find Tom staring at her intently. There was a new respect in his eyes. Pleasure suffused her, and it was all she could do to prevent a telltale blush. Damn it, she chided herself mentally, appalled at how easily she'd let him affect her; she didn't need his approval or even his liking her to proceed.

"So, where do we go from here?" Tom leaned back in his chair, one elbow hooked casually behind him, over the top.

Merritt lifted both palms. She wished there were an easy answer. "I suppose we start with his grades. Since we know John's capable of doing the work, we're simply going to have to provide an environment where he is forced to hit the books every day with no distraction."

Gianni discreetly delivered the sweet brandy-laced

coffees brimming with whipped cream. His half reproachful glare told her he thought it was a terrible choice after the veal. Inwardly, she agreed. However, what was done was done.

"Which is another problem." Ellen Porter sighed, looking more beaten than ever before. "My schedule's so crazy right now, and there's no way I can cut back or bow out."

Tom covered Ellen's palm with his own. The tender understanding of his gaze made Merritt ache for such sibling closeness of her own. "Regarding that, both Ms. Reed and I can help, Ellen, so don't despair." He turned back to Merritt. "That is if you're as serious as you say about helping John."

"Of course." Merritt had the feeling he was putting her on the spot for more than just Johnny Porter's sake. "What can I do?"

"Tutor John for an hour after school every day." He stilled his sister's mute protests with another flex of his large hand. "I'll foot the bill. And help fill in on weekends."

"I'd be glad to tutor Johnny. Ethically, though, I can't accept a fee." When Tom looked as if he would protest, she added, "Just seeing John succeed academically again would be payment enough."

Ellen's eyes brimmed with tears. "I don't know how to thank you."

Merritt was about to say "Spend a little time with John" when she caught the warning in Tom Hennessey's eyes. "Don't give it a second thought." He added protectively, "Relax and enjoy your coffee. Then I'll see you and Ms. Reed home."

As it turned out, Ellen was called back to the bank for the second time that night. "The problem we thought we had fixed wasn't," she admitted, shrugging into her coat after returning from the phone call at the front desk. "Either that or they've punched in the wrong commands and messed up the system again. I've got to dash. Fortunately, my neighbor's agreed to keep John, so at least that's one problem I don't have to worry about tonight." Her face, however, was still etched with the maternal concern about not being home.

"You really don't have to see me home," Merritt concluded personably as soon as Ellen had left. Abruptly Merritt realized she didn't want to spend even five minutes alone with Tom Hennessey. His steady gaze was too sharp. And she'd been alone too long to fool him slightly about anything, or pretend even cursory ease.

"I want to. Did you drive?"

"I walked." Merritt blushed slightly at the disapproving arch of his brow.

"At night?" Gallantly he held her coat.

"I just live a few blocks down the street." Merritt lifted the heavy length of her hair and let the ends spill like raw silk over the upturned collar of her calf-length tan wool coat.

"I'll walk you." Tom led the way toward the door. "It'll give us a chance to talk, and I for one would enjoy the night air after that international mix."

Merritt grinned. "Sorry. I just ordered the first thing that popped into my head."

"Obviously, you don't drink much."

"No."

"Good, neither do I." He shot her a measuring, sidelong glance, adding chivalrously, "Unless of course you'd rather ride. My car's in the lot out back."

"No," Merritt said softly in the awkwardness that fell between them as they paused outside the canopied restaurant door. "I like to walk at night, especially in brisk autumn air." She liked strolling past the lights of the brick houses, lingering in the crush of fallen leaves, the breeze stirring her hair and chilling her nose and cheeks.

Tom nodded, clasping her gloved hand in his own. He slowed his pace slightly after a moment to accommodate her stride. "I love this weather, too," he confided. "When I walk or drive through residential areas this peaceful, I always try to imagine what's going on inside the houses." He grinned. "Most of my mental images resemble Norman Rockwell paintings. You know, remarkably cheery pictures of a family, complete with dog and cat, all gathered around the fireplace, gray-haired Grandma knitting diligently, Grandpa smoking his pipe, lots of well-scrubbed happy children." He turned toward her sternly. "The problem is, Merritt Reed, this is no storybook-safe era. And the streets are not necessarily safe at night anywhere, even in Hyde Park."

Merritt kicked at a loose stone. It felt odd, having her hand encased so familiarly by a man she hardly knew. And yet, it was comforting, as if she had known all along he would volunteer to see her home, and she would acquiesce with very little resistance. "You sound like a cop," she teased, for a moment forgetting her aversion to the profession and anything connected with it, the disastrous effects it had wreaked on her life.

"I am."

Merritt felt as if she'd been flung headfirst into the murky depths of a bottomless pool. "Tell me you're joking."

It was the wrong thing to say. His teeth clenched; his jaw jutted out defensively; every muscle in his body tensed. "I guess this much I should have expected," he said tautly at last. "God knows it's happened before."

"Tom, I'm sorry. I—" Merritt barely realized they had stopped walking. She could only feel her heart pounding against her ribs. Her knees were trembling. Sweat clung to her cold hands.

Noticing her reaction, fear, the line of Tom's mouth gentled. He drew closer, his glance openly curious. Experimentally he trailed a hand up the length of her arm and used the other to slightly lift her chin. "What's going on?"

Merritt gazed into the compelling lines of his face. Seconds passed. "I'm sorry. I didn't mean to offend you," she said. *No, it can't be. I won't let it happen to me again. Not with the first man I've even been remotely interested in since Eric's death.*

"Then explain that terrified look on your face," he demanded softly, eyes still searching her face. When she refused, the hand under her chin dropped. "All right, so much for the subtle approach. What have you got against cops?"

"Nothing!" The denial came much too fast. "What a ridiculous thing to even imply!" Merritt pivoted and started briskly away. The man was getting too close, starting to dig too deeply into wounds that had been permanently closed for over two years, wounds she had no intention of reopening or examining.

"Is it? I wonder!" Tom followed with pantherlike speed, catching her arm and pulling her back against him so abruptly, she ran into the wall of his chest. Merritt was assailed by the provocative fragrance of his skin, the light scent of shampoo in his hair, the sweetness of brandy and cream on his breath. "You wouldn't be the first, you know. Everyone likes cops when their home has just been burglarized or they've been mugged or accosted or simply scared out of their wits. But when it comes to one-to-one relationships outside the duties of the badge—" He cut himself off sharply, apparently having said much more than he intended.

Merritt, feeling close to tears, wanted only to escape. "Please. I've got to go." She tried unsuccessfully to yank free of his grip.

"Do you? Honestly?"

Merritt shivered as if suddenly affected by the chill of the autumn night, yet she knew in reality it was only the memories encompassing her reluctant, vulnerable heart. Defensively, she met his gaze. Without warning, Tom Hennessey looked so much older, tired, disillusioned. It was an onslaught of occasional despair Merritt knew and, unbeknownst to him, understood only too well. "It's just that you don't look like a street cop," she said softly at length. "The times I saw you before, no badge, no uniform. No gun."

At her conciliatory tone, the tenseness seemed to leave his frame. Tom smiled at her, looking affectionately down into her upturned face. His gaze drifted thoughtfully over her lips, then traveled back up to her eyes. "I'm not a street cop. Though the badge and the gun are usually both there beneath my blazer. I'm a detective." Resuming a casual grasp on her arm, he turned and guided them onward in the direction of the next block and her home.

"Well, I'm familiar with the television variety," Merritt teased ignominiously, trying to inject lightness back into the exchange. "What do you do? Run around in a rumpled raincoat, solving mysteries and ducking out of fights?"

Laughter rumbled deep in his chest. "Not quite. Try dusting for fingerprints, interviewing people after a robbery, and checking up on stolen goods. I do the follow-up on the missing person reports, sometimes help locate runaway kids."

"Sounds mundane," Merritt murmured, "and very necessary."

"It often is dull," Tom replied cheerfully. Using the

grasp he held on her arm, he whirled her to face him
once more. He was serious, reflecting. "Frankly, I prefer it that way."

Thinking about the violent way Eric had died, Merritt could believe it, only too well. She glanced to the
sidewalk beyond, letting her dark lashes shutter the
poignant memories from his view, then took a step
back, away from him. If she wasn't careful, the whole
conversation and especially Tom's tenderness would
make her cry. Once started, she didn't know if she'd be
able to stop the onslaught of emotion or the horrid
facts of her life and Eric's death that went with it.

The next thing she knew her back was brushing the
bark of a nearby oak. Tom followed, his warm strong
arms enfolding her and holding her near with a slow,
sensual deliberation that telegraphed his intent. A shaft
of pleasure pierced her and she trembled beneath his
regard.

"Merritt," he whispered, "don't drift away from me
like that. Don't shut me out, not when we were just
beginning to get close." His head slanted accommodat-
ingly, paused, as if waiting for her to reject his advances. When no words of protest were issued, his
mouth moved dreamlike and heaven soft over hers.

She had known he was going to kiss her. She had not
been prepared for the shattering magnetism of the
caress, the seeking, probing quality of his lips lightly
touring hers as he physically requested permission to
continue. His gentle consideration erased the last of her
defenses. With a soft moan that was part whimper, part
plea, her lips parted and she welcomed him into the
velvet sweetness of her mouth. Suddenly she needed
to be made to feel like a woman again, to be desired,
loved, and emotionally whole. She needed the proof of
being alive.

Tom clasped her to him, molding her to his shape.
He threaded his fingers through the wind-whipped

tangle of her hair. His mouth moved across hers tantalizingly as his tongue teased along the upper part of her mouth, explored the sensitive corners of her lips. His hand tilting her head back, he moved his other palm lingeringly across her shoulders. The tips of his fingers, probing and seeking, defined her spine, her waist, her hips.

A molten need shot through her and her own body ignited with a thousand and one sensations. Merritt deepened the kiss, fiercely entwining her tongue with his. Wantonly she explored the contours of his mouth, the sharp edges of his teeth, the soft texture of his lips and the definitive outline of his mouth, and the slightly abrasive surface of his just-shaven mustache and chin, the roughness that declared him male. When they drew apart slightly for air, she was trembling with desire. Knees weak, she leaned into the muscular cradle of his arms, rested her cheek against the smooth leather of his coat.

"Look at me." The whisper was soft, compelling.

Wordlessly Merritt shook her head. She buried her face in his shoulder, still fighting for composure, for breath. She'd never felt like that before—that needy— not even in the days of her courtship with or marriage to Eric. She didn't know why the spark of passion had been ignited, or even how, just that it was, and as volatile a force as it seemed to be, it frightened her. She didn't want Tom analyzing her emotions, or delving into the facts of her past she had yet to really understand or even accept.

"Damn it, Merritt, look at me." His voice was rough with passionate impatience. Cupping a long finger beneath her chin, he tilted her head up. He was taller than she by several inches, but her heeled boots put them almost nose to nose. There was no avoiding his measuring gaze, nor the thwarted desire in his eyes. "You felt something just now," he asserted, his look reminding her of the ardor she had exhibited. "Admit it. Give in to it. Even curse it. But don't pull away from me like that, don't distance yourself."

She drew herself up stiffly, wondering dimly how she had managed to get herself into such a mess. "I didn't mean for that to happen."

"You could have stopped it. I gave you plenty of opportunity." He wasn't angry, merely pointing out the facts.

Yes, she could have, but she hadn't. "Then chalk it up to the romantic atmosphere tonight." Calmly she tried to shrug off her heated response to his embrace. "The stars, the darkness, the crisp, almost wintry breeze."

"Was that all it was?" If so, he didn't share her assessment.

She supposed they'd never know. Because now that she was thinking rationally, she knew she had to keep him at arm's length from that point forward. To love him, knowing he held such a potentially dangerous job, would only mean heartbreak in the end. And she'd had enough of that. Sadly, though, Tom was precisely the sort of man she could fall for. He was strong-willed, committed to his family and those that he loved.

"You wouldn't have kissed me like that unless you meant it, Merritt."

She seized on her only defense. "How can you be sure?"

He looked stunned by her denial, then triumphant. Knowing she'd overplayed her hand, she tried to step avoidingly past. He detained her with a resolute grip on her wrist, guiding her back until she faced him once more, toe to toe. Dropping his grip on her wrist abruptly, he lifted his hand to her face, gently traced the line from cheekbone to chin with the back of his palm, as if committing her silhouette to memory. His fingers dropped to the dark strands brushing against the collar of her coat. Smoothing the silken ends, he asserted, "I don't believe you." And they both knew there was only one way to find out for sure.

Merritt's heartbeat accelerated. Her breath caught and faltered as laboriously as if she'd just completed a five-mile run. If he kissed her again, she knew she'd lose whatever emotional defenses she had regained. "If you're looking for an invitation into my bed, you can forget it. I'm not that abandoned—or casual about affairs of the heart," she said quietly.

His gaze held hers steadfastly, even when she glanced away. "I wasn't asking for that."

Wasn't he? Then what did he want from her? she wondered. And why was he going to be so hard to either evade or dismiss? Could it be ego, that she'd somehow offended his male image of himself by pretending to dismiss the passionate sparks that had passed between them? Or was there something more to his insistence? Could he feel as inexplicably drawn to her as she felt to him? It was an astonishing thought, but one she refused to let herself pursue. When Eric had died, she had sworn there would never be another man in her life. Until now, she had kept that promise.

"Can't we be friends?" he asked patiently.

Now that she knew he did police work for a living, her first instinct was to simply say no and leave it at that. But she didn't want to hurt him. "And that's all you want from me, friendship?" she asked warily.

"For the moment, yes." He held out his hand and they resumed walking, venturing halfway into the next block before he spoke again. "Which house is yours?"

"The next one." Merritt pointed to a well-kept white frame and red brick house.

"I'd like to come in," Tom said as they crossed the front yard.

Merritt refused gently. "I'm sorry. I have an early day tomorrow." Much more of his questioning, and her fragile composure would crack. And she didn't want to embarrass herself or him with hysterical confessions about a man who'd been dead two years.

She pushed past Tom and started across the sidewalk, up the tree-lined path to the steps. Tom followed pleasantly, one easy stride matching her every two. "I suppose you're right." He leaned against the doorframe as Merritt struggled to put her key in the lock. He yawned briefly, barely suppressing a teasing grin. "It wouldn't be wise to invite me in. It might lead to coffee or conversation."

Or more kissing, her conscience pointed out. Her hands trembled under his indolent perusal. Straightening languidly, he removed the keys from her hand and slid one neatly into the lock, then another into the deadbolt above. She could tell by his expression he was enjoying her discomposure. He probably felt she deserved it for her misrepresentation of her earlier response. With a gentle shove from the flat of his palm, the windowed door swung free. Before Merritt could step inside, his arm had once again encircled her waist. His thighs pressed against hers. She felt the persuasive pressure of his girded muscles all the way to her toes. If he'd been trying to communicate openly before, through touch and talk, now he was trying to seduce. Knowledge of that fact, however, only seemed to make her all the more susceptible. She swayed against him, off-balance, fighting her own traitorous thoughts, the wish to kiss him just one more time and see if the experience was as erotic and memorable and moving as she'd first supposed.

"Then again, I've never been known for being that gallant," he murmured, his mouth trailing back over hers, "so why start now?" From the determined set of his mouth, Merritt expected a ruthlessly passionate kiss. She got tiny nibbles and featherlight intensity, the warm brush of a tongue, the slight nip of his teeth. His lips traced the nape of her neck, drifted across her cheek, before moving ever so slowly back to her mouth to linger on her trembling lips. The last of her resistance dissipated, obliterated by the sheer physical need of womanly passions gone two years unslaked.

Merritt's arms wound around Tom's neck. Despite her determination to never so much as go near a policeman again, she laced her fingers through his hair and brought his mouth fully over hers. Telling herself it was an experiment, nothing more, she stood slightly on tiptoe to make the contact more equably exact. He gave as good as he got, and minutes later, both were breathing even more raggedly than before. Realizing she was playing a dangerous game, Merritt drew back to study his face. She was tingling from head to foot. He seemed equally unnerved, but his encircling arm seemed to be molten steel against her shoulders and back.

"Still want me to leave?" Tom whispered against her ear, lips brushing the sensitive shell. Merritt shivered, burying her enflamed face even further into the cool fabric of his coat.

"Yes," she lied devoutly. The truth was she wanted him more potently and completely than she had any man, and that confused her because Tom was a relative stranger, a very nice man, but she hardly knew him well enough to permit him entry into her house, let alone her bed. And still, she wanted nothing more than to take him by the hand, lead him into her home, and let the fates decide what happened next. Maybe sanity was eluding her.

Tom drew back. Tenderly his lips brushed her brow. The warmth of his breath mingled in the mussed strands of her hair curling against her face. He kissed the tip of her nose. "Could I see you again, then, on a strictly personal level—no school or nephew business allowed?"

The million dollar question. Merritt hedged. Now they were back to familiar territory—the need for a division between one's personal and professional life. "I don't know. I don't usually get involved with families of students."

"I'm only an uncle, not a parent."

"But you're stepping in for one."

"Only temporarily, until Ted is back in town or Ellen gets more fully in command." He adjusted the collar of her coat, his fingers moving sensually against her neck. "I'm moving too fast for you, aren't I?"

"Yes." Merritt sighed in relief, feeling about as sophisticated as a six-year-old, but she couldn't help it. As far as she was concerned, making love with a man meant commitment, and neither of them was ready for that emotionally. And she didn't want to be hurt again, or even sexually involved.

"All right." Tom stepped back. He studied her contemplatively, then broke into a slow sultry smile. "How do you feel about dressing up? Or down, as the case may be?"

Merritt choked on her own inhibitions. "What?" she asked, when the tears cleared her eyes and throat.

Tom laughed. "I'm inviting you to a Halloween party the Policeman's Benevolent Association is giving on Saturday. The funds are going to be used to finance the Blue Santa operation we do every Christmas. You can go as anything you like."

"Strictly platonic, no pressure?" Merritt qualified.

"I promise I'll behave befitting my station." He held up both palms in a gesture of surrender.

Merritt wasn't fooled by that evasion. "What are you going to go as?"

Tom shrugged his shoulders and refused to tell. "That, my pretty, you will have to find out for yourself." He cackled in mock ghoulishness. Taking for granted she would go, he pivoted and started lightly down her front porch steps. "Pick you up at seven. Be ready."

"Wait a minute." Merritt crossed the porch after him. "What should I go as?"

Tom turned, walking backward over the lawn to the curb. "Surprise me," he counseled.

Chapter Two

Merritt surprised Tom, all right, maybe too much so. "Unless you want your face to look like a roughly sculpted relief map of China, Tom Hennessey, you had better hold still." Merritt bent over his form and gazed with artistic concentration down into the arresting lines of his face. Tom lounged against her bathroom sink, one hip on the countertop. He had dressed in a red devil leotard that covered him from ankle to neck. A shimmering red silk cape was knotted insouciantly over his broad shoulders and a silk hood was cradled in his hands. The rented outfit was fine. The problem was that he looked too all-American to be in the slightest demonic. And since Merritt had dressed as Little Bo Peep, a little extra costuming was in order for him to live up to his half of the deliciously daring duo.

"Sorry. I'm not used to black makeup on my face." He grimaced, squinting up at her through one eye.

"You'll get used to it." Proficiently Merritt painted on a wicked-looking goatee. "Greasepaint would have been easier to use, of course, but this homemade concoction should do almost as well."

Her date sighed, shifting restively against the feminine hand cupping his chin. "Spoken like a true educator." He laughed, raking her costume with sparkling jade-green eyes. "And leader of the flock."

"Very funny, Detective." Tilting his face back ever so slightly, Merritt inked over both brows calmly. "For the record, this is the first time I've ever tried out my artistic abilities on anyone else's face." She smeared waterproof black mascara onto his upper lip. "I think that's as real a mustache as we're going to get with this stuff." She also hoped it wouldn't wash away with the first party drink of the evening.

Tom exhaled a long minty breath. "Pity they never get easier, isn't it?"

"What?"

"First dates."

Merritt sighed. "I'll agree with you there." Though the decidedly juvenile activity had done much to lighten the atmosphere between them.

Tom swiveled partway around to peruse his newly painted image in the mirror. "Hmm, I do look evil now, don't I?"

Together, they looked like something out of a very bad X-rated film. Merritt, her hair wound in Shirley Temple curls, wore a blue-and-white print dress with short puffy sleeves, a full swirling skirt and layers of frothy white bloomers and petticoats that peeked out from beneath the hem of her dress. A white cane wrapped in blue ribbons stood next to her front door. As she stood next to Tom, their disparate images reflected in the bathroom mirror, the effect was appallingly ludicrous. Merritt got the giggles and Tom joined in. "If not first prize, then definitely the talk of the evening," he expounded when he could breathe again. His assessment proved all too true.

The fund-raising celebration was in full swing by the time they arrived at the rented hall. Cowboys and dance-hall girls cavorted with Batman and Robin, Superman and Lois Lane, and a proliferation of very sultry Antonys and Cleopatras. There were other devils, too, but no Bo Peeps. "See, I told you it was original," Merritt murmured as they paused to help themselves to some spiced cider and doughnuts.

"Very becoming, too," said a male voice at her elbow. Merritt turned to confront a white-blond giant in ragged green garb. His nose had been broken at least twice. Merritt guessed his heritage was Swedish. "Let me guess," she said. "From the valley of the jolly..."

"Green Giant," they all finished in unison.

"Introduce me to your friend, Hennessey." The green-garbed man reached around Merritt for some punch, then reached into his pocket for a flask and added something clear to his.

"Merritt, Artie Kochek. Artie, this is my date, Merritt Reed."

"That much I guessed." Artie sent his friend an amused, assessing look, then turned back to Merritt. "He treating you right so far?"

"So far," she agreed.

"Great. The man's not been known for his overwhelming kindness to women, you know."

"Art—" Tom's brows raised in part warning, part plea.

"Just kidding." Art sobered, adding, "The real reason I came over, Hennessey, is the captain's looking for you. Something about switching the assignments of the men working under you. He thinks he has just figured out where everyone should go."

Tom groaned, finishing the rest of his cider in a single draught. "Where was he?"

Art pointed in the direction of the bandstand. "Can't miss him. He's dressed as a white knight. At least that's what I think he's supposed to be."

Tom touched Merritt's arm, leaning closer to whisper in her ear.

Her senses reeled at the close contact. "I'll be right back," he murmured. To Artie: "Watch what you say to my date. And if you dance with her, be sure it's not too close."

Artie grinned as Tom strode off, devil tail swishing determinedly behind him. The giant held out his arms and executed a gallantly formal bow. "Shall we, Ms. Reed?"

Merritt smiled and put down her cup. "Why not?"

The music was swing. Art Kochek had all the grace of a lumbering elephant stepping on tacks. After his third tromp on her Mary Janed foot, Merritt suggested they wait out the rest of the dance and have some more punch. "Fine with me," Artie said, removing his flask.

"How long have you known Tom?" Merritt asked, watching other couples whirl around the dance floor.

"About six or seven years," Art calculated with a heavenward glance. "We trained together at the academy. I was just out of high school. Tom was just getting out of the service after a three-year tour. Difference was he was a college grad. So after his obligatory year or two on patrol, he went into management, started moving up in the ranks, eventually began working as a detective. I stayed on street patrol and am now one of the lucky dudes to be working the motorcycle division."

"Do you like your work?" Merritt munched on a sugar-coated doughnut as the band lapsed into a slow song.

Artie gestured offhandedly. "It's more traffic tickets and tow aways than anything else now, but, yeah, I enjoy it. I enjoy the excitement." A trickle of cold fear ran down Merritt's spine. "You know, the thrill of never knowing what's going to be going down next, the life-and-death excitement," he finished in mock theatrical tones.

Merritt paled even more. "All right, Art, what have you been saying to my date?" Tom walked back up to join them and slipped a proprietary arm around Merritt's waist. She leaned into the encouraging warmth.

"Nothing. I think it's the stuffiness of the room," Merritt soothed. With the security of Tom's arm around her, she felt the color come back into her face.

"Maybe a breath of fresh air?" Tom asked.

"Maybe a dance."

"Speaking of which, I'd better find *my* date," Art decided. "See you guys later." He strode off.

Merritt relaxed into Tom's arms as he led her out onto the dance floor. They circled and spun slowly to the strains of "Tenderly." "So what were you really talking about?" Tom whispered at last.

Merritt glanced down at the patterned tile floor. "Police work, the dangers."

"Don't let Art upset you." Tom frowned, gazing distantly out at the crowd. "What we do is mostly routine."

Merritt shot back before she could think, "Tell me, does that count if you're the one person who makes the fatality list?"

Tom stopped dancing, stood holding her tightly in his arms. "I hope you're not one of those women who complain about the dangers involved in a cop's work," he said quietly, his gaze fixed on her own.

"Sorry," Merritt mumbled into the soft red fabric of his shirt. "Years of being on the debate club."

He laughed softly. His grip and the fact that he did not resume dancing right away said he wasn't sure he was entirely convinced. "I'm almost afraid to ask your political affiliations."

Merritt cringed. "Please don't." With effort, she kept the conversation for the rest of the evening on a deliberately light tone. She met several more men Tom worked with, their wives, girlfriends, fiancées. She even met his superior, Captain Fielding. Unfortunately for Tom's sake, he was every bit the stuffed shirt Artie Kochek had implied earlier.

After the dance ended, Tom walked Merritt to her front door. "Sorry about the business and pleasure aspect of the dance tonight." He paused, letting his gaze trail over the finely sculpted lines of her face in the dim glow of the lone porch light. He'd taken off his hat, left his cape and tail in the backseat of his car. Casually Tom raked his fingers through his wavy hair. "But I figured you'd be more comfortable at something more impersonal," he said.

He'd read her feelings correctly. Merritt glanced up at her artistic handiwork, needing time to work out her feelings before she let the man draw her even further into his dangerous spell.

"Waterproof mascara's sometimes a little difficult to get off," she stated matter-of-factly, placing a bracing hand flat against his chest to ward off any sudden attempts at a good night kiss. "Mixing it the way we did with the eyeliner—unless you have cold cream or eye-makeup remover on hand—?" He shook his head negatively. "I think you had better come in, then," Merritt decided. "It will only take me a minute to get that off. Without the proper cleansers and feminine expertise, you'd probably be at it half the night and scrub your skin raw in the process."

"You're probably right about that." Tom followed her happily into the living room and strode behind her down the hall toward the bath. Merritt rummaged through the medicine chest, finally pulling out cleansers, cream, and soap. "I'm not sure which one of these is going to work." She was acutely aware of his interested gaze upon her, though she couldn't read what he was feeling in the expressionlessness of his face.

Tom lounged against her bathroom countertop, watching as Merritt walked to the linen closet, then returned with a clean washcloth and towel. Turning on the tap, she set to work scrubbing the angled goatee.

"How's it going?" Tom asked, his back to the mirror. He was watching the gentle persistent motions of her arm as she worked the cleanser-soaked cloth against his chin.

"Okay." Merritt peered closer. "Though I think the

makeup is clinging to your whiskers a bit. Either that or the morning shadow or growth coming in is much darker than your eyelashes and hair."

A beleaguered sigh rippled the length of his fit frame. "Now I am definitely afraid to look." He closed his eyes as Merritt finished up his chin, parted his lips slightly as she worked over his upper lip, the corners of his beautifully chiseled mouth. Merritt leaned closer to reach his eyebrows. Her hips rested casually against his inner thigh. Her breath when exhaled rumpled the uppermost reaches of his layered hair. She could see the silvery streaks in it, illuminated by the bathroom light, and was keenly aware of the baby shampoo scent of his hair, the provocative fragrance he wore. Without warning, two hands were determinedly clamped around her waist. Tom drew her more closely into his embrace, so the length of her body was leaning down perilously close over his, her legs caught between the sinewy cradle of his thighs.

"You're afraid of me," he whispered wonderingly at length, when she started. "Why?"

Merritt had wedged her arms between their chests reflexively the moment he had made his move. She kept them firmly in place so complete body contact could not be made. Beneath her splayed palms she could feel the increasing heavy beat of his heart. "Not afraid," she qualified breathlessly at last, pushing determinedly away. "Just reluctant to get involved."

Tom followed her wordlessly from the bathroom and walked slowly down the hall. Merritt was already to the front door when his stride matched, then overpowered, hers. *He's a cop,* she reminded herself firmly. *A man whose work places him in jeopardy every day. I can't afford to get involved with a man like that, emotionally or any other way.* "It's been a lovely evening." Merritt's smile was pasted on artificially as she reached for the doorknob.

"Full of good causes," Tom agreed. He took a step
nearer. Blood pounded through her veins. "Not even a
good night kiss?" he taunted when Merritt would have
moved away.

She swallowed. "It's...late."

"Let me see. We're back to 'inadvisable' again,
aren't we?" Tom prompted, encircling her waist with
one strong arm. "Why don't we just concentrate on
what we feel this one time?" Delicately, deliberately,
he moved her forward until they stood waist to waist.
Merritt's head tilted up in confusion. "Just what I
thought," Tom murmured. "Afraid." His mouth fluttered across hers. Merritt's hands went to his chest,
fighting him, holding the intimacy at bay. But her lips
had a volition of their own, and they parted under the
gentle sensual pressure, accepted the probing, parting
sensation of his tongue as it moved first between her
lips, then teeth. He tasted of cider and sugar and cinnamon. His chin was still warm and slightly damp from
the cleansing. His hands moved around her, slowly up
and down the length of her back, from shoulder to
waist to lower spine. Merritt was engulfed in a need so
intense she burned.

"God, you're exquisite," he murmured against the
fluttering pulse in her neck. "I wouldn't hurt you, I
swear."

"But you do want to make love to me," Merritt finished. "Just like that." Ice laced through her voice. She
didn't want to be just another casual fling. She wanted
it to mean as much to him as it would for her. She
wanted it to be more than just an exchange of heated
caresses and overused lines.

Tom drew back, studying her with half-hooded eyes.
The passion was still a palpable force between them,
heating their torsos wherever contact was made, quick-
ening her pulse. "Yes, I want to make love to you,
Merritt," he admitted softly. The force of his physical

longing was a hypnotic drug. His hands moved gently up and down the length of her spine, generating tiny electric impulses that eventually made her shiver. "But as for it being just like that, I—"

With effort Merritt extricated herself from his embrace, scarlet color flooding her face. He was taking too much for granted, steamrolling her into a new liaison when part of her still felt, unbeknownst to him, very much another man's wife. "Please leave." Merritt reached for the knob.

Around the circle of brass, his fingertips covered hers. They were warm, implacable. His voice carried a softer, more hesitant plea. "What's going on here, Merritt?" he asked. "Are you involved with anyone else? Still married or in the throes of a divorce?"

She turned, moving away from the door, slipping her fingers out from under the imprisoning warmth of his hand. "No."

"But someone else did live here. A man."

Merritt whirled. "How did you know that?"

His mouth curled into a semblance of a smile that didn't begin to encompass his eyes. "I'm a detective, remember? Your medicine cabinet. It had a few items in it that didn't make sense. Forgive me for looking, but while you were searching for the soap, I had nothing better to do. The top shelf had men's cologne, an old cake of scented soap on a rope. Looked like the kind of deal you'd give someone for Christmas and they'd promptly forget to use. Lower, there was a can of shaving cream and a twin-bladed razor."

"I use that for my legs." Scarlet color engulfed her from head to toe. How dare he pry into her private life like that, invited into her bathroom or not!

"The rest?" Tom remained implacable, hands crossed against the broad surface of his chest. "Or are you going to tell me you prefer a more masculine scent?"

Merritt turned away. Her fingers dug into the palms of her hands. "I'm a widow, all right?"

Silence fell between them, but she was afraid to turn back, afraid he would see the pain still mirrored in her eyes every time she thought of Eric's death. "Can we just drop this?"

"No, we can't." His tone was just as sarcastic.

Sick of the interrogation, she whirled. "Why not?. What does any of this matter to you anyway?"

"It matters to me because it obviously matters to you." Tom moved an inch nearer with every tautly issued word. "You're not over the man yet, are you, Merritt?"

Her chin snapped up defiantly. "Up until now I haven't lifted a finger to try."

She'd meant to anger him, and send Tom away. Her admission did just the reverse. Abruptly Tom's expression had gentled. A sigh rippled his long, lean frame. Pliant fingers moved up to knead the stiffness from her shoulders, tilt her chin up to the surprisingly sympathetic light in his circumspect look. "There's no harm in loving someone, dead or alive, Merritt. I just want to know how you feel, where I stand."

Tears blurred her eyes. "I'm attracted to you. That hasn't happened in longer than I can remember. I thought I was over Eric, at least to the point I could date."

"How long has it been?" The caress of his voice was so soft and understanding, it sent another tear fleeing haphazardly down her cheek.

Her throat constricting with emotion, Merritt turned away. She brushed at the humiliating moisture still lining her face. "Two years." How could she have done this to herself? she wondered. How could she have done it to Tom?

"And you're still unable to even think of another

man." Anger edged into the discussion. Merritt knew he felt she had led him on unfairly. Part of her knew she should have at least imparted somewhere along the line that she was a widow. After a moment he spoke. "In the time since...Eric's...death, you're telling me there's been no one at all."

Merritt nodded her head affirmatively. "That's right."

He walked closer, circling around so she had to look at him. "Why me?" The words were taut with an emotion she couldn't identify. "How did I get the honor?"

Merritt raked her hands through her hair, tossing out the silk ribbons that had held the length back from the crown. "You were persistent. I thought it was about time I got out." Maybe Tom Hennessey was simply the sort of man she hadn't met or even remembered seeing in so long. "I don't know. I haven't really thought about it."

"And his belongings?" The words were clipped.

"I kept a few things after his death, true. Mostly photos and legal papers, a few very precious odds and ends. They're boxed away in the attic. As for his after-shave still being on the top shelf of the medicine cabinet, I'm not much for cleaning storage areas in general. The bulk of my life is wrapped up in my work, the students I teach. I imagine if you look at the decanter close enough, Detective, you'll see it's coated with dust an inch thick. As for the soap on the rope, you were right, I simply forgot it was there."

Her anger seemed infectious. He seemed to think he'd been deliberately misled. "How nice to know you don't savor the aroma nightly."

Merritt didn't react. For a moment neither did he. A muscle working in one lean cheek, he started for the door. "Well, this is the first time I got to be stand-in for a very real ghost." He paused in the portal. More chilling than the drafts of glacial night air was the look in his eyes. "Let me know the next time you want a properly 'haunted' Halloween date." The door slammed fiercely behind him.

Chapter Three

Monday morning found an exhausted Merritt in the teachers' lounge, helping herself to breakfast, courtesy of the assorted vending machines. Guidance counselor Blanche Beck walked in, took one look at the conglomeration of hot cocoa, fudge nut brownie, and box of chocolate-covered raisins, and shut the door behind her. "Okay, Reed, what gives?" The tawny-skinned young woman pulled up a chair, then ran a hand through her silky ebony hair.

To deny a problem existed would be pointless, Merritt knew. Their resident Ph.D. knew every one of the Alomar elementary staff inside and out, and she had a fair working knowledge of every student in attendance, too. "I met a man." Merritt shook a few more calorie-laden chocolate-covered raisins into her hand.

Blanche leaned over, spirited the box from her pal's hand, and tossed it backhandedly into the trash. "You'll thank me later," she told a mock wide-eyed Merritt, "when all of that doesn't go to your hips. Now, more about the man. Who is he? What is he? Is—he attractive?"

"His name is Tom Hennessey. He's the uncle of a student of mine." Merritt moved her cocoa out of the way of Blanche's chiding index finger. "As far as being attractive, he's got his faults. One eyebrow is perhaps a sixteenth of an inch lower than the other. Or maybe he just tilts it that way. He grows a beard at an astounding rate, probably sixty whiskers an hour. His nose has a tiny crook in it slightly above the bridge. The jaw is probably far too square to photograph really well, though why anyone would want to preserve for posterity such an impossible man—"

"Devastating, hmm?" Blanche walked over to buy some coffee from the machine.

"You got it." Merritt took another healthy chug of her cocoa.

"And?"

Merritt suddenly lost all desire for her fudgey binge. Crumpling the remains of her breakfast into the trash, she walked over to stare out the window into the still-deserted suburban streets. "We went out Saturday night. Actually, I've run into him a few times before that." She swallowed, recounting the painfulness of their parting words. "The upshot is he told me to get rid of a ghost—Eric's." She turned to face her best friend, the only other person who really knew what she'd been through after her husband's death.

"I'm sorry." Blanche walked over to slide a comforting arm around Merritt's shoulders. She gave her co-worker an affectionate squeeze, then drew back to look into Merritt's face. "Are you going to see him again?"

Merritt shrugged, fighting back bitter tears. "I don't know. Part of me wants to. The other part—"

"Feels disloyal to Eric for even thinking about it."

Merritt nodded, brushing a tear from her cheek. They continued to slide unchecked as the first school bus pulled up into the parking lot outside.

"Tom Hennessey's the first man you've dated, isn't he?" Blanche affirmed. Merritt nodded. "Well, give it time. You'll get used to it again."

"What if he doesn't want to wait it out?" She hated to admit how numbing a possibility that was. In reality, she barely knew the man. Already the compulsion to be with him, near him, was overwhelming. "I could hardly blame him. God knows I acted like such a fool."

"If he really cares, he'll help you work through it." Blanche handed her a Kleenex, then waited until Merritt had composed herself again. "Come on. We've got a full day ahead of us and this is no way to begin."

The rest of the day went much better, as Merritt knew it would once she got immersed in her work. "Okay, we're going to be starting a unit on family life today and how it can be affected both adversely and positively." Merritt passed out mimeographed sheets still damp and scented with ink. "Statistics show only one out of seven households today contain the traditional nuclear family of father, mother, and children. The rest are comprised of any variety of workable, livable combinations." Merritt strolled to the chalkboard and with the class's help began making a list of the possibilities. "We're also going to be studying what can happen to the nuclear family when a family member becomes ill, or there is a death or a divorce."

"Is that what they mean when they say 'broken home'?" Kristin Stratton asked, seriously concerned.

Brian Anderson interrupted. "Nah. A broken home is like when a house breaks in two. When it gets hit by a tornado or something."

Merritt had learned the best way to deal with Brian was to simply agree with him. She added somberly, "Or a flood." There was a pause. The class clown seemed temporarily at a verbal loss, so Merritt continued. "To answer your question, Kristin, yes, sometimes divorced households are referred to as broken homes. I prefer to think of them as restructured environments or households." She wrote the key words on the blackboard, paused while Brian Anderson looked up *restructured* and *environment* and copied the definitions on the board for the class. "But I'm talking about more than just negative changes. We're going to talk about what happens when someone's dad or mom gets transferred and the rest of the family *doesn't* want to move, or about mothers who go back to work. We're going to read books, have group thinks and team debates, and use similar or related themes for our creative writing assignments this six weeks.'' She went on to give the homework assignment and answer the questions as to the work sheet due the next day.

As scheduled, Johnny Porter remained after the final bell. They went over his extra work for the day, the section of his math book he formerly had failed. Merritt graded papers while he worked, then went over what he'd done with him step by step. Given one-to-one attention, it didn't take him long to catch on, and Merritt was glad to see he'd easily upped his unit test score to a low B with the extra tutorial help.

But she could tell by the look on his face that something more was troubling him. ''Something on your mind?'' Merritt straightened a stack of tests, securing them with a rubber band.

Johnny placed an open palm on the corner of her desk. ''That unit on family life.'' The tall blond youngster refused to meet her eyes. ''Are you doing that just for me?'' He knew most of what they had studied was not in their social studies book.

Merritt rose, tossing down her red grading pen. She felt an honest question deserved an honest answer. ''Partly. Your situation certainly started me thinking about it. But my life has been affected by similar circumstances, too. My parents relocated to a southern state several years ago, and now live in a retirement community in the southwest. My older brother is in the service and is completing a tour of duty overseas. He likes Europe so much I don't think he'll ever return to the States for more than a cursory visit.''

''Yeah, but you must have expected that,'' Johnny argued, stalking restively toward the board. He fidgeted with a dusty eraser in the tray, sending up clouds of yellow smoke. "After all, kids grow up and leave home—"

"And parents sometimes retire to lead a life of their own." Merritt smiled. "You're right. That much I did rather expect. I didn't expect my husband to die when we'd only been married three and a half years." Johnny glanced up sharply, obviously dismayed, and Merritt touched his shoulder comfortingly to let him know she wasn't distressed. "It's all right. I'm over it, mostly. Most of the time I don't even think about it. The point is none of us ever expect anything bad or tragic to happen to us. When it does, we're often thrown, disillusioned. We get angry and it makes it hard to concentrate on the things that really matter."

"Like my schoolwork." Johnny took the hint.

"Among other things. But you're right. You do need to apply yourself more. And the fact you're doing extra work after school is certainly a step in the right direction."

"It won't change my family life," John argued. "And neither will studying about divorce or separation. It won't bring my dad back home again."

For the first time Merritt sensed the depth of his hurt. She trod carefully. "It might help you to handle it, John. And even if it doesn't, it's bound to help someone else. Because let's face facts. The divorce rate in this country is anywhere from thirty to fifty percent, depending upon where you live. The rate for some sort of trouble in any given marriage is even higher. Everyone here is going to face what you're facing to some degree—the fact that their mom and dad no longer get along. Maybe some will divorce. Some may split, move to the opposite sides of the country and never see one another again. And some may eventually be able to work things out before it ever gets to court." Her voice softened compellingly. "I don't know what's going to happen to you or your folks. I do know, as your teacher, it's my responsibility to see you get the best education possible and move on to the next grade, without losing your place in the gifted studies program."

"I'll second that." Tom Hennessey's voice interrupted them. Merritt glanced up to see him lounging in the doorway, his photo badge clipped to his left shirt pocket. "How's he doing?" Tom walked into the room, shadow-boxed silently with his nephew, and then pulled him in for a brief macho hug.

"Much better." Merritt smiled, attempting to keep things between her and Tom on a strictly professional level. "I think John will be caught up in no time and be performing at his usual high level."

"I'm sure Ellen will be glad to hear that," Tom agreed pleasantly.

At the mention of his mother, John's mood changed dramatically. "Don't count on it," the sixth-grader muttered sullenly beneath his breath.

Tom and Merritt exchanged a mutually concerned glance over the child's head. Merritt shook her head, signaling it wasn't the time to compare notes. Tom turned back to his nephew, adopting a positive tone.

"Well, what do you say, kid? Ready to go? I've gotta get back to work, and your mom's been called back in to that bank downtown." Johnny grimaced unhappily and Tom added, "You're supposed to have supper at Kristin's house. Ellen will pick you up there."

"Much more and the Strattons are going to think I live there," John muttered fiercely, collecting his backpack and coat.

Tom attempted a joke. "Look on the bright side, sport. At least you're not stuck with my cooking or another Big Mac on the run."

"I want my mom and dad back together again." John strode angrily out the door. "I don't care if my

mom never cooks again. I don't care if they fight. I just
want us all under one roof. And there's nothing any of
you can say that's going to make me change my mind
about that."

Tom shot Merritt an alarmed glance, started to
speak, then stopped. Conveying her a look that seemed
to promise he'd be back, he sighed, pivoted, and
stalked resolutely after his disgruntled nephew.

Not surprisingly, Tom Hennessey returned to the
school a scant half an hour later. Merritt was finishing
her lesson plans for the next day. "I thought you were
due back at work," she observed, using a pleasant but
matter-of-fact tone to hide the nervousness she felt
whenever he neared. It had been raining steadily most
of the day and the sound of the icy precipitation drumming on the roof of the deserted building only added to
her feeling of isolation.

He roved closer, barely seeming to even breathe. His
expression was grimly serious. "I called in and got
someone to cover for me the rest of the shift. I'll go
back in and pinch-hit for them later." He paused, then
went on reluctantly, his voice low and subdued. "I
talked to John. He said you started a unit on family
life-styles today." Tom glanced at her accusingly, as if
he could hardly believe her callousness.

Merritt read the judgment in his eyes, once he realized his nephew's report was indeed factual. It was
even worse than the derision they'd held the last time
they'd met. Her chin lifted angrily. Why did he habitu-
ally assume the worst about her motives? "Yes, we
did." Rising from her chair, she pulled on her blazer,
slid the lesson plans into the center desk drawer, and
pushed in her chair. Aware he was still watching her
indignantly, waiting for an explanation to be delivered
posthaste, she lifted her hair casually from beneath the
collar, took her time smoothing the silky mass over her
shoulders. She would not lose her composure with

him, no matter how irately he behaved. It was unprofessional. They weren't on a date now. He wasn't in her home, waiting for the correct moment to bestow a good night kiss. They were discussing a student who concerned them both.

Apparently mistaking her silence for indifference, Tom prowled closer, his hands splayed defiantly against his waist. "Because of John?" The words were ground out between clenched teeth.

"For many reasons," Merritt replied stiffly, trying hard to ignore the flat, uncompromising line of his mouth, the deliberately metered rise and fall of his chest as he took in irate breath after breath. "All of which I explained to John right before you came in."

"Well, he sure as hell doesn't understand, then," Tom shot back acrimoniously, a muscle working furiously in his cheek. "Because he just told me he thinks you're making a spectacle of his family deliberately."

Merritt sighed and looked away, fighting to contain her anger. How like a layperson to assume he knew the reasons behind her every educational move! "If you had done any reading on the subject at all, Mr. Hennessey, you'd realize Johnny probably already feels singled out." Her spine stiffened and she glared at him aggravatedly. "All children who are victims of a divorce or separation do, and generally with darn good reason! No one ever talks about it. No one ever says 'This is what may happen to you. This is what has happened to other people so you are not alone.' How can we expect our children to cope, if they first aren't given the tools with which to do so? Every child in my classroom knows John's parents are separated. As it happens, three other children are also in homes where the parents are having difficulty. One lost a younger brother last year in a boating accident on a family picnic. Another has a grandparent who is terminally ill. They are all managing, grant you. Somehow children miraculously do. But not very well. As for the unit on family studies, John was right, it is not included in their usual textbook studies. I have, however, implemented it before, usually toward the end of the school year as opposed to the beginning. The topic matter is timely, controversial, and provides much food for thought among my preadolescents. It also makes for very good additional assignments along the gifted student lines, as there is a wealth of material for them to sift through."

By the time she'd finished, he looked extremely chagrined. More, amused by the fact he'd jumped to conclusions. Color flooded Merritt's face as she realized just how passionately she'd been speaking. Mortified, she tried to step past. He moved with her, steadfastly blocking her way. Before she could try to bypass him again, he said, "I'm sorry." He captured her hand and touched her wrist lightly, familiarly. Feeling her resistance, he circled the limb pliantly and caressed it with fingers and thumb. His voice was as soft and mending as his touch. "I didn't mean to accuse. I'm just worried about John. Forgive me for overreacting?"

How could she not? Merritt's shoulders relaxed. She leaned her weight into the sturdy frame of her desk. Her heart seemed to be pounding at double the normal speed. She wished fervently he'd release her, at the very least stop touching her so gently and seductively. And yet at the same time his gaze was so sincerely apologetic she couldn't bring herself to move away. She exhaled a ragged breath. "I know exactly how you feel. I'm worried about John, too. He seems to be getting more upset and withdrawn as time progresses, not less."

Tom's grip on her dropped. He sighed heavily and stared out at the dusky afternoon. "Maybe I'll disregard Ellen's instructions in this case and give my brother-in-law a call," he mused quietly. "Maybe if Ted made a special trip down to see John..."

"Certainly he'd feel less abandoned," Merritt concurred.

Tom's gaze lingered on her mouth, the teeth worrying her full lower lip. A sigh rippled the length of his muscular frame. A genial light shone in his eyes. "Do you have any plans for dinner?"

Slowly Merritt shook her head. *Don't get involved with this man,* her heart warned. *He'll break down all your defenses and leave you hurting and heartbroken again.* Because of the dangerous nature of his profession, and the security she sought, she knew an affair with him couldn't end any other way.

Tom glanced at his watch. "Well, about all I've got time for is a quick sandwich and a cup of coffee. But if you wouldn't mind the eat-and-run approach to a weeknight date, there's a lot I'd like to make up for, a lot I'd like to discuss."

Merritt nodded her agreement. What harm could come of one dinner? "I'd like that very much." Under his interested gaze, she picked up her briefcase and purse and removed her winter coat from her locker. "How are the roads?" Merritt asked calmly as Tom helped her into her coat. It looked bitterly cold and desolate out, not the kind of weather anyone would venture out in willingly. The schoolroom windows were frosting up, the panes rattling slightly as the wind outside picked up.

"They're fairly slick." Tom's hand lingered on her shoulder as he talked. Warmth engulfed her and it was all she could do to keep the hot blush of desire from her cheeks. He continued bemusedly, "Though all of the main thoroughfares have already been salted."

"Is it still raining?" She turned to face him, fastening the button at her sternum. The scarf was tangled beneath the collar, so Tom reached up and extricated it gently. He seemed thoroughly distracted. "It was sleeting lightly when I came in. Snow is predicted for later this evening. Did you drive?"

"My car's in the lot." Merritt sighed, thinking of the treacherous roads. Much as she wanted to go out with Tom, she hated to risk driving on icy streets. As far as she was concerned, driving in the snow was even worse. When Eric had been alive he'd always seen she got to and from work and errands safely. Now she was on her own; though, sadly, she was no more confident in that one regard.

Tom sensed her trepidation. "My car has snow tires on and chains in the trunk if I need them for added traction. Since it's only a couple of blocks from here, why don't I follow you back to your place now. I'll drive us to the restaurant, then drop you off at your house afterward. That way you won't have to drive after dark alone."

Relief poured through her. "Always the safety-conscious cop, aren't you?" she teased lightly, remembering his lecture about darkened city streets.

"There are times when I'm a man with the same weaknesses and desires as any other." He sighed heavily, touching his thumb to the softness of her lower lip. "Tonight, however, I have only your best interests at heart, and that means getting you home unscathed. So we'd better get going. Salted or not, those streets aren't going to get any better."

The drive to her home was uneventful. Merritt drove haltingly, never exceeding twenty miles per hour. Tom followed dutifully, then waited, his Camaro running, for her to park her Volkswagen in the drive and dash back toward him. Icy rain splattered the interior of his car as she jumped in. "Wicked night," she observed.

He sighed, agreeing. "Which probably means a lot of auto accidents later on."

"You're not worried about your own safety?" She

faced him curiously. At five thirty, the streets were cloaked in misty pewter gray.

He shook his head. "One of the first things a patrolman learns is how to get around safely in all kinds of weather. The department gives a free course in defensive driving, you know. It wouldn't hurt you to take it."

Was he making a derisive comment about her lack of confidence earlier? she wondered. His face was so impassive it was hard to tell. "I'll think about it."

"Do that." His mouth twisted wryly and he shot her a teasingly provoking glance. "But until then, Ms. Reed, do everyone else a favor and stay off the wintry streets!"

After consulting with her briefly, he selected a gourmet hamburger shop several miles away. Because of the inclement weather, the restaurant was sparsely populated. Over dinner they discussed everything from the latest movies and books to the weather. Finally, Tom's halfhearted absorption with the other patrons, the salt and pepper shakers on the table, and the nighttime traffic outside the windows ceased. He took a deep preparatory breath and faced her boldly, as if mentally bracing himself for whatever she might say or do next.

"I'm sorry about my reaction the other night," he began reluctantly. "I knew when I asked you out you weren't... well, you didn't go to bed with every man you met."

That was putting it lightly, Merritt thought, toying with the clasp of the handbag on her lap.

"I shouldn't have started anything," Tom continued, jaw tautening with the effort the admission cost him.

Merritt hesitated, equally at a loss. "I never meant to lead you on. I do need time to sort out my feelings and adjust to being single again."

"And I'm going to need to understand. You, your

past, where we go from here." His hand reached across
the table to twine with hers. The warmth felt solid and
comfortable and strangely compelling. "Tell me about
your marriage," Tom said softly at last. "Tell me about
Eric."

"Eric and I were high school sweethearts." She
sighed. It seemed like it had been a lifetime ago. "We
began dating when we were both sixteen. From that
point on, there was no one else for either of us. We
went everywhere together, even selected our college as
a team. Between our junior and senior year we got married, and lived in a small efficiency apartment on cam-
pus. I was satisfied, content to go on with my studies.
But Eric was restless. Eventually, because of increas-
ingly tight finances, he dropped out of school to take a
full-time job. I kept going to school. The plan was that I
would finish and teach. He would use the time to get
his bearings and decide what he wanted to do, then go
back, pick up the necessary classes, and graduate."

"But he never had a chance, did he?"

Merritt sighed. "No, I wanted to stay on and get
some additional training so I would be able to teach in
the gifted program. By the time I had finished, Eric was
more reluctant than ever to go back, despite my urg-
ings. He said one more year of working, of just being
together and being able to relax without worrying about
grades or exams, and then he'd go back...." Her voice
trailed off. She glanced down at the fist in her lap. It
was white with the strain of clenching and unclenching.
Talking about Eric's death, their life together, always
made her tense and unhappy. She didn't like thinking
about what they'd lost, the unfairness of it all. But
then, she mused with a bitterness born of harsh experience, no one had ever promised her that life would
be fair. That was always something she had just assumed.

"You loved him a lot, didn't you?" The question

was quietly put. Merritt couldn't tell what Tom was feeling.

"Yes." She drifted off again, thinking of all the crushed dreams, the reality of living alone, the horror that haunted her still. She found it so hard to trust anyone now. Merritt straightened abruptly as the waitress appeared to freshen their coffees.

"Tell me about you," Merritt encouraged. "I know next to nothing about you. Have you ever been married? Lived with anyone?"

"I'm divorced."

"I'm sorry." Merritt took a sip of her coffee.

He flexed his shoulders, then settled back further into his seat with a deep, half-humorous sigh. "Don't be. Carin never understood police work, my desire to 'serve and protect' relative strangers from the dangers of the street. She wanted me to quit, do something less noble and better paying. Eventually, she realized I meant what I said when I told her I had found my niche for life. She packed her bags, most of the furniture, all of the joint savings, and left. Except for the signing of the divorce papers, which was handled through our respective lawyers, I haven't heard from her since. Don't really expect to." About that much, at least, he seemed to have no remorse.

"Any children?"

Tom shook his head. "That's my only regret. I love John like my own, but he is only a nephew, after all, with his own set of parents, warring though they may be. The way I work, well, let's just say I'd never ask a woman to marry me again."

"Not even if you loved her?"

Their gazes collided. He seemed taken aback by the raw honesty in her voice, the need to have him promise something more than just the moment if they were to get involved.

"I don't know," he said softly at last, turning to face

her more squarely. His gaze drifted lower, to the curve of her chin, the slope of her neck, the open collar of her silk shirt. "Until now, there's never been even the remotest possibility I might become involved."

Was he saying he could love her, given time? The possibility lifted her spirits and gave her hope for the future. For the first time since Eric's death, the horizon did not seem bleak. She knew she'd never stop loving her husband, but what they had was over now. She did have to go on. But perhaps she would not have to be alone. He wouldn't have wanted that for her, she knew.

The sleet was coming down ferociously when they left the restaurant. They dashed to the nearby car, took shelter there for long shivering moments as Tom coaxed the diffident motor to life. "I'd better let it warm up a little bit," he decided, a worried frown crossing his face. Seeing her shivering, he asked, "Are you cold?"

"Yes." Her hands were like icicles, and she'd left her gloves in her car.

"Me, too. Here, let me warm you." With the offer, he moved. His right arm slid behind her head, around her shoulders. The other slanted across her and swung her around and toward him until they were just inches apart, matching breath for recklessly indrawn breath. He placed her palms on his chest, unbuttoning his coat, then his blazer, to slip them inside against his chest. Her fingertips curled against the smooth cotton of his shirt. She could feel the drumming cadence of his heart, the heat of his skin.

Again, his tender regard strayed to her mouth. Of their own volition, her lips seemed to part. She was drifting nearer, tilting her head back, more fully under his, anticipating, wanting, yes, needing his kiss. The future be damned, Merritt thought, responding to the salty taste of his lips over hers. She wanted to live that moment, she wanted to be there with him.

Around them the night had darkened to pitch-black. The parking lot had been cleared of all but three or four scattered cars. The sounds of traffic on the street seemed another world away. With a last, slow shake of his head, Tom nipped at her mouth softly, let his lips flutter across hers, teasing, brushing, tormenting. Her lips blossomed open and Merritt gasped softly as a wave of pleasure encompassed her, and then again as the velvet sensation slitted out into her limbs.

The hand cupping her shoulder tightened possessively. His tongue traced the inner softness of her lips, the edges of her teeth, then gradually grew rougher, more unrestrained. Merritt heard him murmur her name endearingly, and then became progressively aware of little else except the taste of him, the gentleness of his touch, the mastery of his kiss, and the changing pressure of his lips. One minute he was coaxing, the next demanding, and the inadvisability of the place only added to the allure. When he moved back at last, as if to draw away, Merritt's hands curled into his lapel. "Don't stop," she whispered imploringly against his tantalizing mouth.

With a groan, Tom shifted her back into his embrace. He kissed her aggressively, as if no longer caring what anyone else might say or think, as long as she knew how he felt—enamored. She received his caresses blissfully, moaning softly, running her hands across his chest to his arms, to his waist. Tangling his hands in her hair, he crushed her against him, demanding incessantly until she was returning his kisses with equal abandon. Her senses were spiraling when he released her minutes later. His breath was ragged against her hair, his mouth hot and open against her neck. "I think," he said slowly and with great effort, "we had better get you home." He sighed reluctantly, straightening. "Either that, or risk being here all night."

Merritt wished fervently the embrace had not happened there, that they had not been forced to stop because of a lack of privacy or poor timing. She wanted to be loved again, before she had time to think of all the reasons why she shouldn't be. More, she wanted to love someone in return. But Tom was right, they did need to leave. "I think you're right." Shakily Merritt moved back into her seat.

His laughter filled the warmth of the car. "Don't look so crestfallen," he murmured, reaching across the console to give her another quick kiss. "This isn't anything that can't be continued later, that is if you're still sure it's what you want." Their eyes met. She thought she had never seen such tender concern in a man's eyes. "But I want you to think about it first," he added gently, "and make absolutely sure you're doing what's right for you."

Merritt sighed. Perhaps he knew her better than she thought.

It was sleeting heavily as Tom guided his car onto the street. Swearing eloquently beneath his breath, Tom switched first to the weather, and then eventually the police station on his shortwave radio. "Do you mind?" He shot her a quick glance, tuning it in.

"That probably is a good idea." Merritt forced a smile. Inside, she felt like a huge chunk of ice, tossed right back into the shivering deep freeze.

Moments later, a multicar pileup was reported on the interstate. Tom glanced at the street signs, and then at his watch. "With traffic the way it is, they're going to have a devil of a time getting rescue units in. I'm gonna have to swing on over and lend a hand." He slanted her another concerned glance. "I'd offer to drop you off first, but there isn't time. And there's no telling what they're dealing with there. You'll have to wait in the car."

Merritt nodded.

When they arrived, the prognosis was very bad.

Seven cars had been involved in the pileup, and only one squad car had managed to slice through the congestion. Traffic was backed up for miles, visibility was only a few feet. The injured were being removed from the tangled wreckage, taking cover wherever possible, from whomever was willing to help. Tom parked his Camaro on the shoulder, then, badge in hand, strode forward to assist.

For a moment Merritt stayed in the car, fighting the memories and the darkness of the night, the fear inherent in reliving any similar scene. And then reaction took over. She pushed from the car, moving forward to help.

A two-year-old had been thrown against the dash. His face was cut and bleeding. Once the child was lifted from the car, Tom nixed the idea of laying him on the gasoline-soaked ground. His small coat-covered limbs were already turning blue from the numbing cold. His mother was unconscious, her face and arms badly abraded. Tom knelt over the small boy, checking for injuries, accepting with thanks the blanket another person proffered. He swiveled when he saw Merritt, and wrapped the small child up in her arms. "Merritt, take the child back to the car. Turn on the motor and the heater full blast."

Merritt concurred, protesting as she cradled the small motionless form to her chest. "But—"

"To move him's a risk, granted. To leave him out in the weather is to guarantee shock and a trauma-related death."

Merritt moved obediently in the direction of the car. The boy was light. It was easy enough to lay him gently across the seats. Her winter coat added to the child's warmth. She sat with him until the rescue squad arrived. The paramedics agreed with Tom's decision as they moved the boy onto the stretcher.

Merritt nodded. The rescue efforts continued. With

the boy gone, she got out of the car, stood shivering and leaning against the front of it. More people were transported by ambulance. Miraculously, only a quarter of them were seriously hurt, most had been saved by securely fastened shoulder straps and seat belts, according to Tom. Wreckers and fire trucks arrived and the three-lane pileup was slowly cleared. Through it all Tom remained calm, authoritative, in perfect command. Merritt admired his devotion and expertise. She resented like hell the memories it brought back. Eric, craving the excitement of the night and the dangerous city streets. Eric, foolishly insisting he stay with a job the income from which they no longer needed.

And it was then Tom pivoted and strode slowly back to the squad car in front of her, reaching into the open window to grab the squawking radio microphone. Then someone called his name, and again he turned, looking back over his shoulder in the direction of the low male voice.

Memories Merritt had sought to bury for years came rushing back. The night exploded with sirens she heard only in her mind, a sudden telltale blast, a vision she had dreamed repeatedly but only witnessed by other people's pieced-together accounts, and then all was treacherously still, black.

Tom's voice drifted reassuringly down through a haze of spiraling gray-and-black sky. Merritt felt herself being lifted into the warmth of the car. The bucket seat was snapped back into recline. "I think she'll be all right," Tom was saying in a soothing tone. "It was probably just the shock, the accident, caring for the boy. I probably shouldn't have asked her, but..."

"Who would have figured another car would have had a blowout on top of all that ice?" another man murmured.

"All that glass," said a third. "Shattered from here to..."

Eventually, Merritt became aware of something hot being pressed up against her lips. Tom was kneeling beside her, his arm around her shoulders. Around them, red lights of all sizes and heights continued to blink on the vast array of emergency vehicles. "Try and sit up a little," he soothed. "Take a sip or two of this coffee. See if that will help."

It burned her lips, then her tongue and throat. "I'm fine." Merritt struggled to sit up through the haze.

"Sure?" Tom's face lowered gently to hers. Worry etched fine lines around his eyes and mouth, lines that had not been there previously, even when handling the small injured child.

Merritt nodded weakly.

Tom gave her hand a quick squeeze. "Okay, hang on. They've about cleared this place out and we ought to be able to leave in another five or ten minutes. And then I'll get you home."

The door closed. Merritt shut her eyes, shivering against both the blast of cold wind that assaulted her face and the tears that ran unchecked from her eyes.

"You're still shaking," Tom observed as they walked into Merritt's darkened house. She turned to switch on a light, hoping he wouldn't notice the lines of the tears from her eyes. No such luck. He zeroed in on her distressed state almost immediately. With one hand he removed her coat. The other pushed her gently into a chair. The seat seemed to come up to greet the back of her knees. Merritt knew she was close to fainting again.

"Do you have any whiskey or brandy?" His voice came at her through a misty gray haze.

Merritt gestured vaguely. Tears misted her eyes. "Never mind. I'll get it."

He strode into the kitchen, switching lights on as he went. Seconds later he returned with a bottle of bourbon and a glass. Merritt blanched even more when she realized he intended the drink for her, not him. Since Eric's death, she had rarely allowed herself to drink, and never at home alone, fearing she would become even more depressed.

"No." She pushed the small tumbler of amber liquid away. "No." The liquor had been her husband's. "I don't want it."

Tom pushed it back. The steel in his voice matched the determined glint in his eyes. "You need it. Don't argue with me."

Because she had no wish to faint again, she sipped the liquor slowly. Tom knelt in front of the overstuffed chair. His eyes searched her face as if trying to make some sense of her heightened reaction that night. She was relieved to find he still seemed as mystified as before.

After a moment, still at a loss, he shook his head. "I'm sorry I asked you to help me tonight. I guess I should have known better, dragging a civilian into that mess." He raked a hand agitatedly through his hair. "If I'd known that sort of thing would have upset you so, I—"

"It wasn't the accident," she stated bluntly. She didn't want him blaming himself.

Tom's eyes were level with her own. "The child, then?" he guessed.

She knew she could never explain without recalling even more explicitly the events of Eric's death. And that would only distress her more. She finished the bourbon in a single gulp, gasped as the alcohol tore through her throat. Tears stung her eyes, but eventually the trembling in her arms and legs desisted. Still, she felt ridiculously weak and shaky. Determined to regain her composure, she held out her glass to him. "I'd like some more, please, if you wouldn't mind." If she'd been one hundred percent certain her legs would have supported her, she would have got it herself.

With another confused shake of his head, Tom got up, poured her some more, and then walked into the kitchen for a glass and some ice for himself. "Beginning to feel better?" he inquired, strolling back into the room.

"Yes."

They drank in silence. Aware of his gaze, Merritt shut her eyes and put a hand protectively to her brow. She prayed he wouldn't ask anything more. "Don't you have to get back to work?"

"I told them I would be taking you home. As it happens, enough volunteers are out now. Or at least for the rest of the night, unless it worsens considerably." He sighed. "I'll probably take another double shift tomorrow, guessing at what the roads will be like." Merritt opened her eyes to see him drain the last of his drink. "Motorists can't wait to get back out once it snows. Cabin fever. That results in a rash of wrecks it takes the Division of Motor Vehicles three months to untangle. Not to mention the rescuing and paperwork *we* get to do."

Merritt grinned weakly, crossing her legs. "Then think of the overtime pay."

Tom walked over, set his glass aside, and then removed the glass from her hand. "I'd rather discover what is taking the life out of you." His hand moved to twine with hers, and then he knelt beside the chair. "What happened out there tonight, Merritt? What was the real reason you became so upset, if not the child?"

Merritt pushed past the familiar warmth of his hand and stumbled to her feet. She'd expected to be in complete command of her surroundings; since sitting she had felt better. But as she leapt to her feet the world careened dizzily around her, as upsetting and undependable as before. His arms closed around her, to prevent her from falling. She reached out blindly for his chest, then hid her face in its solid warmth. "Don't interrogate me about this." Her voice was muffled against his coat.

Tom's hand stroked the wind-tangled mass of her hair. "All right," he said softly. They clung together several moments longer, her arms locked about his waist, his palms gently stroking her back. Merritt was never sure exactly when the quality of the embrace changed from one of comfort to desire. Only gradually did she become aware of the more caressing quality of his touch, the pronounced rise and fall of his chest as he took in unaccountably shallow breaths. A tremulous feeling had started deep inside her. Through the mists of latent hysteria and inhibition-robbing whiskey, the need to be loved strengthened, shutting out the dark memories of the past, confining her only to the moment, the man. She wanted to continue what they had started earlier, in the car.

Tom tenderly disengaged himself from her embrace. "If you're sure you're going to be all right now, I'd better go." He glanced humorlessly toward the door. Though clearly reluctant to leave, he didn't want to be accused later of taking advantage of a woman who was exhausted and upset.

"Please stay with me, at least for another hour or so." She met his gaze beseechingly, unwilling to tell him how much she feared being alone. As long as he didn't have to return to work, what reason was there for him not to stay?

"I think you ought to try and get some sleep, Merritt." His voice was harsh in the silence of the room. He wanted her. God, how he wanted her. But he couldn't even consider making love to her when she was that distraught.

"I wish it were that simple." She laughed tremulously, running a hand through her hair.

"It is that easy," Tom stressed deliberately, taking her arm in a firm grip and leading her toward the stairs. "With two glasses of whiskey in you all you have to do is go up and lie down. Sleep will come."

"You don't understand," she said as they reached the bannister. She pivoted to face him, leaning against the wall. "I suffer from insomnia," she said very low. "I've had trouble falling asleep since Eric died."

He looked stricken, as if maybe he shouldn't have recommended the alcohol. Wordlessly he dropped his grasp. She hated the sudden chill where his warmth had been. "I'm sorry. Do you have anything to take for it, any medicine?"

"No, I didn't want to risk developing a dependency on any drug. Unfortunately, that's not the worst of it." Her eyes fell to the faint trace of beard lining his chin, the column of his neck. "I have nightmares, bad ones."

"About Eric?" It hurt him to think she was still involved with her husband emotionally. And yet knowing her, he would have understood less if she hadn't grieved terribly.

"Sometimes I dream about Eric, sometimes not." Weariness overwhelmed her. She wondered how her life had gotten so complicated and so empty. "Half the time I can't even recall what I've dreamed. I simply wake screaming, shaking. If I go back to sleep immediately, they inevitably recur, so usually I read or work on lesson plans until I can forget. So you see, by staying, you won't be interrupting my rest. I wouldn't be getting any regardless."

He wondered how she could be so accepting of the misery life had dealt her. "Have you seen anyone about the insomnia?"

"I talked to my physician. He said the dreams were a result of stress and that they would probably slack off when I recovered from Eric's death."

"And have they?"

"For the most part, yes. Unless I'm overtired or overwrought."

"Like now."

"Yes."

Tom could feel the blood pounding through his veins. The mute appeal of her gaze reached out to him. She looked so fragile, so sad. "I still think you ought to rest," he said bluntly. If he stayed, there was no guarantee he'd be able to keep his distance physically.

"No."

He sighed, letting exasperation cover his susceptibility. "I'll go upstairs with you. It's either that or I'll call your physician," he threatened mildly when she still hadn't moved.

The resistance drained from her. "You don't leave me much choice, do you?" She took the lead resignedly and they moved to the bedroom on the second floor. Tom suspected that she had redone the master suite. It was decorated in a soft feminine style, all dusty rose silk and chiffon, and smelled faintly of the jasmine scent of her perfume. Despite his determination to remain sexually aloof, he could imagine her lying on the bed, draped in a negligee or sporting only his shirt or wearing nothing at all. The sensual images tormented him. He turned away, wanting only to escape before he took advantage of the situation and of her.

"Merritt, I shouldn't be here with you," he muttered roughly, as if furious with both her and himself. He glanced down at her through half-shuttered eyes. His conscience warred openly with his desire.

"Not even if I want you to be?" she whispered softly. The life-and-death atmosphere an hour before had reminded her of how very little time anyone really had. And she had wasted so much of her life the past two years, pining away for a man who would never return, would never love her again. And for what reason? Surely Eric would never have wanted that for her. "Stay with me, Tom, please."

Was he taking advantage of her? Tom couldn't tell. She looked as if she knew what she was doing and saying. Her words weren't slurred. She stood steadily on her feet. But the night had been traumatic for her. And she'd made it clear when they first met that she didn't make love with a man casually. No, he had better leave. He would hate himself in the morning, but at least he'd be able to live with what he'd done.

"Tom—" As if sensing his resolution, she moved slightly, blocking his way to the door. He swallowed, tension throbbing in his groin. She glided forward, wrapping her arms loosely about his shoulders. His hand laced through the thickness of her hair against her neck. He had meant to hold her back; he ended up holding her close.

"I don't know if my wanting you is right or wrong," she whispered softly. "Tonight I don't care. I just need to be held. Please don't deny me that. I've had so much taken from me, Tom, so much. Don't let me lose this, too." To her horror a lone tear began to slide down her cheek.

The show of emotion affected him like no seduction could ever have. He drew her close, wanting nothing more than to protect and cherish her as she deserved to be, if only for that one moment.

She stood on tiptoe, her lips brushing his in the first tentative contact. Her hands braced on his shoulders, she drifted languorously with the sensations he conjured with his mouth. He was sunlight in a world that had been dark for so long. He was reality. He was love. He was everything she had ever wanted. When she deepened the kiss she melted into him, letting her body show him all the pliant stirrings she felt. With a groan, he surrendered to her need, his palms aligning her more fully against him. They kissed again, each subsequent caress more fervent than the last, until Merritt was leaning against him, her every curve closely juxta-posed to his.

Pulses pounding, she reached over to shut off the ceramic light so she might see him only in the glow from the streetlights spilling into the room. The dark-ness made him seem even more formidable, the force of his masculinity making her catch her breath. She uttered a trembling sigh, afraid now, not of the past but of him, of being with a man again. He held her closer, letting her know it was all right, that he understood her fears, without saying anything. When he finally drew her back away from him, her heartbeat had slowed to a manageable rate. "You're clear on what you're doing," he said quietly.

"Yes."

She'd been guarded with him for so long, the knowledge she yearned for him so freely was exhilarat-ing. And yet he knew that craving, when combined with his own ardor could prove their destruction. The passion between them would be like a wildfire raging swiftly out of control. He hesitated, his thumb tracking her temple with light mesmerizing strokes. "Merritt, you're so beautiful. I don't think I could stop... once..."

"I understand." There was so much warmth flowing through her now it was hard to believe an hour earlier she'd been standing out in the sleet, watching them remove injured passengers from the wrecks, listening to the sirens and the crackle of a short-wave police ra-dio, the smell of spilled gasoline permeating the air. If he left, she knew the memories would come rushing back. "I want you to stay with all my heart, Tom. I want you to make love to me." She would worry about the possible ramifications of that act later, when everything wasn't so sad and frightening.

Tom broke the embrace and waltzed her backward

toward the bed. "I shouldn't be here," he said roughly, forcing her to sit down. The room spun with the unexpectedness of his actions. She clutched at his jacket, dragging him down with her. He lost his balance abruptly, stumbling forward, falling onto her, the bulk of his weight being concentrated on his forearms, which he placed against the mattress on either side of her. "Merritt, you don't know what you're doing," he said grimly, trying in vain to extricate her fingers from his lapel, but she tenaciously refused to uncurl them or relinquish her grasp.

"Yes, I do." For the first time in her life she was letting passion rule her actions, letting it erase the bitter memories of the past. "I need to be loved, Tom. Everyone does. Why is that wrong?" During the skirmish her skirt had twisted up past her knees. Having no answer for her question, he reached for the hem, intending to straighten her skirt and pull it down. From the moment he touched her soft, open thighs, he knew he was lost in a need every bit as blind and overwhelming as her own. His hand closed over her and she shifted slightly, moaning and whimpering deep in her throat. He stroked her reverently, then with growing agitation, his hands sliding up over her hips to her abdomen, and down again to the joining of her legs.

A thousand reasons crossed his mind as to why he should get out of there before hurting them both, but the feeling of her body pliantly ensconced under his persuaded him otherwise. He'd been lonely too since his divorce. And if the solace they sought in each other's body eased the despairing quality of her monastic existence the way it had eradicated his own.... Oh, God, why not admit it? he thought. He wanted her. He might even be falling in love with her. Certainly no woman had ever tangled up his emotions the way she had.

Slowly he unbuttoned her blouse and slid his hand

inside. He could feel the rapid beat of her heart, the
softness of her breasts. She was watching him, wide-
eyed, subdued. Waiting. Wanting. Cursing his own
weakness as well as admiring her dauntlessness, he unfastened the front clasp of her bra, drawing the material
aside. His palm closed over a blossoming peak, moved
over lightly to explore the twin crest. She groaned
softly at the contact, arching up into him until he felt
his loins were on fire. Her mouth was offered up to him
as the pressure of her hand on the back of his neck
brought his head slowly down to hers. As their lips met
the last of his cautious resolve fled. He wanted and
needed her as much as she seemed to need him.

His thighs pressed into hers. His hands slid beneath
her, cupping her to him, reveling in the crushable contours of her prone form. The moments spun out time-
lessly as she met him kiss for demanding kiss. Her
thoughts were lost to the passion infusing her, his to
the magic she created, the maelstrom of their passion.

They drew apart, watching one another mesmeri-
cally. It was understood then there was no going back,
neither of them wanted out. Neither was capable of resisting the turbulent forces that had thrown them together, nor the sweet lure of love that kept them locked
in an embrace.

Merritt removed his shirt. He removed her clothes,
then stood disrobing methodically as she peeled off her
own stockings. When they were both naked, they lay
together on the bed. His hands slid caressingly over her
hips, down her thighs, to the backs of her knees, the
curves of her calves, the slender bones of her ankles.
Shivering with sensation, she let her fingertips explore
his solid thighs. He encouraged mutely, stroking as she
stroked, kissing as she kissed, caressing and loving and
learning until she thought she would go wild with the
unassuaged ache deep inside her. With a groan he
caught her against him, burying his face in her hair. His

mouth invaded hers roughly, possessively, urging her to new, ardent heights.

"Tom, please—"

He gathered her to him gradually. She welcomed the plundering heat, the final joining, the merging of passions and hearts. Release came with blinding intensity. Tom shuddered against her, within her, then held her to him tenderly, his breath warm and real against her neck. Tears sliding from her cheeks, she clung to him, trembling, wanting the moment never to end. But of course she knew that like everything else, not only that it would, but that it must.

Tom traced the moisture on Merritt's face. She thought she'd never seen such gentle caring on anyone's face. "Did I hurt you?" he asked softly at last. A sigh rippled through him as lines of worry creased his brow.

They were lying against the pillows, Tom on his back, Merritt draped across his chest, her face buried in the crook of his arm. "No." She could smell his cologne mixing with the musty scent of their lovemaking and their perspiration. The fragrance was heaven to her love-starved senses. It had been so long since she'd been held, she thought, so terribly long. But it wasn't right to make love without commitment, not for her. And in that sense, she knew, she had done them both a disservice. Still, she didn't regret their passion. It would have been a lie to even try. "No, you didn't hurt me."

"Then why the tears?" He drew a finger down the tip of her nose to her chin to midchest. She tingled wherever he touched.

"It's been so long, I guess. The physical release—" She stammered and blushed. She didn't have to tell him how eagerly she'd responded, nor how fiercely she'd clutched him to her at the end.

He traced the last of her tears, restfully smoothing the moisture away. "Then you're over what you saw tonight. The wreck." He took a deep breath, adding tautly, "The trauma, the blood..."

"Tonight, yes." What she'd never be over was the memories the crisis had evoked. Sirens blaring in the night... the sound, like a gunshot, ripping out through the stillness... the black, keening despair that had followed.

She shuddered and he held her close, asking, very low, "Had you ever witnessed any similar tragedy?"

She shook her head. "Only one other life-and-death situation that occurred as a result of a traffic accident. I wasn't there when it happened; though. By the time I arrived, the victim had already been taken to the hospital." It had been Eric. "Only the police and the wreckers were left to clear the tragedy from the public road."

Tom sensed she didn't want to discuss it further. He drew her closer, his arm tightening around her protectively, as if he could shield her with his warmth. His lips brushed hers, then again, communicating both tenderness and renewed desire. "I want to hold you like this through the night."

But it didn't happen as he planned. Sometime later, Merritt woke to find him talking softly into the phone beside her bed. He had pulled on his jeans and was standing barefoot and bare-chested beside her window. One arm pulling back the drapes, he was gazing out into the snow-filled night. "Yeah, looks pretty bad out here, too. No, until they at least get the major roads cleared and salted I don't think I'll be able to move my car. But if you send someone with four-wheel drive over... Yeah, I'll be waiting for you. Thanks."

He turned, startled to see she was awake. "I'm sorry I woke you." He padded back to the bed. Kneeling on the carpeted floor, he drew a hand through her rumpled hair, pulling her near for a soft, meaningful kiss. He placed another kiss on her brow, then her temple.

"But the roads are pretty bad. Not much accumulation of snow yet—just a couple of inches, but it's solid ice underneath. A lot of people are stranded and the department needs all the extra hands it can round up."

"You're going in?"

"Yes." He didn't apologize for his dedication to his work. "I was awake anyway. I might as well be of some use."

He had been, more than he knew. He'd brought her out of her extended mourning and she appreciated it more than he would ever know. "Thanks for staying with me tonight."

"There are going to be a lot more nights like tonight," he promised.

Would there? Merritt felt a cold shiver of fear trickle down her spine. "Cops lead a dangerous life," she said evenly.

Tom paused, every fiber of him tensing with the casually uttered statement. "Does that bother you? You mentioned it once before."

Yes, Merritt wanted to shriek, *it upsets me more than you could ever possibly know.* "It's just that it never ends."

"What?"

"The crazy hours, swing shifts, dedication to helping people you don't even know." Some who didn't want and had never asked for your assistance.

"I guess sometimes it's a twenty-four hour a day job," Tom mused, glancing over at her. Though his eyes raked the sheet-draped length of her, Merritt sensed he was aware only of her sudden emotional withdrawal, her reflexive need to isolate herself from the intimacy they had just shared. He paused in the process of buttoning his shirt, reaching over to draw a finger up her arm, to the curve of her shoulder against the patterned sheets. "Merritt—"

"I'll make you some coffee before you go." Merritt

rose, belted on a robe. She needed to hang on to the memory, to cherish the moment for what it was, because deep in her heart she knew she would never allow their love affair to continue. The possibilities for getting hurt again were too great.

School was canceled the next morning because of the snowy and icy streets. Around eleven, a light snow began to fall, with several more inches predicted. Merritt had nothing to do except pace her small home, sip coffee, and lament over the lesson plans she was unable to complete and the papers yet to be graded. All were still at school. She strode to the window, watching thoughtfully as a snow plow and salt truck passed. Tom's car was still parked at the curb in front of her house. Her VW was in the driveway. Fifteen or twenty minutes of shoveling snow would clear the cement path enough to enable her to get her car out. The elementary school was only a few blocks away. Perhaps if she hurried, she could get there and back before even another full inch of snow was on the ground.

Hurriedly Merritt donned old jeans, a sweater, and heavy boots. She put on a parka, hat, mittens, and scarf, then started out the door. Grimly she studied the condition of the newly cleared street. Though it had just been salted, the going still looked treacherous. Merritt knew she should head on back inside, but the thought of being cooped up for a day without her papers spurred her on. She had to get her mind off Tom Hennessey. And the only way to do that was to work.

Once she'd cleared her car off and gotten it out of the drive, she found Halpin Avenue fairly easy to negotiate. The car only slipped twice, and both times Merritt was able to right the careening vehicle. The third time was not as easy. As she turned onto Alómar Drive the wheels suddenly, inexplicably, locked and the car slid sideways, oblivious of her attempts to right it. An oncoming Jeep just missed her, and still her car careened in a zigzag fashion over and down the next hill.

Merritt refused to give up. She jerked ferociously at the wheel, then tried stomping on the brakes. Too late, she realized; though the second road had been cleared, it evidently had not been salted, either earlier or moments before, and the new snow covering it had made it slicker still. The VW careened crazily down the incline, gathering speed with every foot of icy street. The car crossed to the opposite side and it sailed past a fire hydrant, jumped the curb, then finally ground to a halt at the base of a nearby tree.

At the impact, the maple sapling bent an obliging forty-five degrees. Merritt's head smacked against the wheel and then jerked sharply back. "Ouch! Damn!" Tears clouded her eyes and it was a minute before she could fully recover, another two before she could even remember how to unsnap the safety harness around her waist and get out of the car. The world tilted dizzily as she stood. Merritt paused, one hand on the roof of her car, while she waited for the vertigo to pass.

"Blast it all, anyway!" she swore, stomping forward with a determined shake of her head. But her ordeal wasn't over yet. In her agitation to inspect the damages, she slipped again on the icy sidewalk and bumped her forehead a second time against the open metal doorframe. If Mother Nature was trying to teach her a lesson, she decided ruefully, rubbing her forehead, she'd more than made her point!

"Are you all right?"

Merritt was dismayed to see a uniformed cop coming up from behind her. She swiveled to see the blue-and-white patrol car parked at the other side of the hill. The red lights were already flashing. "I'm fine." She swallowed, swaying uncertainly, wondering how much of the fiasco he had seen.

"I was right behind you all the way, about fifty yards

back." He grinned, shaking his head at her lack of driving skill. "You're supposed to turn into a skid, not away from it."

Merritt blushed. "I know. I panicked when my car began picking up speed as I . . . slid down the hill." Her fingers clutched the open car door tightly. What was the matter with her, anyway? It was over. She was safe. Her legs could stop shaking.

"Lesson number two," the cop continued, already scribbling down the number of her Ohio license plates. "Never brake on ice. That will only lock the wheels, especially as hard as you evidently hit them."

Merritt moaned silently, nodding. "Right." She glanced at her car, then at the pad in his hands. "Are you going to give me a ticket?" He probably had grounds for negligence at least or reckless driving. Not to mention stupidity for even venturing out.

"Lady, you're going to have enough trouble just paying for the damage to your car and that tree. Just hope those homeowners don't sue you for damage to their property. Do you belong to any of the auto clubs here in town?"

Merritt shook her head. On her salary, even that was too much a luxury to afford. Besides, before this, she'd never had so much as a flat tire.

"Well, then, I'll call in and see who I can get to come out." The cop smiled at her paternally and patted her on the shoulder. "Given the condition of the streets and all the fools out trying to drive, it may be a fairly long wait."

She accepted the prediction resignedly. "I'm not going anywhere."

The leather-jacketed cop was still radioing for a tow truck when the second patrol car came slowly down the hill. Just what she needed, Merritt thought miserably, face and hands already numb from the stinging cold. More of an audience. Her dismay increased mightily when she saw who got out of the car. Tom Hennessey, this time dressed in the regimental dark blues of the street cop. She'd never seen him in uniform before, and it was a mesmerizing experience. The dark color and clinging well-cut cloth made him look leaner. The set of his hat low over his brow, the gun on his hip, the badge and leather jacket covering his chest, made him a force to be reckoned with. More, he didn't look the least bit pleased to see her, and she could tell by the grim set of his mouth and his unrelenting stare he had recognized her on sight. Oh, glory.

Swiftly Merritt turned her back, leaning against the hood of her bashed-in car as if that would give her the strength to confront him. Maybe if she covered her face and pretended not to recognize him, she hoped unrealistically, he wouldn't insist on encountering her face to face.

"What the devil do you think you're doing out trying to drive in this?" His ferocious voice emanated from a distance of three feet away.

Merritt swallowed at the barely controlled derision in his words. She whirled to face him glibly. Because there was no reasonable defense for her foolhardiness, she ignored his question. "What are you doing in uniform?"

His jaw was rigid. He looked not the least bit appeased by her cordial tone. "It's customary when one drives a squad car. I'm required to be in uniform when I work in the streets. I keep a spare in my locker at the station."

"Oh. Well"—she took a deep bolstering breath—"you look nice." A bit gruff perhaps...

He stalked closer and rebuked her with a glittering stare. "I could care less how I look right now, Merritt Reed, and you know it." His expression was implacable as he continued, very low, "And you didn't answer my question. What are you doing out in this kind of weather?"

No one had ever spoken to her in such a censuring tone in all her adult life. His superior attitude fired her temper. She snapped back acrimoniously, "What does it look like I'm doing?"

Frosty flakes of snow were accumulating on the bill of his visor. Hands loosely circling his hips, he bit back a smugly amused grin. "Wrecking your car. Waiting for a tow truck. And cold-bloodedly murdering someone else's tree."

His lampoon infuriated her. Unfortunately, she knew it was true. She had crushed that poor maple...

"Did Joe issue a citation?" he asked gently, his anger dissipating in the chill air.

"No." Embarrassed, Merritt glanced away. People were peering out of the windows of their houses. More were donning coats and coming out to act as spectators in an ever unfolding drama. Weariness swamped her. "How did you know I was here?" More to the point, she wondered, how often did Tom work the streets? When they'd first met, he told her he was simply a detective, investigating routine occurrences.

He rubbed a hand tiredly across the back of his neck. She realized abruptly he couldn't have had more than two or three hours sleep at the very most, if that. Shadows beneath his eyes emphasized his fatigue. "I was at the station house when the call came in for a wrecker and assistance. They gave out your license plate and name." He exhaled his disappointment raggedly, shifting closer, his voice confidentially low. "What on earth prevailed you to be so dumb? I thought I made it clear to you last night that this is the one thing a civilian should not be doing."

His censuring words, no matter how quietly issued, intensified the dull ache behind her eyes. "Enough," Merritt ground out irritably. "So I acted stupidly. It wasn't the first time I've been impulsive and I hardly think it will be the last. I don't know what you're so upset about, anyway! It's not as if you have to pay for it!" He was acting like an irate husband, for heaven's sake, as if he had some claim to her.

Her words struck a chord, a wrong one. He moved closer, his eyes sparking with more fury and emotion than Merritt had ever seen him display. His frosty breath punctuated the air with every tersely gritted syllable. "It is not enough! Don't you realize you could have been killed if you hadn't been wearing a seat belt? For that matter you could have killed someone else, a child playing on the streets—God knows there are enough of them out here with sleds!—another motorist, yourself! Damn it, Merritt, wasn't the tragedy we saw last night on the interstate enough?"

Merritt paled. She knew the frustrations cops worked under, the fatigue Tom had to be dealing with. And he was right. She hadn't had any business to be out driving on the slick streets once the travelers' advisory had been issued.

"I'm sorry. But I worry about you. Can't you understand that? I care about what happens to you."

Her heart soared with the confession. But before she could say more, Joe was intervening, shouting, "Hey, Hennessey! The wrecker's here!"

Tom lifted a hand in acknowledgment. "Thanks, Joe!" He turned back to Merritt, moved closer, one arm touching her arm lightly. He seemed to be very conscious of both his uniform and the gathering crowd. Tilting her head back with a light, leather-gloved hand under her chin, he examined her face. "Are you all right? You look pale. What's that bump on your forehead?"

Swiftly Merritt brushed her feathery bangs over the painful bruise. "Nothing. I just bumped my head a little when I was getting out of the car, that's all." Her jaw jutted out stubbornly. She refused to admit to the jolt of the crash after the chastisement he had just issued. If the bruise still hurt when she got home, she'd call Blanche. "Ouch!" She recoiled angrily when he tried to inspect the bruise.

Tom frowned, handing the clipboard of accident reports to the other cop working the sectioned-off street. "That settles it. You're going to the hospital."

"I am not." She drew herself up to full height, reaching just to the bridge of his nose. "I hate emergency rooms."

"Tough." He started to take her arm, but she shrugged out of his grip.

He grimaced, warning, "Merritt, that lump on your head has to be checked out. Head injuries are nothing to be scoffed at."

"You're overreacting."

"Am I?" he questioned, his deep sensuous voice sending shivers down her spine. His eyes probed her relentlessly and she tingled even more. Despite everything, their night together had been a moment she'd remember the rest of her life. "I suppose there's only one way to find out." His hand cupped her chin and sensations darted between them like red-hot sparks. *He's a cop,* she reminded herself firmly. Life-threatening danger was a part of his everyday life. Eric's death had almost destroyed her. As much as she wanted to, she couldn't risk it happening again. She couldn't let him get closer to her than he already was.

"Thank you, no," she refused firmly, fire flashing in her defensive gaze. She swallowed at the disarming smile he sent back, adding, "My health is my responsibility, not yours."

"Want to bet?" Both hands clasped his waist.

"Tom—" She took an uneasy step back, dismayed to find the VW at her back, trapping her escape.

"You're going, Reed, if I have to sling you over my back, haul you to the squad car, and strap you in myself!" he gritted between clenched teeth.

He meant it. Her heart racing, Merritt regarded him

with belligerent silence. Not even Eric had ever dared
try and tell her what to do. The second cop cleared his
throat and turned to the gathering crowd, explaining,
"Uh...they're evidently...old friends."

"New friends," Merritt corrected, never taking her
eyes from Tom's face. She had never seen him so in-
domitable. Part of her was thrilled he cared; the other
part felt only annoyed at his macho surveillance. Did
he think she was incapable of taking care of herself?
Was he setting a precedent, trying to show her who was
boss? If so...there was only one way to nip that in the
bud, and that was to treat him as patronizingly as he
was treating her.

Tom was still waiting for her to make up her mind.
"Well, what's it going to be? Do I carry you to the
squad car or do you walk?"

"Neither!"

He sighed, looking chagrined. She could tell he
wasn't relishing the idea of a scene. "I'm not going,
Hennessey, so forget it."

"Think again, sweetheart."

Her gasp of protest was choked off as Tom picked
her up into his arms and, turning, stalked steadfastly
toward the patrol car. Unless she wanted to make even
more of a spectacle of herself than she already had, she
had no choice but to encircle his neck with her clasped
hands. "Bully," she muttered beneath her breath,
unable to help but notice how warm and solid his chest
was against her breast.

"When it comes to your well-being, you're damn
right," he agreed. "And just so you know, I'm en-
rolling you in that defensive driving class at the first
available opportunity. You're taking it, like it or not."

There was no arguing with his tone. Merritt fell silent. Once in the car, she closed her eyes. Drowsiness
overcame her as he drove and peace reigned between
them once again.

The hospital emergency room was understandably

crowded. Tom sipped coffee and leaned against the wall wearily as they waited for Merritt to be seen. An examination revealed a mild concussion and whiplash. Muscle relaxants were prescribed for the latter, the care for the former was discussed. "Even in minor concussions such as Ms. Reed's, I don't like the patient to be alone for the first twelve to twenty-four hours," the white-coated resident determined. "On the other hand, there's really no reason to admit you, if you can find someone to stay with you, watch for any dizziness, nausea, confusion, a severe headache, or pain."

"It's no problem, I'll stay with Merritt," Tom generously volunteered. The resident shot him an amazed glance. "We're more than just rescuer and rescuee," Tom informed dryly, indicating his patrolman's garb.

"Oh." The doctor nodded discreetly, handed her a written prescription and diagnosis, insurance forms, then indicated the way out.

"You've got a lot of nerve," Merritt chided grumpily after they'd signed all the appropriate forms and left. Her headache was still raging, and she felt faintly sick to her stomach. She didn't want to be with him if she was going to throw up.

"I've also got the rest of the day off, since I worked all day yesterday and most of the night. Don't be stubborn, Merritt. You need someone to help you and it might as well be me." He guided her out of the emergency room, toward the parking lot and patrol car beyond. "Besides that, I want to do it. I will have to go back to the station house, though, clock out officially, and drop off this car. Artie's agreed to meet us there. If it's all right with you, he'll drive us back to your house. We can stop off at my place on the way. I'll pick up a change of clothes, my shaving gear."

What could she say? He seemed to have everything all planned out. And she didn't have any way to get back home, other than to call a cab. And in this weather she knew there would be none available. "All right," she acquiesced finally. Her hand clasped his briefly. "Thanks."

He drew her near, his fingers clasping her upper arm, and bestowed a tender kiss on first her lips, then the fluff of bangs covering her bruised temple. His eyes glowed down at her with a soft, protective light. "Oh, Merritt," he whispered, relief sweet in his voice, "don't you realize there isn't anything I wouldn't do for you after what happened between us last night?"

She was beginning to. Wordlessly she let him hug her to him. They stood clasped together only momentarily, but it was long enough to send adrenaline pumping through her heart and tears of joy glistening from her eyes.

Artie and Tom discussed the major accidents, fires, and weather-related catastrophies as Art drove them from the station house to Tom's apartment, then to Merritt's. The snow had halted temporarily, with only an additional inch and a half accumulation. The streets were still treacherous, though, and Merritt felt only relief when they arrived at her house and let themselves in. Art came in for coffee, then left almost immediately to go back to work.

"You look exhausted," Tom observed softly. "Why don't you go on upstairs and rest? I'll wash up these dishes and then check to see where they've towed your car."

Too tired to argue, she went up to her bedroom, kicked off her shoes, and lay down on her bed. She must have fallen asleep almost immediately, because the next thing she knew it was almost dark and Tom was sitting on the edge of the bed. "How are you feeling?" he asked gently.

Merritt groaned, a hand adjusting the heating pad under her neck. "Stiff."

Tom produced the muscle relaxants the doctor had prescribed and a glass of water. He watched concernedly as she swallowed a pill. "Better?" he asked anxiously as she lay back down.

Merritt laughed weakly. "Give the medicine a chance to work."

"Sorry." He clasped his hands nervously between his thighs. "I've just been worried about you."

She shaded her eyes with her hand. She knew she must look a mess. Maybe that was what he needed, though, to see her at her worst. Maybe then he wouldn't be so romantically inclined. And she wouldn't be so dangerously close to throwing caution to the wind and loving him anyway, with all her soul and heart. Somehow, she managed a droll tone. "Save your worry for my car." And how she was going to manage to pay to have it fixed.

"I've got a friend who owns a body shop nearby," Tom offered, glad for the chance to be useful. "If you want, I could call and see if they'll repair the alignment, front fender, and dented side. Their rates are reasonable. And I can vouch for their work."

"Would you?" Her insurance company would account for all but the deductible, she knew. And it was imperative the VW be repaired as soon as possible.

"It would be my pleasure."

When Tom went downstairs to make the calls Merritt got up, feeling only slightly disoriented, and went to the bathroom. A glance in the mirror confirmed her suspicions. She did look pale and exhausted. Sick or not, she decided, there was no reason for her to look that bad.

Tom spent the next forty-five minutes on the phone counteracting all the damage Merritt had incurred when she wrecked her VW. Finished, he took the stairs quickly, and strode down the hall, anxious to share the results with her. "Merritt?" he called lightly, ambling into the room as casually as if he spent time there every day.

He halted dead in his tracks as she emerged from the bath. Her face was flushed from the steamy air. She was wearing a fluffy robe that brought out the deep blue of her eyes and some sort of white lacy gown beneath that. Her hair was twisted and pinned up loosely on the back of her head, tendrils escaping around her face. He thought he'd never seen her looking more beautiful or more vulnerable. Desire stirred deep within him, making him forget what he'd been about to say.

"I thought maybe a bath would help me feel better." Her voice was soft, melodious, but she faced him with all the wariness of a child caught out of school. He wanted to cradle her close in his arms until the haunted look in her eyes dissolved, but something frantic in her expression kept him at arm's length. He realized she was half-afraid of him physically as well, and that dampened his ardor as well as his spirit. Was she regretting the fact they'd made love? Or just afraid he'd try to approach her again?

Tom could smell the sweet jasmine of her perfume, and it stirred his senses pleasurably. "Did it make you feel better?" His tone was matter-of-fact, as was his expression, but inwardly he was remembering the glow of her naked skin, the way it had felt beneath his hands, the cries that had sounded deep and low in her throat when she'd reached fulfillment, the fierce way she'd clung to him then and trembled afterward.

"Yes. I feel much better." She smiled, breaking into his thoughts. "I was going to come downstairs for a while. I hate to think of you sitting there all alone. It's not exactly the greatest way to spend your time off."

"It's no sacrifice, believe me." His voice was husky with the irony. "There's no place I'd rather be right now." She flushed, and he paused, wondering how to put her at ease. "Are you hungry?" He didn't think she'd had much to eat or drink for several hours.

"Yes," she admitted cheerfully, as if surprised by her own recuperative powers. She brushed past him, leading the way toward the hall. "You must be starved. I don't know what I've got downstairs in the kitchen, though. I hadn't planned on getting snowed in or having company, so I'm afraid it will be strictly potluck."

When they reached the stairs, he placed his hand steadyingly on her waist. Though she didn't verbally acknowledge his touch, she leaned into his grip slightly, as if grateful for the support. Once in the kitchen, she sat down almost immediately, explaining when he sent her a quizzical glance, "I'm still a little wobbly on my feet if I'm up too long, or walk too far. It's okay, though, it's just a slight dizziness. To be expected for a day or so." He frowned and she reached up to release the barrette holding her hair, smoothing the tresses slightly with her fingers as it cascaded down around her face and shoulders. She yawned, looking drowsy again. "I think there's some canned soup in the cupboard and half a loaf of French bread from the bakery in the freezer."

Tom didn't like the imminently fragile way she looked. "I think I can manage here. Why don't you go in and curl up on the sofa?"

"You're sure?"

"Yes."

She left and he sighed in relief. His desire for her had been making it very hard to concentrate on anything but Merritt. He'd never needed or wanted a woman the way he wanted her. He had to keep reminding himself she was in no shape for lovemaking, either physically or emotionally. It was too soon. *Face it,* he thought, amused by his own never-ending concern, *you're falling in love with Merritt Reed.* She was in his thoughts, day and night. Making love to her had surpassed any physical liaison he'd ever experienced. His only regret was that they'd begun their intimacy so impulsively. He'd needed more time alone with her, both before and after. And now, he was afraid he'd lost more ground with her than if he'd never given in to her needs and his desires and touched her at all, because there was something different in the way she looked at him now, something wary and untrusting and afraid. He didn't know what he'd done to cause it. He didn't know how to correct it. He only knew in her presence he felt as tongue-tied and fumbling as an adolescent boy, and twice as anxious to please. More, she was capable of making him more furious than any woman ever had in his life.

Methodically he prepared the meal, then carried the tray into the living room. Merritt had very nearly drifted off to sleep while watching the news. She sat up when he entered, and made a valiant attempt to spoon up the soup he'd prepared. He swallowed several spoonfuls, more interested in watching her than in what he was putting in his mouth. How could she look so beautiful, he thought, so soft and warm and cuddly, after all she'd been through?

"I heard you on the phone earlier," she said. "What were you able to find out about my car?"

"It's been taken to a holding compound for the moment, but it will be towed to Hank's body shop in the morning. They'll have it for you in two to three days. I also talked to the property owners. They've agreed not to sue for damages to their yard if you'll replace the tree you bashed in as soon as the weather permits next spring."

She exhaled in relief. "I don't know how to thank you for everything you've done. I guess I didn't act that way at first, though. I'm sorry if I made you angry at the scene of the crash."

He felt the blood rush to his ears as he remembered his own volatile actions. If anyone at headquarters found out about the way he'd first bullied her into going with him, and then carried her to his patrol car in front of a crowd of spectators, no less, he'd be in for the razzing of his life, not to mention a refresher course from his superiors in basic procedure. "I overreacted myself, par for the weather and the day, I guess." He rubbed at the crease in his pants, admitting more honestly, his voice low, "When I heard you'd been in that wreck today, well, let's just say I had a bad moment or two." He had panicked. If her condition had not been reported as relatively unscathed, he would have torn the city apart trying to get to her. As it was, it had been a tense ten minutes as he'd driven across the precinct, and he'd prayed fervently for her safety and health the whole time. For the first time he knew what she might have felt when her husband died. If Merritt had loved him, half as much as he cared for her now, it was no wonder it had taken her a long time to get over his death.

"I'm sorry I worried you." She glanced up at him sheepishly, but the glint in her eyes said she was pleased he had been concerned. Abruptly she put her hand to her forehead and drew in her breath.

"Headache again?" he asked.

She nodded. Paleness overwhelmed her face. There were lines of strain around her mouth. "I think," she decided carefully, "I had better get back to bed."

"Does it help to lie down?"

"Yes. It's even better if I can go to sleep."

"Can you walk that far?" He wished she'd let him carry her or do something. He felt so helpless, standing there, watching, knowing she was in pain. "If you're dizzy—"

"Thank you, but I think I can manage." She forced a smile. Nonetheless, one hand loosely encircling her waist, he strolled her as far as her bedroom door. "I'll check on you later," he said. "And don't worry about the kitchen. I'll straighten that and do the dishes for you."

He raced through the kitchen chores, then paced the living room floor silently through the duration of a situation comedy. An hour later he went up to check on her. She was sleeping so soundly his heart pumped. *Oh, God,* he thought, panicking, *please let her be okay.* "Merritt," he coaxed gently, sitting down on the edge of the bed beside her, pressing the back of his hand against her cheek. He was relieved to feel the breath moving in and out of her at regular intervals. "Wake up, sweetheart."

She groaned and rolled over into the covers away from him. "I'm too tired to talk to you now, Tom. Go away," she demanded irritably.

He knew by her highly irascible tone she was as fine as anyone who had been awakened from a sound sleep. He nearly laughed out loud in his elation. "I can't. I have to ask you a few questions."

"At this time of night?" she asked sleepily, rubbing her eyes. "Ouch!" She put a hand to her head as she started to rise. "What time is it?"

"Nine." He reached around behind her and gently positioned the pillows behind her head. He'd never been one for sickrooms, but he had to admit he was enjoying this experience—as nerve-racking as it was—to the hilt.

"In the morning?" she commanded groggily, looking toward the drawn drapes and softly glowing lamp.

"Now."

She groaned and lay back down on the pillows. "I know what the doctor said, but this is ridiculous. Really, I'm fine."

"Then it won't hurt to check," he insisted firmly.

She bristled, clapping her hand back over her

temple. "If this keeps up, I'll never live through the night."

"What street do you live on?"

Without opening her eyes, she intoned sarcastically, "Easy Street. Now can I go back to sleep?"

He tensed slightly, not sure whether she was teasing or really confused. If it were the latter, it could be serious. "Merritt, I'm not playing games with you. I need some straight answers."

She sighed. Her eyes blinked open. She looked at him, amazingly alert. "Okay. Halpin Avenue is the name of this street." Behind the dull throbbing of her temples was a feeling more urgent coming to the fore. Didn't Tom know how sexy he looked with the top few buttons of his uniform shirt undone? she thought. His nearness set her heart to pumping adrenaline into her bloodstream at an astounding rate.

"Two more questions, then I'll let you go back to sleep, I promise. What's your last name?"

"Reed." She wanted to touch him. As ill-advised as it was, she wanted him to sleep right there beside her, crawl beneath the covers with her and cradle her close to his chest. But he wasn't even smiling now, and she knew their distance was really for the best.

"What do you do for a living?"

"Teach sixth grade."

"Remedial students?"

"Gifted. That was a trick question, and three queries, not two," she reproached huskily.

He grinned, relaxing, and returned her surveyal with a bold narrowing of his eyes. The lace of her gown flared innocently up around the slim column of her throat. He could see her nipples outlined against the sheer cloth. *When you're well again,* he promised silently, *I'm going to make love to you until you writhe against me, whispering my name.* "I guess you're still in full command of your mental faculties," he assessed at last.

"Knowing me, would you have expected anything less?" she retorted spiritedly. He thought not.

Tom went back every hour or so thereafter, keeping check on her through the night. Just before seven the next morning, he woke her one last time. Not because he had to, but because he wanted her to know he was leaving, and he wanted to say good-bye.

Merritt rolled over, placing her head under the pillow as if for protection. "If you ask me my name, address, and place of birth—or anything else related to my life—one more time, Thomas Hennessey, I am going to scream," she warned.

He laughed huskily, resting his hand on his chin. "I promise. No more questions."

Merritt removed the pillow and sat up, running a hand through her sleep-tousled hair. The motion pressed her breasts unknowingly against the thin cloth. With difficulty he tore his eyes away and back to her face. Somehow he kept his hands to himself. To touch her then, after such a night, would be to resign himself to convincing her to make love with him regardless of the complications later. And if he did that now, he'd lose her for sure.

"How are the roads?" Merritt asked, stifling a yawn.

"Better—no school, though," he admitted. "How do you feel?"

"Much better." She gave him a sunny smile.

"I'm glad." God, he wished he could stay.

"Are you leaving?" She glanced at his sport coat and tie.

He nodded. "I've got to get to work."

"Regular shift?"

"Yes." A frown crossed his face. "You seem to know a lot about the way I work." Either that or she was extraordinarily intuitive and accepting.

"I knew someone once who was a cop," Merritt said

lightly, glancing back at the clock beside her bed. He sensed she wanted to get up, but wouldn't until he had departed. He stood reluctantly. "Is there anything you need or would like me to bring you, since you're temporarily housebound without a car?" He didn't think she needed to see the doctor again, she looked so much better, but if she did, he would see to that, too.

Merritt shook her head. "No, I—I'm fine." She looked as if she wanted to say more, but didn't.

"You're sure?" Tom studied her silently. Merritt nodded. He leaned forward to brush her brow in a good-bye kiss. She drew back slightly, tense again. "I'll be in touch," he said. And then he left.

Chapter Four

Artie Kochek was drinking coffee behind Tom's desk when Tom entered his office. "Hey, pal, that was some rescue you orchestrated yesterday afternoon." Art grinned, clasping his hands behind his head as he continued. "Quite the talk of the station house, the way you carried her off in your arms."

Women were the source of much clever repartee around the station. Tom didn't want Merritt's name bandied around. He grimaced, tension snaking through his frame. "Knock it off, Kochek."

Artie grinned, crumpling his used paper cup and tossing it into the trash. "Hey, you know I didn't mean anything by it," he apologized seriously. He studied his friend complacently. "So, it's that serious."

For him, yes, Tom thought. The trouble was, he didn't kow how Merritt felt. Clearly she needed a man in her life, someone to love who could and would love her back, but did she really want it to be him? Or had he just been a convenient stopgap along the way, someone with whom to vent a lot of pent-up emotion and sexual desire?

Art was still watching him smugly, waiting for him to reply. Tom sent him a warning glare. "I'm not in the mood for this, Kochek."

Art held up both palms in surrender and sauntered out.

"Sorry I brought it up. She seemed nice enough, I'll admit, though how anyone, however great looking, could make a macho guy like you lose his head, I'll never know."

That was Artie, Tom thought, always having to speak the last word. Sighing, Tom walked over to pour himself a cup of coffee. Merritt was holding back on him, holding out. He knew she needed time, she'd made that very clear from the first. Strangely he found himself unwilling to give it. He sensed giving her even another week alone would mean her return to total self-sufficiency. It pained him to admit just how much he didn't want the barriers coming back up between them, barriers that he had just begun to tear down. But he wasn't sure what to do about it, or how to proceed, and that bothered him even more. Merritt was an enigma. And she didn't seem to want that to change.

The day passed slowly in a nightmare of traffic reports, weather-related deaths, and trivia to follow up on. By seven that evening Tom was chomping at the bit. The fact that Merritt was not answering her phone added to his unease. Tortured by his concern for her, he drove to her house immediately after work. He needed to see her. He needed to make love to her again, to make sure what they had shared had been as meaningful for her as it had been for him.

Darkness had fallen in Hyde Park. A two-inch layer of snow glistened in the yellow glow of streetlights and the scent of burning wood filled the air. Merritt was the only person out on the street. She was bundled up and shoveling snow from her front walk and steps.

As Tom parked against the curb, incensed she had been so indifferent to the state of her own health, Merritt froze. Abruptly she looked as nervous and unsure of everything as he felt.

"This some sort of new therapy for whiplash?" His

voice cut the silence between them as he approached her.

Merritt forced a smile, looked at the ground, then away. "Cabin fever," she admitted, resisting his probing gaze. "You know how it is when you're cooped up in the house all day."

Tom had felt precisely the same way at the office, but it had nothing to do with the winter storm that had forced them indoors. "Here"—he strode toward her authoritatively—"let me do that for you."

She held the shovel closer to her chest, instead of relinquishing it. "No, Tom, really, I can—"

"Too late." He cut her protestations short with a shake of his head. The shovel was already adeptly in his hands. He made short work of the chore Merritt had been fussing at, but she didn't look as if she appreciated his intervention. He was annoyed by her lack of gratitude, puzzled as to what he had done to incur her wrath.

"Thanks." She dug the toe of her boot into the piled-up snow next to the walk.

From the moment he'd seen her that first day at school, he'd known she was an exceptionally capable woman—beautiful, accomplished, wonderful with children. Later, listening to her discuss John's problems, he was filled with admiration for her dedication and skill. Finding out she'd been married before hadn't been as much relief as torture, though it had explained a lot about her nearly virginal reserve. He hated to think of her with another man. He hated to think she might still be in love with her husband's memory, might always be, or that she would never feel as deeply about anyone else as she'd felt about Eric. Eric...

Tom turned up his collar against the cold, wishing fervently she'd ask him in. "I assume all this activity means you're feeling better now."

"Yes." She moved restlessly, shivering and stomping the snow off her boots.

"Got any plans for this evening? Anything I can help you with?" He met her eyes directly, hoping to communicate his concern for her.

"As a matter of fact, this is only a temporary break," Merritt begged off reluctantly. "A friend of mine dropped off some papers from school. I have lesson plans to prepare, papers that need to be graded."

So, she didn't feel up to company. He supposed he could wait another day or two to be alone with her, as disappointed as he was. "I see." He nodded agreeably, not wanting to push her too fast or too hard. "Tomorrow night, then."

"I'm sorry, Tom, I—" Floundering, Merritt glanced at the layer of white shimmering on the leaveless limbs above.

Her clumsy lies infuriated him. If she had a grievance, if he'd done or said something, why didn't she just say it? He found himself delivering an ultimatum before he had time to think. "If you don't want to see me again, Merritt, just say it." His tone was as bored as he could make it.

Merritt winced, as if he'd struck her. "All right." She straightened, retrieving her shovel. "If you want the truth, I'd rather not." She met his gaze in the most honest exchange of the night. Never had she been more remote.

Tom swallowed. It felt as if the wind had been suckerpunched out of his gut. He'd expected a confession, a tearful list of recriminations maybe, but never this. "You're going to have to explain that one to me."

For a second his stunned tone seemed to penetrate her defenses. But the next instant all the barriers were up. She was glacial widow, hiding behind years of hurt—hurt he had done nothing to inflict. "I don't owe you anything," she said icily, apparently having taken exception to his sardonic glance, "except maybe thanks and a return favor or two for all your help the past couple of days regarding my health and my car." Her stormy glare reminded him she hadn't asked for anything of him, he had volunteered, and so willingly.

Merritt looked miserably at the ground, battling the tears that threatened to overtake her at any minute. She'd made such a mess out of everything, first turning to him and encouraging his affections when she knew a relationship between them would never work. Now she was falling in love with him, and he seemed to have some sort of macho, possessive feelings about her, and it was only going to get worse as time went on. After worrying about it all day she'd decided to end it now, as cleanly and simply as possible, because there was no way, once she started depending on Tom, she'd ever get over losing him. She'd barely recovered from Eric's death, and he'd never stirred in her the passion Tom had evoked. She'd adapted a hard tone because it was her only defense against his analyzing gaze. Much more of his gentle prodding, and she knew she would crumple. She'd do whatever he asked, even take him into her home and her heart. "Look, Tom, I...we made love. Albeit a little rashly, but it was...nice..." Her fumbling explanations were only making it worse.

"Nice?" he echoed, chagrined. "We make love for the first time and it was merely...nice?"

"Well, what do you want me to say? That I saw sky-rockets and stars?" Which would have been, she admitted inwardly, a much more accurate description.

Tom's jaw had stiffened, but his eyes mirrored the depth of his hurt. "I'm sorry." She sighed, penitent again, placing a mittened hand to her brow. The whole exchange was making her temples throb. "It's just that I'm not ready yet to get heavily involved with a man. I thought I had made that clear."

"With me?" Tom found himself asking bitterly, abruptly recalling her initial reaction to his choice of professions. "Or just a cop, any cop?"

Merritt didn't want to deny it. "If you want the truth, Tom, all right. I don't want to become romantically involved with a cop." Maybe he would accept her decision more readily if she leveled with him. "I don't like your hours, the danger." Merritt searched vainly for even further excuse when he seemed to demand it. The only thing she could think of was even more of a lie, but she knew it would serve her purpose in breaking off his growing attachment to her. "I don't like your pay."

Silence fell between them as her voice fell dully. Tom stared at her as if he were seeing a stranger. With difficulty she swallowed the tight knot of emotion in her throat.

"Well, you certainly can't be accused of leaving me with any illusions, Ms. Reed." Tom turned, a muscle clenching along his jaw. His mouth compressed in a forbidding line. "Call me if your car slides into another tree. But you can forget about the compassion. Because with the animosity you've just established, I doubt I'd be able to summon up anything but cold contempt!"

Her heart breaking, Merritt watched him stomp back to his car and drive off. The knowledge that she had done the best thing for both of them proved very little comfort, either that night or the following days.

For the rest of the week Merritt was up to her neck in superlatives, state capitols, and base tens. Predictably, she did not hear from Tom. And though she knew it was best for both of them, she was still quite depressed. So much so she couldn't get enthused about the sixth-grade choral program.

Scheduled during the PTA meeting, it was held in the auditorium. Merritt was in charge of ushers, program distribution, and seating. She was wandering the drafty school lobby a few minutes before curtain when Johnny Porter and his family came bursting in. "Hi,

Ms. Reed!" Johnny slid to a halt just short of her. "Wanta meet my dad?"

To say her student was in high gear was the understatement of the year. Privately Merritt wondered how he would ever make it through the program without knocking at least one person off the wooden risers in his ebullience.

"Hello, John." Merritt ruffled her lanky student's hair affectionately and gazed up at the man beside him. "Mr. Porter."

"Hello, Ms. Reed. How nice we finally get a chance to meet." Though cordial and polite, of the same light hair and tall lanky build as his son, the successful lawyer seemed not to want to be there at all. Ellen Porter looked tense. An artificially bright smile was on her face. She stepped forward and shook Merritt's hand, weariness mirrored in the cornflower blue of her eyes. "We're all looking forward to the program."

"Speaking of which..." Merritt commandeered a stack of programs from the nearby table and handed one each to Johnny's parents. She turned to John. "Hadn't you better let your parents get a seat? And you, young man, had better spring on around backstage." The students had been expected to report a half an hour earlier.

"Yes, ma'am!" John saluted her impishly, then dashed off. Murmuring something disapproving about John's unusual rowdy deportment, Ted Porter took his estranged wife's elbow and led her through the door. Still observing Ellen's tense, unhappy demeanor, Merritt leaned against a nearby table. The next instant she was aware of a low drift of provocatively male cologne. Simultaneously the music began and the auditorium lights lowered. As student ushers pulled the doors shut Merritt glanced up into Tom Hennessey's ruggedly attractive face. For the moment they alone shared the dimly lit lobby. "Well." His gaze drifted appreciatively from the top of her hair to the toes of her pumps. "Fancy meeting you here, Ms. Reed. I thought you would have been up front, directing the choir."

And she'd expected him to be out somewhere investigating a robbery or pitching in on patrol. "Tom." Caught off guard, the word was a husky whisper, tremulous with emotions she thought she had successfully repressed. "What—?"

"Ellen felt the need for moral support. I'm late getting in because I had to park the car. I'll admit, though, I also had hopes of catching you alone."

He was extremely confident of his charm, too much so, considering the way they had parted. Exasperation rippled through Merritt's slender form. "I thought I had made it clear I didn't want to see you again." If there was anything she didn't want it was to be taken for granted.

"First of all—" Tom crashed through her cursory illusions with a voice that could have cut glass. His tone lowered even more dangerously as he moved her back toward the wall. "I'm here for John's sake. He wanted us all to see his program. As for the other—" With a smile, he put a hand against the wall on either side of her. His gaze roved caressingly from her head to her toes. "I've missed you. And that was something *I* didn't count on."

Merritt hadn't anticipated the tripling of her pulse and senses whenever he was near, the overwhelming desire to touch, talk to, and stay with him. He was a cop, she reminded herself firmly. Even if they could work things out, they'd never have a real future together.

Tom read the rejection in her gaze. His mood darkened. In retaliation, his tone grew smoother. "You're looking tired," he commented with a temper-prodding arch of his light brows. "As if you've been having trouble sleeping. Something pricking at your conscience, Ms. Reed? Something you conveniently *forgot* or neglected to tell me, perhaps?''

Merritt ducked beneath his outstretched arms, paused to smooth down her skirt and greet a few other late-coming parents as they brushed by and slipped into the darkened auditorium beyond. "Believe me, Mr. Hennessey, there is absolutely nothing to keep me up nights," Merritt muttered fiercely. How dare he comment on her appearance, anyway. And as for Eric...

Tom grinned. "You're right," he agreed smoothly. "This is no place to catch up on old times between... friends. I'll talk to you later." He started toward the auditorium doors, program in hand. "No, you won't..." Merritt started to say, but he was already gone, striding through the doors.

The program went well, with only minor mistakes, most of which were not visible to the audience, Merritt was sure. Afterward, she and all the other teachers were deluged with well-wishes, congratulations, and occasional complaints from students' parents and friends. Ellen and Ted Porter waved from a distance, but did not stop by on the way out. Merritt experienced a startling stab of disappointment when she observed Tom Hennessey also slipping out the side entrance. Darn it all, despite the friction between them, his suspicions, she had wanted to see him again.

"Don't look so down," Blanche commented on the way out. "After all, no one got sick, fainted, or fell off the bleachers. The parents were reasonably pleased, and the PTA enjoyed record attendance for a meeting so far this year."

"Right." Merritt walked with the school's guidance counselor. They collected handbags and coats from the lockers in the staff lounge.

"Was that Johnny Porter with both his parents?" Blanche asked, pausing to get a Coke.

Merritt nodded.

"Uncle, too?"

"How'd you know?"

"Well, true, you're not eating chocolate. But you didn't help yourself to any of the cafeteria punch and cookies, either. And you spent a fair amount of time gazing restively around between greeting parents. Let me guess. Which one was he? The hunk in blue tweed?"

Merritt nodded. "The tall distinguished-looking man in the three-piece suit was John's father, Ted Porter." She turned up her collar against the cold as she walked out the door. "Who knows, maybe they're going to reconcile. Johnny sure was happy tonight."

"And wild," Blanche added, tugging on her gloves. "Not necessarily in a positive way."

Merritt's student occupied her thoughts the rest of the solitary drive home. Though progressing more successfully academically, John had a long way to go to regain his former A-student status. Her house was completely dark when she pulled up in front of the cement walk. Merritt emerged from the car, briefcase and handbag in one hand, keys in the other.

Tom Hennessey was waiting for her on the stone balustrade of the rectangular front porch, sitting casually, his long legs stretched out in front of him. Merritt's heart seemed to stop momentarily. His audacity and composure in the wake of her emotional confusion and physical indecision infuriated her. "What are you doing here?" Her voice was low and trembling. Half of her wanted him out. The other half wanted him there. The truth was, she didn't know what she wanted. And he knew it and was preying upon it.

"I believe I indicated earlier I'd come by."

Merritt swallowed, increasing her grip on her keys. "You said—"

"I'd be seeing you later." He rose insouciantly from his perch, flicking a piece of lint from his tailored

slacks. Stars lit the midnight velvet backdrop of the sky.
The scent of burning hickory filled the air. They were
completely alone once again, as if both time and the
world were temporarily standing still for just the two of
them. It was too romantic a scene for Merritt to risk
seeing him again. She was feeling too vulnerable. "Unfortunately, Mr. Hennessey, I've got plans."

"Grading papers?" His eyebrows rose.

Merritt's teeth clenched. He wasn't making it easy
for her. And why? Because she had suffered the poor
judgment to sleep with him once? She moved to brush
past him toward the door, wishing with all her heart
she'd had the foresight to leave the outdoor light burning when she left. "You know what they say: An educator's work is never done."

He laughed at that, his voice low and enticing. Merritt couldn't manage the lock. Eventually, he took the
key from her hands and navigated the lock with just
one easy flick of his strong wrist and nimble fingers.
"This apparatus would be a breeze to pick," he decided, moving on to the dead bolt above. "Good thing
you had the second installed."

Merritt resisted the urge to tell him Eric had said the
very same thing. Eric. Would the rest of her life be
lived with his memory and nothing, no one more? The
door swung open into the darkness of Merritt's house.
She turned, blocking the passage.

"I've got a few things to say." Tom cut off her next
excuse. "However, if you'd prefer to go over them
here on the porch, it's fine with me, too."

The gentle threat worked. Her emotions in a tumultuous whirl, Merritt led the way. Why did he have to be
a cop? Why couldn't he have been something safe and
sane, like an accountant or teacher or street cleaner?
"Coffee?" Her voice held a distinctly polite chill.

He followed lazily, smiling like a mountain cat.
"Yes."

Merritt flicked on a light, tossed off her winter coat, and stalked into the kitchen. "Cookies, too, I suppose?"

"Actually, I'd prefer a sandwich." Nonchalantly Tom tossed off his suit coat, loosened his tie and the first button of his shirt. His cuffs were unbuttoned with the same indolent ease and rolled neatly to just below the elbows to reveal strong sinewy forearms. He pulled out a chair, sat backward, his arms folded one on top of the other across the top. "I had dinner at Ellen's and she can't cook. Never had the time or the inclination to learn."

"You disapprove?"

He shook his head, not the least disturbed. "Sexism is not among my faults. Surprised?"

"No," Merritt said quietly. Again, tingles of unease pricked at the back of her neck. She felt like the mouse, trapped in a corner, just waiting to be devoured at the cat's specific ease. Routinely Merritt prepared the coffee. "How are things at the Porters?"

Tom was quiet for a moment, watching her remove a loaf of whole wheat bread from the freezer and place four slices into the toaster to warm. "Do you care?" He seemed curious, not judgmental.

Merritt whirled, her hands bracing the countertop behind her. "Of course I care. Why would you even ask?"

Tom shrugged, getting up to move closer. "You have a way of distancing yourself from people or anyone who might trod too close, both figuratively and literally."

It was an effort for Merritt not to move away. But running then would have only proved his point. Deliberately she removed roast beef, condiments, and lettuce from the refrigerator to her left. "I believe we were talking about John. Is his father here to stay?" Her tone indicated that if he wanted a sandwich he had better lay off.

Tom sighed heavily, thrusting both fists into the pockets of his trousers. Watching her make the sandwiches, he leaned against the counter. "No. Ted's here to meet with Ellen about finalizing their divorce with Dominican Republic speed."

"I'm sorry. Does John know?"

"Not yet." Wordlessly Tom carried their plates to the table while Merritt poured the coffee.

"Well, that accounts for John's wild yet tense elation tonight, Ellen's strain," Merritt mused. "How do you think he's going to react to the news when they do tell him?"

"Badly."

They ate in silence, each reflecting on a little boy whose home was being torn apart, his world disrupted, his heart broken. Yet, seeing Ellen Porter and her husband together, Merritt couldn't see that staying together would have made things any better for the disparate couple. Nor apparently could Tom. When they'd finished their impromptu meal, Merritt got up to pour more coffee for them both. "Why didn't you tell me your husband was a cop?" Tom asked the minute she'd returned the glass decanter to the warmer. "Why didn't you tell me how he died?"

Pain laced through Merritt anew. Tears burned her eyes, but she seemed powerless to flee. With lightning ease Tom moved to his feet and came up behind her. Merritt turned to avoid his penetrating gaze. He refused to let her escape, bracing his arms on either side of her. Tears blurring her eyes, Merritt pushed angrily at his chest. He didn't budge. "I want an answer, Merritt," he said roughly.

"Damn you for searching into my past."

"Damn us all. Isn't that the next part? You hate all cops and everything we do? Everything we risk?" He caught the flailing hands against his chest, held her wrists, one in each palm. "I'm not going to die, Merritt. And I'm certainly not going to turn my back or even approach without backup any mildly suspicious felon."

"Eric didn't know—"

"I'm aware of that," Tom said more gently. "And I'm sorry. But that doesn't make me less competent, too. Street cops have a gut instinct about sensing danger, Merritt. Mine was honed in Vietnam. Eric only had the academy and his limited experience on the street." Tom held her closer, waiting until the tears had nearly stopped, until her form had relaxed into the welcoming warmth of his. "Is that why you fainted the other night, at the scene of the accident?"

Merritt nodded. "It was just too close to what had happened to Eric, stopping on icy streets to help after a traffic accident. Only, in Eric's situation, the driver of the offending car wasn't hurt—"

"And didn't have a registration, either. The car was stolen."

"Eric ordered him out of the car and turned back to radio for help." Merritt recited what had become imprinted irrevocably on her mind.

"And was shot as he reached for the mike. I'm sorry," Tom said softly, stroking her hair.

After a moment Merritt pushed away. If he wanted to hear it, he might as well hear it all, so they'd never have to discuss it again. "I got there shortly after it had happened," she confessed shakily, trying without success to control the tremors in her hands. "One of his friends had called me. They'd already removed the body..." It was impossible to say "Eric," she thought, to connect the image of her laughing, fun-loving husband with the lifeless form she had buried. The shudders encompassed her then. "They never caught the guy who shot him," she added, her voice rising hysterically. "In the confusion he just drove off, later abandoned what we now know was a stolen car. So he's still out there, presumably running around free. And Eric, my wonderful, gentle, chivalrous Eric, is dead. Dead because of his crazy desire to be a modern-day Sir Gallahad, a uniformed street cop."

Bitterness settled over them like cerecloth. Merritt expected recriminations, arguments. She expected him to leave. Tom pushed temperately from the counter, moved to close the gap between them serenely, and enfolded her into his arms. With his touch, the flood started anew. Merritt's grief was wet against his shirt.

"I'm sorry," he said softly at length. "Sorry it happened and sorry you had to go through it. But that has little to do with us."

"It has everything to do with us." Merritt pulled away furiously.

"No, it doesn't. And when you get some perspective, you'll realize that."

The conviction in his tone eventually halted her tears. "How did you find out?" Shakily Merritt wiped at her cheek with the back of her hand.

"Artie recalled something about Eric's death, wanted to know if you were related. I looked it up...." His voice trailed off.

"I'm sorry." Merritt glanced away, embarrassed by her emotional display.

"For allowing yourself to feel? It's not *that* you should apologize for, Merritt. It's shutting yourself off from the world the past few years you should regret. It's shutting yourself off from me, not trusting me enough to level with me in the first place."

Tom moved closer, not comforting now, but clearly wanting, willing to take. Merritt's breath was suspended in her lungs as she waited. Part of her still wanted to run; the other half knew she would never flee from him again. His head tilted slightly to the side as if in slow motion. Their breaths mingled as his lips fit serenely over hers. "Tom—" she whispered, and then he kissed her, gently at first, then more insistently. As the embrace deepened his index finger came up to tenderly wipe away a salty tear still trailing down her cheek.

Again, Merritt whispered his name, twining her arms about the width of his shoulders to bring him closer still. The delicate curves of her breasts flattened malleably against the sinewy contours of his chest. His free arm slid down her back to her waist. He paused, drawing back to study her as his hand smoothed the tangled silk of her dark hair from her face.

"I care about you, Merritt," he whispered. "I never thought I'd be saying those words again. But I can't help it. I want you more than life, and nothing is going to change that." The passion he had held so tightly in check was unleashed in a floodgate of emotion. His lips sought hers with aggressive abandon.

A warmth of desire rippled through Merritt, followed by a rush of belonging so intense it brought tears to her eyes. Belatedly, she knew she wanted Tom, wanted to know him again in the most intimate way possible. She needed to be with him; she wanted to wake cradled in the reassuring wrap of his strong arms. She wanted to be vulnerable again, but only to and with him.

Sensing her surrender, Tom reached for the ascot at her neck. Still holding her close, he began the unhurried process of unraveling it. Merritt shivered as the cloth slowly unfurled. Tom watched her reaction, his eyes heavy lidded and slumberous with desire. His hands trailed over her breasts, then skimmed lower, gently cupping the undersides. His thumbs passed restlessly over the flowering crests. His slow touch made her moan and she clung to him.

His mouth skated over hers. Still kissing her, more leisurely, patiently now, Tom unfastened the buttons of her blouse and parted the edges of silk until the blouse dropped from her arms. Tenderly he traced the lacy pattern embroidered on her camisole. Resolutely he pushed the thin straps aside, down the curve of first one shoulder, then the other, until both rested partway down her arms. The weight of her breasts swelled against the silk. The slow unveiling, coupled with the fiercely enamored expression in his eyes, made a wild aphrodisiac on her impassioned senses. She knew he found her as beautiful and captivating as she saw him.

Nipping gently at his lips, she inched her tongue into his mouth, tentatively exploring, enjoying the new role of pursuer. She shifted against him ardently, hoping to inspire him with the same ravaging urgency she felt. Never had she wanted anyone the way she craved him.

"Slow down, darling," he whispered, cupping his hands beneath her hips and aligning her sensuously against him. "We have all the time we need...." Did they? She wondered. But he gave her no more time to think about it. The warmth of his hands encompassed the full circular weight of her breasts as he divested her of the restrictive camisole, leaving it to pool in a circle about her waist.

"I want you," she whispered passionately.

"I want you, too. But I don't want it to be over before we've had time to savor this moment." His gaze met hers, and she swayed toward him, mesmerized. "I don't want you to ever be able to forget...." He didn't want it to be like the first time, born out of need and regretted later. He wanted her to know what she was doing, think about it, consider, and still want him and need him and yes, love him with all her heart.

The warm craving inside Merritt intensified unbearably. Boldly she guided a hand down his body, exploring. He groaned raggedly, shuddering his need, then turned her back toward the counter, pinning her between the hard surface and his length. She gave no protest as his lips trailed down her neck to her breast and closed over one dusky rose peak, laving, caressing, driving her wild with need.

Abruptly his arm slid beneath her knees. Merritt was lifted against his chest. "We should have started this in a conducive setting," he swore, moving just far enough to hook a heel around the rung of a chair. Pulling it close, he sank down into the cushioned seat, bringing Merritt down across his lap as he went. The whole process took two or three seconds. It seemed an eternity to her, and as she looked into his face, she knew he was as driven with conflicting needs as she. The requisite for perfect romance, in setting... the more vital mandate for immediate gratification, to a love too long denied.

He shifted her until she lay back against his arm. Languidly his lips forged a burning trail across the abandoned arch of her neck until she was gasping for breath and control. With a moan, Tom drew back. Merritt's fingertips curled into the sinews of his shoulders. He watched her through eyes darkened and latent with desire.

"Let's go to bed, Merritt," he urged softly. "I want to make love to you. I want to hold you. But I want to do it in some decently comfortable place, now I know you're really amenable, not half-bent over a wooden kitchen chair."

Merritt straightened, blinking as if emerging from dreamworld into reality. Reality merged with the past in a horrifyingly bizarre way. Eric had said those same words, she recalled. "... in some decently comfortable place... not half-bent over a kitchen chair..." Oh, God, what was she doing, even contemplating falling in love with another cop? Was that part of the reason she was so enamored of Tom, so swiftly? Because he reminded her in some very vague way of Eric? Or was the similarity only a farfetched coincidence? Was she making more out of the situation than need be? Realistically, it wasn't such an odd thing to say. Nor, knowing her, was it an odd occurrence. She'd never relied on the bedroom setting to deliver a kiss or indulge in a needed embrace. They were adults, for God's sake, they were all adults...

"What's the matter?" Tom was watching her tensely, a new look of terror in his eyes.

Merritt shook off the memories. Starting for the stairs, she absently adjusted her clothes. Why was she letting the past get to her, now of all times, unless it was a subconscious roadblock to her relationship with Tom? She couldn't call a halt now, after saying yes with both body and soul only moments before. It wasn't fair to him and it wasn't fair to herself. Her needs and wants hadn't changed.

Merritt forced briskness into her voice. "Nothing's the matter." She took a tremulous breath, fluffed the ends of her hair. "Switch off the light, will you?"

Tom grabbed her tenderly by the arm and pulled her back into the kitchen light instead, positioning her there so she had no choice but to face him, holding her there firmly when she clearly would have run, at the very least evaded. "Wait a minute," he said roughly. "This isn't Be Kind to Cincinnati Policemen Week. I'm not looking for a sexual handout. If your heart isn't in it, Merritt—"

He wanted her to say it was. She couldn't lie, not after everything honest that had just passed between them. Even if she had tried, he would have seen through her and she knew it.

"What happened in the last twenty seconds to change your mind?" he asked softly, attempting visibly to hold on to his flaring temper and mask his hurt. "Was it something I said? That dumb joke—"

Merritt shrugged off both, not wanting to wound him. But the silence was even more deadly as he jumped to his next conclusion. "It's Eric again, isn't it?" His voice was taut with frustration.

How could it not be? she thought wearily. They had

just been discussing his death. They were standing in the kitchen she and Eric had shared and, occasionally, made love in. "I'm sorry." She looked away, flushing fiercely.

"What did I do this time?" Anger eliminated the last of his passion, becoming more virulent in force with every passing second in which she didn't, couldn't, respond. "What did I say?" He stalked dangerously near. His eyes glittered fiercely. "Was I sitting in his favorite chair? Was that it? Drinking coffee from his favorite coffee cup? What? Tell me."

Merritt felt the blood drain from her face. She put a hand up to shade her eyes. "Tom, don't be cruel." The words were wrenched from her. She didn't want to cry.

"Then you stop being cruel, too. Damn it, Merritt, what did I do? At least have the decency to tell me!"

Merritt swallowed. Silence stretched between them as he waited furiously. "That wise remark about making love in the kitchen. Eric once said something very similar to me. It was an old joke, one we shared a lot." She regretted the words before they were said, but by the same token she knew Tom would not have let her go until she did tell him.

An emotional battle line had already been drawn between them, negating any apologies or explanations she might have given. Merritt was silent, staring at the floor, tears blurring her eyes.

Tom took a shaky breath, looked away a long moment as he ran a hand through the length of his hair. His palm rested on the collar of his shirt. "I guess I asked for that one, didn't I?" he asked bitterly. "Drawing you into my sensual spell directly after discussing your sainted husband's death!"

"Tom—"

"Let me finish, Merritt." His tone roughly underlined every word. He cupped his hands around her upper arms and held her fast. "I care about you. And I know you could feel something about me if you gave yourself half a chance.''

That was true. But he was pushing her. Chin set stubbornly, she turned her head evasively to the side. ''I need time.''

''You've had time, damn it, plenty of it.'' He breathed deeply as if regretting his tone, then spoke more calmly. ''What you need is a new house, Merritt. Look around you. How many memories are stored in just this one room? Where can I, or anyone else for that matter, go without tripping over his favorite chair or erroneously picking up the wrong paper or book or tray or dish?''

She'd thought about selling her home once, but interest rates and higher payments had discouraged her. ''A new house wouldn't help.''

''Maybe not, but answer me this. Would you be able to stand having me watch football here on a Sunday afternoon?''

''I don't know,'' Merritt said tightly, attempting a joke. ''I always hated the Sunday afternoon blitz.''

''That isn't what I meant, Merritt.''

''I know.''

''You can't enjoy living this way.''

''I don't.''

''Then do something about it.'' He moved forward imploringly.

''Like what? Make love to *you*?'' She hadn't meant to say the words at all, much less aloud. But he'd pushed her too hard, too long, and once the bitter accusation had been made there was no retracting it. His face turned to stone. Before he could say something even nastier, she jumped in to have the last word. ''Maybe you'd even like to have one of my dead husband's shirts. Oh, I forgot, I gave them all away. Maybe his pillow, then, his blanket. Would you like to sleep on his side of the bed?''

She'd half hoped he would slap her and end the tension between them. But he didn't, rather only grew calmer. "You're not Eric's possession, Merritt," he stated empathically. "Making love to me isn't a betrayal of anything the two of you might have shared. That's over now, finished."

Intellectually, she knew that. But her feelings weren't so clear. Part of the problem was that she had never stopped thinking of herself as Eric's widow. She still used his name, clung to the memories of their past which they had shared when her present life seemed most futile. For a long time that knowledge had been all that had kept her going, but she didn't have the words to explain to Tom the pain she had been through. Nor was she sure he could understand, even if she tried.

Silence stretched between them, this time unbridgeable.

He slammed out of the room, grabbing his jacket as he strode. "Call me when you decide to join the world of the living, if you ever do." Clearly he had his doubts.

Merritt let the tears fall heedlessly over her cheeks. She wept until she felt she had been completely dehydrated, but eventually her attention was riveted back to the point Tom had made. She walked over to the rack of coffee mugs, turned it until she selected the one that had been Eric's favorite. She examined it wordlessly for long minutes, then walked over and quietly pitched it into the trash. Next went his Cincinnati Bengals beer glass, his mint julep glass from the Kentucky Derby.

Eric had collected a lot of souvenirs. They were all over her home. Merritt spared not an item. And it turned out to be a very long, difficult, but finally accomplished task.

Chapter Five

A chef's apron covering her clothes, Merritt strolled the cafeteria kitchen, inspecting her students' work for the Thanksgiving Feast. Apples were being peeled and diced for sauce, green beans snapped and washed. Kristin headed up a group scraping pumpkin from a shell. Brian Anderson and Johnny Porter worked over a scratch recipe for cornbread. Parents had been invited to share the early evening meal at which students were celebrating the end of a social studies unit as well as the coming holiday, and learning to apply culinary skills. All in all, Merritt was pleased with their group spirit and cooperation, until the fight over the cornbread broke out.

"Hey, I said it was my turn to stir!" Brian insisted loudly. Color flushed his face. Angry sparks dominated the normally mischievous blue eyes. He had a point, Merritt knew, as John had been deliberately hoarding the bowl for the last ten minutes.

"John—" Merritt started toward the quarreling boys. "Brian's right. It is his turn."

"Is not." Johnny Porter's lower lip went out truculently. His hands clenched the wooden bowl and spoon.

Merritt walked closer, placing a hand gently on John's shoulder. Before she could soothe him into relinquishing his grip, Brian muttered disparagingly, just loud enough for the class to hear, "Jerk. Just because your parents are getting a divorce—"

That did it. Both bowl and spoon went flying. Johnny's fist contacted with Brian's jaw, knocking him backward into the table. He got up with a howl, and rushed right back at his closest friend, head butted down into Johnny's stomach. John yelled and landed a fist on Brian's head, then another. Merritt struggled desperately between the flailing hands, arms, and legs. Kristin screamed, and then rushed forward to help intervene. Everyone else in the class soon followed suit. Seconds later, the boys had been parted. Panting, bleeding, still hurling insults, they were quite a sight and only marginally more calmed down when they were hauled bodily to the principal's office ten minutes later.

"What do you two have to say for yourselves?" Mr. Tierney demanded.

"He started it." Sporting an angry red welt across his chin, Brian pointed an accusing finger at his friend.

John scowled, eyes straight forward, and said nothing. The principal looked at Merritt. "Ms. Reed?"

"Brian's right. John threw the first punch," she said calmly. Shooting an irate glance at Brian, she added, "But it was after a rather heartless remark. One Brian knew better than to make, all things considered."

Brian's face suffused with red. He clenched both fists against the seat of his chair and looked down.

"I see. Ms. Reed, I'd like to speak to you alone." He waited until they had shut the door to his private office before he continued. "You know what the penalty for violence is in this school. I'm going to have no choice but to suspend them both."

Merritt cringed. "Please, I know it looks bad, but—"

"You're darn right it does. What if one of those children had been seriously hurt?"

"If you suspend John, he'll fail the semester. Brian's grades will be pulled down to a marginal level. Both would be in jeopardy of being dropped from the gifted program."

"If they can't behave any better than that, then perhaps they should be."

"Sir, Johnny Porter's been going through a bad time personally. His parents are divorcing. He's dealing with a lot of anger. Obviously, today things got out of hand, but I assure you it won't happen again. As for Brian, yes he's mischievous, but not violent or aggressive on any regular level. The Thanksgiving holiday begins tomorrow evening. If you could just give them a break this one time. Let them off with a warning?"

"One full day's suspension instead of three, Ms. Reed. Along with a five-thousand word essay from them each on the inappropriateness of violence in the schools. Also, both will have to be barred from the class dinner this evening. I'm sorry. But that's the best I can do."

"It wasn't fair, Ms. Reed. John and Brian had a right to be here tonight. It was their class dinner, too," Kristin Stratton complained as she helped Merritt set out the assortment of class-baked and parent-donated dishes comprising their Thanksgiving meal.

Merritt sighed. She felt much the same way herself, but there was nothing she could say to the child at her side without appearing disloyal to the school's hierarchy. "John and Brian knew better than to fight today, regardless of their differences over who got to stir the cornbread. Now, I'm sorry they are not here, too, but those are the breaks."

"It's still not fair," Kristin grumbled rebelliously, looking over at the principal as he chatted with a small group of parents. "Brian says he's going to be grounded for the rest of his life and probably won't get anything for Christmas, either. Johnny's parents don't even care about him!"

"Kristin!" Merritt chastised automatically, burning her hand on a chafing dish full of green beans decorated with almonds.

"Well, it's true," Kristin retorted. "John told me so himself!" The student flounced off to gather with her dressed-up classmates.

Merritt struggled over class-baked pumpkin pies that were a suspicious shade of greenish orange, and slightly lumpy in texture. "Need a hand? Or just a new cook?" said a male voice beside her.

Merritt glanced up to see Tom juggling a bakery box in each hand. The breath left her lungs in one agonizing whoosh. She trembled, recalling how she'd hurt him the last time they'd met. She'd never seen him that angry. So many times she'd wanted to call him. Afraid he hadn't or could never forgive her, she'd resisted the urge. But watching him stare back at her as if entranced, she knew nothing had changed. He still wanted her as much as she wanted him, practicality be damned. "Tom, hi," she whispered, feeling herself pale.

"Ellen said she was committed to bringing two walnut-and-raisin pies, whether John was able to be here or not," he said matter-of-factly. Edging closer, he brushed her arm with the side of his wrist momentarily. The action was deliberate and it sent tingles all the way to her toes.

"Not at all," Merritt croaked nervously as she set the boxes aside. She'd imagined them meeting again many times, but never at so formal or dutiful a function as a class dinner over which she was presiding.

Tom smiled reassuringly, teasingly pretending to mistake the reason for her unease. "Don't worry. The pies Ellen sent are store baked." Tom glanced back at the class-made pies. "Judging from the competition, though, Ellen probably could have baked her own. God knows she's no Julia Child, but—"

Merritt tried to wipe the wry grin from her face, but failed. As she wheeled to face him reprovingly the pulse pounded in her veins. "Cut it out. One of the children might hear you," she hissed conspiratorially. "And though I know you're teasing, they might not."

"Sorry." His apology was prompt. She hated to admit the way he could make her heart stop with just a glance. But it was so good to see and talk with him again. Relief balmed her nerves.

"Rough day with John, hmm?" Tom's voice was the softest caress. A smile hovered over his mouth. He wore the same heavy lidded expression as when he was contemplating kissing her. She flushed warmly at the thought, knowing she was feeling the same, but the thought of the audience around them kept them a discreet physical distance away from one another. *Oh, Tom, how I've missed you,* she thought.

Merritt nodded regretfully, rubbing the tension from her neck as she reminisced over the day's events. "I'm sorry your nephew was suspended. For the record, I tried to get both boys off with just a warning, though neither of the boys is aware of that."

"From what I hear they did get off easy, considering their behavior." A weary sigh rippled through his tall muscular frame. "It must have been some scene. This where it happened?"

Merritt nodded. "The brawling took place next to the refrigerators. I guess we were lucky no one got hurt. Certainly there were plenty of knives and vegetable peelers in the vicinity. How's John doing?"

"He's disappointed, naturally. Sulking steadily, too, according to Ellen. But I imagine that will pass."

"You didn't see him?"

"He was in his room, working on his five-thousand word essay, when I dropped by. Need some help?"

"If you wouldn't mind filling those paper cups with apple cider, and bringing out the cartons of milk from the refrigerator."

"Will do. What time is this feast supposed to end?" He favored her with a devastating smile.

Despite herself, Merritt flushed with pleasure. "Probably around seven thirty or eight," she answered shyly. Then she cautioned, "I have to stay until everything is put away and locked up, though."

"Clean up committee of one, hmm?"

"More or less, since it is just our class." She paused, looking down at her hands. "Would you like to stay? As my guest?"

"Lady"—Tom grinned—"I thought you'd never ask."

"Tell me, are all class dinners that dull?" Tom asked as they strolled hand in hand toward the parking lot.

"Most are even worse," Merritt admitted. During others she did not have his pleasant, personable companionship to get through the process. "Though to be honest I don't imagine it's much better for the parents. Trying to make small talk about the PTA and class projects, the common conversational ground disappears fast for all but the most gregarious in the group."

"I can imagine. Go somewhere for coffee with me?" The request was quietly issued. He seemed not to exhale at all as he waited for her reply.

"I don't know." Merritt paused under the intensity of his gaze.

"A restaurant. Somewhere quiet." His voice lowered beseechingly as his hands closed compellingly over hers. "I need to talk to you, Merritt. There are some things I have to say. Some things that need clearing up."

"All right." Elation overruled common sense. Trying to get a grip on her soaring emotions, she warned, "But it will have to be early. I've got class tomorrow."

"As early as you want."

The restaurant he selected was only a block away. Quiet, inexpensive, it was the perfect place to talk. "Okay, Detective, what is it?" She propped her chin on her entwined fists, elbows resting casually on the table.

"About the other night—"

Merritt straightened. "Tom—"

"I need to say it, Merritt. I pushed you. I'm sorry."

Merritt glanced at the potted plant next to the cashier, embarrassed. "It seems to me that was just as much my fault as yours. My life has been an emotional roller coaster the past month. I guess maybe I have just tried to bury too many things before they were adequately dealt with." The next came with a great deal of difficulty. "I'm not sure I should see you anymore, at least not until I do get some of these...issues resolved." Nervously she rearranged the silverware on the paper napkin next to her plate.

"I'm not sure you ever will resolve them unless you do see someone like me." His fingers moved across the table to twine with hers, stop the agitated action, and force her glance up to his. "Someone who cares. Someone who'll question and prod and occasionally fight back." When Merritt didn't disagree with his assumption, he asked abruptly, "Do you have any plans for the holidays?"

Merritt shrugged. Blanche had asked her to share the holiday meal with her family in Columbus, but she had hedged. She also knew she didn't want to spend another Thanksgiving in the Hyde Park house, alone or with anyone else. She said, "Is this an invitation or a proposition?"

"A little of both?" He grinned predatorily. "I have this house in Spring Valley, a little town about fifty miles north of here. I'm still in the process of fixing it up. I thought maybe you'd like to go, too. I could do with a little tasteful advice."

"You're taking quite a chance. You might not like anything I would suggest." Merritt smiled at him disarmingly.

His eyes roved her thoughtfully. He favored her with a tender smile, "I'll take my chances."

Merritt was so aware of the man she could almost feel the electrifying caress of his fingertips gliding over her own passion-bared skin. She knew by the lengthening of his breaths, the suspended attention, and hooded glance he was making love to her in his mind. "How long would we stay?" Her voice was irritatingly breathless.

"As long as you want. I've got two days and two nights off. It's the longest stretch of free time I'll have for a while. "I need to get away," Tom continued to explain casually. "And this is one of the few places I'm able to relax. I'd also like to get to know you better, without interference or further family calamities of any kind. What do you say?"

He sounded so pragmatic. Merritt's pulse was racing. "Will Ellen be able to manage without you?"

"John's father is back for the weekend. It's about time Ted started holding up his end of the parenthood contract."

"All right," Merritt said softly, then wondered long after he'd taken her home and dropped her off with only a short, casual kiss if she'd made the appropriate decision.

"Tell me about your property," Merritt prompted the next afternoon after they'd been served a Thanksgiving dinner with all the trimmings at an old restaurant north of the city. Tom paused to pour them each a glass of Chablis.

"I suppose it seems out of character to you for a city cop to invest in a small town domicile."

"Yes."

"Well, don't expect anything too elaborate," he joked lightly. "There's still plenty of room for improvement on my minifarm. And that estimation includes the house.''

"How did you acquire it?'' Merritt leaned back in her chair, relaxing in the pleasant atmosphere. "And isn't it a little far to come, considering you live and work over an hour's drive from here?''

Tom shrugged. In honor of the holiday, he'd worn a navy wool suit. He looked exceptionally handsome, and the knowledge he'd made the effort specifically for Merritt was an elating thought. "I still have my apartment in town, though admittedly that's been little more than a place for me to eat and sleep since my divorce. And as for the distance, I welcome it, if you want to know the truth.'' His gaze roved the lines of her silk shirtdress approvingly, lingered on the heart-shaped pendant suspended at her breasts.

"When Carin and I divorced, we sold our home in Oak Hills. She took her share of the profits and moved to Washington, and now works for a District of Columbia law firm. I took mine and bought this place. I'd already rented a small efficiency near work during the initial separation, and was bound there by a lease. Tax-wise, I needed to reinvest in real estate or face losing some of the profit I had gained. It was a kind of therapy for me the first year alone. Tearing out walls, repainting, stripping floors, clearing out some of the underbrush and weeds from around and beneath the front porch.''

"And now?'' she asked curiously at length, wondering if he was still in need of exorcising his ex-wife's memory, the dying ashes of their failed marriage.

Tom read her tension correctly and smiled reassuringly. His hand covered her own. "Now the farm is more of a weekend home than an investment, which is precisely why I asked you to help decorate it.'' Merritt flushed with pleasure at the promise his low voice held.

She needed to be friends with Tom, needed the emotional support he was capable of giving. She wouldn't worry about possible problems, not today.

The conversation during the rest of the meal was confined to possible budgets, suggestions, color schemes, and decors. After all the help he had given her during the aftermath of her car wreck, it was a joy to be doing something in return for Tom.

They drove out toward his ten-acre farm at dusk. Nestled in a fenced-off section of heavily treed land was a two-story white frame farmhouse and small barn. "I see what you mean by rustic," Merritt noted duly, taking in the peeling white paint and multihued shingles of the patched roof and porch. Inside, however, was a pleasant surprise. The floors had been refinished to a beautiful shine; the kitchen bore a new coat of paint; wallpaper accented the gleaming white cabinets. A parlor with fireplace and chandeliered dining room completed the downstairs. Upstairs were four small bedrooms and a single bath, complete with claw-footed antique tub. "Tom, this is marvelous."

"I was hoping you'd say that." He set her overnight case and bag down into the only bedroom with a mattress and box spring. The rest were conspicuously bare. And though the room had been recently wallpapered and painted, it sported only nailed white cloth against the windows. "Among other things, I need drapes." Tom grimaced. "But I can't afford to order them from a department store and furnish the place all at once, too."

Working from a limited salary herself, Merritt understood his dilemma only too well.

"We could run up some priscilla curtains and sheers," Merritt suggested. "Similar to the ones in my living room, but in a different fabric, something more masculine."

"You'd do that for me?" He looked amazed.

"Yes." Merritt blushed shyly, astounded to find how strong the compulsion was to assist him.

"Sounds good to me." Tom rubbed his hands together enthusiastically. "When do we start?" From anyone else such a request would have sounded presumptuous, from Tom only genuinely, boyishly excited.

"Tomorrow, if you're game. Unless I'm mistaken a town of Xenia's size will probably have several fabric centers as well as discount stores. Maybe we'll be able to find something there, since it's only a ten-minute drive from Spring Valley."

"In the meantime," Tom suggested affably, "how about a brandy by the fire?" Lacing an arm affectionately around her waist, he led her back downstairs. Merritt watched as he shrugged out of his coat and constructed a fire, admiring the flex of his muscles as they stretched across the smooth soft cloth of his shirt. "I really appreciate your offer to help with the drapes," Tom murmured when they were comfortably ensconced before the fire.

Merritt relaxed in the cradle of his arm, her face resting against his familiar warmth. "I wouldn't be here unless I wanted to be."

"But?" He detected the wariness lacing her tone.

"Let's take it slowly, one step at a time. Be friends first." She traced the hair feathering the back of his hand, admitting prudently, "There's still so much I don't know about you."

"Such as?" he asked softly, his eyes inscrutable.

"The reasons for your divorce, how you feel about your ex-wife and getting involved again." He'd acted possessively. But he'd never really talked about marriage.

Tom sighed, tension snaking into his frame. "Carin worked for the district attorney's office. She helped prosecute the cases I brought in, which is how we initially met. More than anyone, she knew the dangers we faced out on the street. At first it didn't bother her. She felt—we both did—that we could handle anything. But as, time went on, and she saw other patrolmen getting hurt, she began to object. When the job offer in Washington came up, she jumped at the chance to leave Cincinnati and start fresh. An added bonus was the possibility of me working for the same company, as an insurance investigator going after fraud. Though it still had its dangers, it was much safer work, and along the lines of what I had been doing on a more routine level.''

"Why didn't you go?'' Stunned, Merritt sat up, swiveling partway to face him.

He heaved a beleaguered sigh. "Because insurance work didn't interest me in the slightest. Eventually, Carin realized the problem was more than the dilemma of where we would live. She didn't want a cop in her life.'' Tom explained further, "In lucrative corporate law a lot of business is conducted after hours. Let's face it, socially we make things awkward. It's hard to party when you have a cop standing next to you, monitoring the amount of alcohol you're pouring into your bloodstream, watching who elects to drive, who lets themselves be poured into taxis for the trip home. After a while it becomes second nature. And no one knows that better than the lawyers. As a rookie attorney, Carin didn't want that kind of pressure. So we separated, saw each other a few times, spent the weekend together, and tried to figure out if we could somehow compromise and make it work. Not surprisingly, it didn't. Most long-distance marriages don't, at least not the way we both needed ours to. About six months later, I got a letter from her asking for a divorce. It seemed she had met some corporate lawyer who wanted to marry her. She felt they'd have a better shot at making a life together than she and I would, and she wanted her freedom. I gave it to her. We wished each other well. End of story.''

Not quite, Merritt thought, detecting his introspective tone. "Did you love her very much?"

"Once." Tom stared at the floor. Frowning, he got up to stoke the fire. "But that's over now. My marriage is behind me, it has been for three years." He slanted her an assessing look. "What about you?" He strolled back to lounge next to her on the sofa. "Were you always so independent?"

Her mouth twisted ironically. "Unfortunately, no." Absorbed, she watched Tom loosen his tie and the first button on his shirt, clasp his hands behind his head, and prop his feet up on the coffee table. She glanced down at the hands folded primly in her lap. "That's just been a trait I've sought since his death."

He inclined his head toward her. "Any particular reason why? Other than that you found yourself alone?"

She took another sip of brandy, recalling, "Eric died intestate. All of our checking and saving accounts were joint. Everything was frozen until it could go through probate—six months later. If it hadn't been for my paycheck coming in from my job, I don't know what I would have done, and as it was, it was difficult for me to pay the mortgage and buy groceries at the same time." She'd never told anyone this, not even her parents. She hadn't wanted them to worry, or think less of her for being so shortsighted.

Tom's brows rose and fell in wordless empathy.

"I know. It's dumb not to have the foresight to make a will. But that wasn't the worst of it." She shook her head in chagrin. "I'd never done our taxes, either. I had no idea where he kept any of our records. It turned out they were scattered haphazardly throughout the house, the safety deposit box at the bank, the attic, the glove compartment of the car, you name it. The receipts were everywhere but in our files. I'm still unable to locate six months of canceled checks from our first year of marriage and the income tax return for that year."

"Didn't you have any insurance?" Tom asked, the golden glow of the fire picking up the silvery ash-brown lights of his hair.

"We had a policy in his name, that he'd had before we were married. His father had talked him into getting it. But evidently Eric cashed it in to pay for an impromptu trip we took to Florida one spring." She frowned, remembering how exhilarated she'd been when he'd come home waving the tickets after she'd completed her final exams. She'd accepted his story of a bonus from work so readily, she thought, too readily.

"You mean your husband cashed it in and didn't tell you about it?" Tom looked aghast.

She shrugged. "It was his policy, in his name. Technically, I suppose he had the right to do anything he wanted with it."

"And the money he got from the department?" Tom asked. "I assume he got something in the way of benefits."

She nodded. "A small amount, but that took several months to come through, and most of it went to pay for overdue charge accounts, the rest of Eric's school loan, and his burial expenses."

Tom looked stunned to discover how difficult it had been for her financially. Her loyalty for her first husband came back, full strength. She explained, "Eric was very much a live-for-today person. I used to be, too. I trusted him to take care of both of us." She sighed, admitting, "I know, that's an old-fashioned idea—"

His gaze narrowed. "Not necessarily." He reached out to capture her hand.

She withdrew it restlessly. "Yes, it is, Tom. Every woman should be able to take care of herself. More than that, she should be prepared. If I had been—"

"It's always easier to look back and see how much better things might have been."

His understanding attitude helped her to relax again. "I know. But I don't think I can ever go back to being the way I was, Tom. I want to know precisely where I'm going to be ten, twenty, even one year down the line."

His penetrating gaze made her feel unusually short-sighted in regard to her future—again. "Even if it's just keeping your life status quo?" he challenged huskily. "Living alone, teaching school?"

"I guess you're right. I am afraid to take chances now." Identifying the problem, however, did little to change the way she felt or lessen her anxiety about the future. "Frankly, I don't know if that will ever change."

Later, at Tom's insistence, Merritt took the bed upstairs and he took the couch. Over breakfast the next morning, they made plans for the day. "I'd like to take in an auction, maybe visit some of the local thrift shops and see what we can do about furnishing this place," Tom informed, taking a bite of French toast. "I'm pretty handy with a paintbrush and hammer, not so good when it comes to selecting fabrics and coordinating decors."

"I'll be glad to help you in any way I can," Merritt said softly. She'd just have to keep reminding herself it was his house, not hers, and would therefore have to be outfitted entirely in his style.

They shared a second cup of coffee, then companionably cleared away the meal. "Have you always wanted to be a cop?" Merritt asked as she dried a plate.

"Are you kidding?" Tom laughed, dipping his hands elbow deep into the frothy white suds.

"Then this wasn't a childhood calling."

"No. In fact, if you want to know the truth, I was hell on two feet as a kid, which is, unfortunately, precisely why I'm so hard on my nephew John at times. I don't want him channeling his excess energy into mischievous behavior."

Merritt surveyed Tom boldly. "No, I just don't see you as a ten-year-old terror."

"Believe it." He grimaced. "Like John, I was unhappy with the fate life had handed me, pretty unhappy with my situation in general. We didn't have much and my father had died, so he wasn't around, either. I felt like a misfit growing up in an all-female house. And then too I wanted to prove I was a man, that I could take care of my sister and my mother."

"What happened?"

"I got in a lot of fights, broke my own nose as well as someone else's jaw. Yeah," he summarized at her aghast look, "it's not something I'm particularly proud of and I use it to remind myself of what can happen when boyhood scams get completely out of control. The other kid was layed up for a week. After that, my mother put me in group athletic activities year round, so I would have no more chance to test out my abilities that way."

"Then what happened?" Merritt leaned back against the kitchen counter.

Tom's eyes twinkled. "I went to college. Worked my way through on a military scholarship and what my mother could spare. Did my time in the service. Afterward I worked as a CPA for a while, which was, of course, what I had majored in at UC."

"What happened to make you quit?" Merritt finished up the silverware and slid it into the paper-lined drawer.

Tom shrugged. "That is not so pretty. I was in a restaurant late at night, having dinner with a date. A couple of guys came in with sawed-off shotguns and held up the place. They made us all lie facedown on the floor, and then weren't content with the amount of cash they got, so they shot the restaurant owner in the back." Merritt's face had turned ashen. Tom's voice was noncommittal as he talked, as if he'd long gotten used to the facts. The set of his jaw said he would never get used to the horror.

"I couldn't do anything at the time, of course, except lie there and pray I or the girl with me wouldn't be next. Well, we got out of there okay, as did everybody except the owner. The local cops and press seemed to think we were lucky to get out of there with just one death. Having personally witnessed it I felt it was one too many." He was silent again, looking off into space, out the window at the deserted winter pastures beyond to the sparse hickory and oaks covering his suburban property.

"I kept thinking about it. The incident haunted me for days. I just couldn't get it out of my mind. Soon after that, my mother died. With Ellen safely married, and in the process of getting her education, I really had nothing left to lose, no one depending on me. So I went down to the academy and enrolled."

"But now?" Merritt asked, her heart pounding, astounded that he could keep something like that from her for so long. "You have your whole life ahead of you. You could get married again, have children—" She cut herself off, having said far too much.

Tom smiled, querying gently as he took a step nearer, "Whose dreams are we talking about now, mine or yours, Merritt Reed?"

Merritt didn't deny or try to hide the growing extent of her feelings for him. "It's not as if you don't have a profession to go on to." One that would pay even better than the one he had, one that would guarantee normal working hours, and a normal, very safe working life.

"You're right," he said softly. "It isn't a question of survival. It's a question of options. And police work is the one I chose." His eyes met hers levelly. "There are people out there depending upon me, Merritt. It's a job I know I can do well. It's a job I think I will always want to do."

Merritt understood everything he had revealed. Part of her even admired him. The other part damned him incessantly for insisting on continuing in a profession that was literally land mined with danger.

The auction was held in a remodeled barn, which offered small protection against the winter chill. Tom and Merritt huddled together as item after item was paraded out for public view and bidding. Tom lost on a wagon-wheel coffee table, but did gain twin armchairs with stained upholstery. "We can make slipcovers for both of those with very little effort," Merritt whispered in his ear. "And think how nice they'll look before the fire."

"I'm thinking how nice you'll look in one of them, sharing a cup of coffee or a glass of wine," he replied softly, tucking her gloved hand beneath his arm. She reveled in the feeling of intimacy his gesture created, could almost imagine they were decorating the house for mutual future use, instead of as a favor from female to male friend.

Tom bid on a solid pine armoire in need of refinishing, a trestle table, and twin benches for the dining room. "I'm afraid that about does it furniture-wise for today," he said, sighing as he checked his bank balance after the auctioneer had been paid. Arrangements were made for the furniture to be delivered. "Still game for some shopping?"

"Try and stop me," Merritt said.

Together they tromped through several thrift shops for accessories and numerous fabric shops before Merritt was able to find inexpensive material that would match the calico print of his overstuffed Victorian sofa.

It was shortly after five when they turned into the

long graveled drive. "We never did have lunch, did we?" Tom recalled.

Merritt glanced at her watch. "Look, the furniture will be arriving soon. If you'll let me borrow your car, I'll run to the supermarket at the edge of town and purchase and then prepare dinner. It's only fair, since you sprung for breakfast and the dinner last night."

He studied her silently. "The cooking I'd welcome."

"Double or nothing."

"All right," he agreed reluctantly, handing her the keys to his Camaro. Driving his car only deepened the feeling of intimacy growing between them, Merritt noted. Making a cozy dinner for the two of them heightened it even more pleasurably. Merritt knew she was falling in love with him. The fact that he was a cop seemed less and less important. In the face of being with him, loving, caring, it seemed not to matter at all.

Merritt returned with ingredients for beef Stroganoff, a crisp green salad, crusty French bread, and a bottle of good red wine. Tom was waiting for her. The newly purchased furniture was stored in the unused dining room. "And there it's going to stay until I have a chance to refinish and cover it," Tom said, looking quite pleased with his purchases.

Merritt smiled. "I'll bring my portable sewing machine down the next time we come and cover those chairs for you. Running up the living room drapes won't take much longer."

"I don't think I've thanked you properly for all your help," Tom said gently, pulling her to him for a lengthy, very tender kiss. Merritt was shaking when she pulled away. It may have been a figment of her imagination, but she thought at the last moment she'd detected a shudder of pure pleasure rippling through him.

They prepared dinner in the same way as breakfast, companionably and expertly, only occasionally getting in each other's way. They carried their plates in to eat before the roaring fire, shared the last of the wine long after the dishes were done, each reluctant to finish or necessitate their sojourns to different beds. Tom made no move to touch her or kiss her again, true, but she could feel his desire, see the passion etched in the taut lines of his face. "I don't know how we're going to manage it," Tom said roughly at last, "but I realized something today, Merritt. I want you as part of my life."

"I'll always be your friend." She couldn't imagine a life without him, if only to speak occasionally on the telephone or see him for casual dinners or lunch or a walk in the park.

"And I'll always be yours, but I don't think that's going to be enough for us, Merritt." He moved forward, one arm encircling her back, the other turning her more fully toward him. "I want to make love to you," he confessed on a soft, ragged note. "But I want you to desire me, too, and not just on a momentary basis." They sat knee to knee on the sofa, the fire blazing in the hearth before them. There was something new and faintly dangerous in his gaze, something *determined*.

"I do desire you," she whispered. She felt as if she'd been in love with him forever, as if she knew everything about him, and yet at the same time so little, as if he would forever be a fascinating enigma for her to explore and learn anew.

Reaching around behind him, his eyes never leaving the mesmeric hold on hers, Tom flicked off the single lamp. The only sound in the room was the measured sounds of their breathing, the crack and hiss of the fire. The isolation made her feel vulnerable, the intensity of her own desire flooding her with ill-advised languor. "You haven't even kissed me yet and I'm trembling,"

Merritt confessed. A tremulous sigh rippled through her, making her shiver slightly.

"Now you know how I feel," Tom whispered, leaning closer by treacherously slow degrees. A gentle hand came up behind her neck, laced through the thick tangle of her hair, and directed her mouth to his. His lips parted as they brushed against, then over hers with leisure.

Whatever objections she'd been feeling, she could no longer remember. Merritt sighed her surrender, both to him and herself. How could anything that felt so right be wrong? Their need for each other was tantamount to everything else.

His arms tightened. They slid slowly backward, so Merritt lay against the sofa, her hair flaring out around her like a silken fan. Her palms spread out over his chest, beneath the edges of his shirt. The skin was warm, ruffled by the curling tendrils of light brown hair. His eyes were dark with pleasure, his breath warm and fragrant against the heat of her skin. "I want to make love." Merritt nipped tiny kisses into the beard-roughened underside of his chin.

Tom drew back and studied her intently with half-hooded eyes. He wondered hazily if she were smashed, or if the wine had just lessened her usual inhibitions. He read nothing but ardor and love in her gaze. "I want that, too," he said softly, reaching for the buttons on her blouse.

Merritt gasped as the back of his palm brushed deliberately against her breasts, lingered over the taut, swelling nipples. She shivered, not from the cold or fear, but the effort it was taking to hold back. He raised his brows in silent question. She affirmed softly, "I want you to touch me. Yes, like that . . . yes . . ."

"What else?" His palms gently traced the swell of her hips, then slid under her, cupping her tighter against him and the proof of his desire.

She burned relentlessly from head to toe, arching and writhing beneath him. "I want to touch you." She ran her hands through his hair, over his back, below his waist. "I want to undress you." She gazed at him rapaciously, longing to know the muscled contours of his body beneath her hands. She wanted to learn the tenderness of his caress, the rough command of his mouth and hands, and the excitement only he could arouse. "I want you to know how you make me feel."

"Which is?" His warm lips moved steadily down her throat, to the accelerating pulse. He caught her skin lightly with his teeth, then laved it with his tongue.

"Alive." She shuddered in response as his mouth curled around the lobe of her ear. He capitulated with a groan that was half passion, half frustration. His mouth moved over hers demandingly as if the sole act of kissing could obliterate every other person who had touched their lives. His hands tolerated no barriers, his touch no withdrawal or holding back. He kept it up until they were both breathless and pulsing with ardor.

Tom moved so he was resting between her knees, his full weight supported by the forearms he placed on either side of her shoulders. Merritt stared at him contemplatively, excited, aware. Her hands rippled across his shoulders as she welcomed his weight, the insistent shift of his form against her parted thighs. "God, I want you," Tom whispered as his hands slid down across her arms to her waist, molding and shaping the flare of her hips.

"And I want you so much," Merritt whispered. But she knew intuitively he would draw out the passion to the very end, lengthening their ardor, heightening their eventual pleasure.

Lifting her slightly, Tom crushed her to him. His legs moved impatiently against hers, sending waves of passion coursing through her. Aggressively, she lifted her mouth to his, reinitiating the kiss with passion that stunned them both. Bold, hungry kisses followed until they were moving together, against one another, molding, imploring, burning with the heat of their desire.

Merritt tugged at his shirt, watched as he shrugged out of it compliantly and tossed it to the floor. "I want to feel all of you against me," she demanded passionately, running her hands down his chest to his belt. "I want to touch you," she whispered boldly, staring up into the intensity of his eyes. "I want—"

"Me," Tom finished with a satisfied sigh, divesting her of her blouse, throwing it aside to lay beside his shirt.

"What we have now is so good." Merritt sighed. More than she had ever hoped to have again. What did it matter how long it lasted?

Tom paused, bending over her seriously. "Why do I have a feeling there's a catch to that statement if I look hard enough?"

Merritt swallowed. He was waiting for an answer, his mood shifting dangerously as the seconds ticked out. With effort he disengaged himself from her arms and sat up. She'd never seen him look more furious or disappointed. The soft glow of firelight played over the tension-flexed muscles of his back. "Don't tell me you're already setting stipulations on how our lovemaking is going to be, when, where, how often, if ever, again?"

"Tom—"

"The truth."

She glanced away evasively, hating the brutal sound of her next words. "You know how I feel about police work as a profession." Her jaw jutted out stubbornly. "It would be pointless to think past tonight." It would ruin everything they'd felt, the impetuousness of the moment.

For Tom, it was like replaying the first time they'd made love, her later rejection. "I see." He paused, fists clenching. "I didn't bring you here to try and seduce you or pressure you into a liaison," he said tensely. "So maybe this isn't such a good idea."

Merritt sat up abruptly, feet touching the parquet floor. "You're not stopping now?" She stared at him incredulously.

Tawny brows raised as he reached for his shirt. "It seems to me you still have your doubts."

"About tomorrow, maybe, but not today. Tom, I want to make love to you!" She was enraged he had strung her along that far and then simply quit.

Sighing, Tom moved even farther away, ignoring her outstretched arms. He bent to stir the glowing red center of the fire. "Merritt, don't make this any harder on me than it already is. We shared a nice evening. For me, at least, it was a great day, too. But how much of what you're feeling right now is caused by the wine and the fire? How are you going to feel in the morning if we do make love again tonight? Will you want to make love to me again or will you resent me even more than you did the last time? We've come too far to go right back to square one, which is exactly where we would be if this continued." He ignored the mute invitation of parted, love-soft lips and clothing that was still draped in wild disarray. "I can't let you do this without thinking it through. I won't risk all the emotional ground we've gained for one night together. It's not worth it."

At Tom's insistence, Merritt again took the bed upstairs and he slept on the couch. More disquieting than the sexual tension that had gone unslaked was the knowledge that Tom was right. Merritt knew she desired him, she knew she was falling in love with him more rapidly and dangerously than ever before. She wasn't sure, however, they could ever have more than a fleeting love affair. And both she and Tom had just realized they did want more out of life and each other.

The question was, would it work? Were they fools to even think of cementing a relationship that was by all other standards doomed from the start?

They drove back to the city bright and early the next morning. Tom dropped her off at her door. "I wish you didn't have to work today." She grimaced, disappointed. She hated to leave the situation between them so unresolved.

"Unfortunately, I've got to work the rest of the weekend." He drew her close for a light, impersonal kiss. "Holidays off don't come cheap."

Merritt knew. And it meant even more that he had decided to share the time with her. Maybe there was hope for them, after all.

Chapter Six

"Well, Johnny, how was your weekend?" Merritt asked as she fitted a rubber band around a stack of un-graded papers. Hers had been delightful, even if she hadn't seen Tom since he had dropped her off at her home early Saturday afternoon.

Johnny Porter sighed, moved to his feet. Frowning, he shuffled toward Merritt's desk and handed her his completed extra credit assignment for the day. "All right, I guess. If you forget about those five-thousand word essays me and Brian had to write."

Merritt suppressed a grin. "An interesting premise, Johnny. Violence in the schools is inappropriate because of the rising cost of medical supplies?"

"I had to think of something," John shrugged. "And after about the first ten words, I gave up on the ordinary reasons."

"Well, at least you're both off the hook now."

"Brian's not." Johnny stuck his hands in his pockets, wheeled around, and walked toward the windows. "His parents are still pretty upset. Especially his mother. She says I'm a bad influence on Brian and that he can't spend time with me anymore."

Merritt studied the impassive expression on Johnny's face. "Maybe she'll change her mind once this blows over."

"I don't think so," John said soundly. "You don't

know Brian's mother. She gets hysterical about everything. She'll never forgive me for this, Brian either, for that matter. He's the first in his family to ever be suspended even for one day."

"How are your parents taking it?" Merritt got up to stand beside Johnny. They gazed companionably out at the empty school yard.

John shrugged. "Nothing new. Mom's convinced it's all because she's working too hard. Dad says the same thing. He feels guilty about leaving, and after yelling at Mom for a while, he soothed his conscience by taking me out to buy a new Atari video game and cartridges."

Merritt sat casually on the windowsill. Despite the gift, Johnny didn't look happy. "Sounds to me like you've been doing plenty of thinking about this."

He shrugged. His shoulders appeared even thinner beneath the shirt. "I went to the library and did some extra research, used the *Readers' Guide* like you taught us at the beginning of the year. All the magazines had plenty of articles about divorce and the effects on the kids." He sighed, brushing back a lone tear near the corner of one eye. "There wasn't much in the children's section. Just one book by Judy Blume and I already read that. Kristin gave it to me. So I went over to the adult book section." He laughed humorlessly. "They had lots of books on how to handle the children after a divorce." He smirked. "They all said not to overdo it on the gifts."

Merritt smiled at his light sarcasm. If John was reaching out for help, in whatever way, it meant his mental outlook was improving. At any rate, talking about his situation had to be better than keeping it all bottled up inside him, threatening to explode in even more volatile or irresponsible behavior. "What else did you find out?" she asked gently.

"Basically, that Dad's into what they call the 'weekend Santa' phase."

Merritt studied her charge. "How long is the phase supposed to last?"

John shoved his hands even deeper into the pockets of his jeans. "Well, there the books and experience differ, but every kid knows when the parents get divorced, the bribes start. Watch, a couple of days and it will be Mom doing the soliciting, buying me a bunch of stuff I don't need, sometimes don't even want, just so she'll feel she's made it up to me."

"Have you spoken with them about this?" Merritt asked.

"No. Besides, what would I say? Hey, folks, I don't want your money I just want your love? I want us to be a regular family again, with Mom, Dad, and kid?" Tears welled behind the bright blue eyes but did not fall. John lapsed into bitter silence.

Merritt placed a comforting hand on her student's shoulder, wanting to be able to do so much more. She sensed something else bothering the child, but she waited for him to restart the conversation. Swallowing hard, John eventually did.

"Dad says he's getting married again next spring. They want me to be at the wedding."

No wonder he'd been upset, she thought. "What does your mother say?"

"That her marriage to Dad was over a long time ago," John remarked scornfully. "It's all for the best. You know the routine. Regardless of their differences, she still wants my father to be happy, and that there's nothing either of us can do about it, even if we wanted to, and she really doesn't anymore. Mom's beginning to like living alone. And that's what worries me, Ms. Reed. If they don't get back together soon, it might never happen. It might really be too late for us to ever be a family again."

Neither Johnny Porter nor Brian Anderson showed up for school the next day. Since the flu had been going around, Merritt didn't think anything of it. As much time as the two boys had previously spent together, it would have been surprising if one hadn't infected the other.

"Did Brian show up for classes today?" Blanche appeared to ask half an hour after school was dismissed.

"No." Merritt finished stuffing papers into her briefcase and reached for her coat. "Neither did Johnny Porter. I marked them both absent."

"I know. I saw the attendance sheets." The guidance counselor grimaced. "Mrs. Anderson was just on the phone. She's concerned because Brian is late getting home from school."

Merritt froze. "Then he wasn't sick?"

Blanche gestured reluctantly. "Apparently not. I didn't mention that to her, though, until I was sure the attendance sheets were right and had double-checked with you."

Merritt sank down into her chair. "You know what this means, don't you?"

"Another suspension for both, if Johnny Porter was truant, too."

"You want me to call Mrs. Anderson back?"

"No, I'll handle that. You just try and find Johnny Porter and his mother and hope to heaven those boys have a good explanation."

There was no answer at the Porter house, so Merritt called Tom. He swore very low at the news. "Ellen's out of town, not due back until late tonight. No doubt that was what Johnny was counting on."

"Then he wasn't sick as far as you know?"

"No, but he's going to wish he had been by the time his parents get through with him. Darn that kid, anyway. As if Ellen hasn't had enough to contend with the past few months."

"Tom—"

"Just sit tight. I'll run by the house and see if he and

Brian are there. Afterward I'll either call you or run by the school.''

He showed up in person forty minutes later, looking more grimly displeased than ever. "They're truant, all right," he announced the moment he and Merritt were alone. "The house is a mess. The kitchen indescribable. They've got games and Atari cartridges spread across the living room floor.''

Merritt tapped her fingers restlessly across her desk. "Now what, Detective?''

"I guess we go out looking for them.'' Tom shrugged. "That is if you want to go along.''

"Are you kidding?'' Merritt asked, grabbing her coat. "I'm partially responsible for this, since I just assumed both were out with the flu. Parents are supposed to phone the office when their children are ill. They frequently don't. And because of clerical understaffing, we usually just assume—''

Tom didn't seem to think the fiasco could have been avoided in any case. He paused, opening the glass lobby door. "If I know John, there isn't much anyone could have done. Once he gets his mind made up about something, that's it. Beyond which, truant is truant, whether it's one hour, half a day, or a whole week.''

Together, they checked the local parks, city streets, local shopping centers, and small businesses and restaurants. Two hours later both were exhausted. They returned at Tom's suggestion to his sister's house. "Ellen ought to be due back anytime now," Tom informed, tripping over an Atari cartridge on the floor.

Merritt knelt to stack several others and restore order to the room. Johnny hadn't been kidding when he had said his father had tried to buy him off the previous weekend. There must have been fifteen cartridges there. A proliferation of glasses and half-eaten snacks were strewn across every chair and countertop.

Tom swore continually as together he and Merritt

routinely cleaned up the mess. "Normally, I'd wait and see John did this himself," Tom muttered beneath his breath. "But I don't want Ellen to have to walk in on the mess."

Merritt agreed. The phone jangled, interrupting their disgusted reverie. "Hello." Tom listened intently. Frown deepening, he queried curtly, "Where are they now? No, I don't want to pick them up at the store. And forget sparing them any of the usual shoplifting procedure on my account. Give both Brian and John the full treatment. And Frank?" Tom paused. "Don't be in any great hurry to call either of their parents. Let the boys sweat it out a bit first. Thanks. See you in a little bit."

"John and Brian were caught shoplifting?" Merritt asked incredulously as Tom hung up the phone. Both boys might have been mischievous and imaginative, but neither had ever done anything remotely unethical.

"Two hundred dollars worth of new Atari cartridges, if you can believe that. Apparently, they'd had them stuffed inside their sweat shirts, and tried to walk out the door. The whole episode was recorded on closed-circuit television. There's no doubt both were guilty as hell, and evidently having one great time doing it, too."

Merritt slid the back of her hand across her mouth. "Tom, I had no idea either boy was feeling restless. I talked to Johnny yesterday, of course, and he was understandably upset about his father's plans to remarry. Brian, too, apparently was distressed because his parents had forbid him to play with John anymore after that fist fight they had at school."

Tom's eyebrows raised. Apparently, that much was news to him. "Either way, it doesn't excuse this."

Merritt reached for the phone. "We've got to call Brian's parents."

The hand on hers held the receiver firmly down.

"The desk sergeant at the station house will take care of that as soon as the boys have been processed."

"But Brian's mother will be worried."

"Right. And she'll rush in to save her baby before he's even been fingerprinted or booked, if we call her now. You're going to have to trust me on this, Merritt. Let things go the usual way. It will only be fifteen or twenty more minutes before Brian's parents are notified, but believe me, by the time the desk sergeant and staff are through with the delinquents, it will seem like a lifetime to them. Getting mug shots taken and being thrown into a holding cell isn't something one easily forgets."

"Aren't you being just a big rigid?" Merritt ground out.

Tom cast her an unappreciative glance as he tugged at the tie around his neck. "If you hadn't bailed them out the first time, and had given them the full three days suspension for fighting in the first place, they wouldn't be out shoplifting now."

Merritt winced. His criticism stung, even more so because it was at least partially accurate. "Maybe I shouldn't have bailed them out the first time. But they are only eleven years old, Tom. And John's had such a rough time on the home front."

Tom met her stare unflinchingly. "If they're old enough to shoplift and skip school, I think they'll survive this," he said dryly.

"What are you trying to do, Tom? Scare them into straightening up their act?"

"At the very least."

Merritt hated his attitude. "What if the taste of prison life doesn't work, Tom?"

"It will." He seemed very sure of himself. And altogether too unconcerned about what might happen to the boys, she thought resentfully.

"Juvenile detention centers breed delinquents, Hennessey. They don't cure them of the penchant for crime!"

"So now you're an expert on criminal law?" A muscle clenched in his jaw.

"I know sixth-graders and what is right and what is inappropriate. After all, this is their first offense."

"And their last," Tom cut in rigidly, crossing his arms over his chest. "If the sergeant or I have anything to do with it."

Merritt's reservations increased when they reached the police station. Artie Kochek was standing at the front desk, talking to the sergeant on duty. He turned when he saw Tom, a worried, knowing expression crossing his youthful face. "Some Christmas present for your sister, isn't it?"

"Where is he?" Tom gave the high sign to the man in blue on the other side of the desk.

"In the holding tank with the other kid. What's his name?" The sergeant turned to Kochek.

"Brian Anderson," Merritt supplied quietly.

Artie cocked a blond brow, openly curious. "You know him, too?" Apparently, he assumed she was just there to see Johnny.

"They're my students, both of them," she answered in a gritty tone laced with anxiety. She ignored Tom's wish to handle the release. "May I see them? After all, they are partially my responsibility, since they were both truant from my class today."

Air hissed through Artie's teeth as he sent a questioning look toward first the desk sergeant, then Tom. The sergeant and Artie were both amenable, but Tom shook his head.

"Why not?"

"Because I don't want them to think you're bailing them out," Tom said tightly. In a gesture of frustration, he pushed back his jacket and clamped his hands on his hips. His eyes were hard, implacable.

Merritt's gaze drifted down to the photo badge he still had clipped to his pocket, the police number and identification beneath. "Then you go," she suggested quietly. "Just talk to them. Make sure they're all right."

Wordlessly Tom shook his head.

"Forget you're a cop for a second," she counseled despairingly under her breath. "Johnny's your nephew, for heaven's sake!" The next words came tumbling out before she had a chance to think. "How can you be so cold?"

He gave her a dark, warning look. "Don't second-guess me on this one, Merritt. This is my domain. And we've already done it your way, to less than positive results."

"Don't treat my students as if they were common criminals guilty of violating parole!" Merritt's protective instincts got the better of her. With effort, and awareness of the audience they were gathering, she lowered her tone. "Please, Tom. Brian and John have been in here for the better part of an hour. I just want to make sure they're all right."

"They're not off the hook," he cautioned.

"Believe me, I'll make sure they're aware of the gravity of what they've done." Merritt met his gaze in silent plea. After a minute he gave in reluctantly. But frustration, his and hers, still permeated the air.

Artie Kochek escorted Merritt through the maze of cells to the holding room where the two boys were confined. "Is this usual procedure?" Merritt asked, shoving her trembling hands into the pockets of her coat. Never had she been so close to steel doors, bars, and small windowless cells. The feeling of claustrophobia was overwhelming.

"Depends on the offense. Some kids get off with a warning and never see so much as the inside of a squad car. Others, like John and Brian, are given the rude

awakening of the whole treatment. They're fingerprinted, booked, cursorily searched, and if they make it
as far as the Juvenile Detention Center, showered and
deloused.''

''That seems a little harsh.'' Merritt paused against a
metal door.

Artie Kochek looked down at her, no sympathy read-
able in his gaze. ''Where do you draw the line, Ms.
Reed? How else do we let them know what's in store
for them a little further down the line? Don't be so
hard on my buddy. Tom's just doing his job. If anything, you ought to be thankful he didn't exercise his
unofficial option of pulling a few strings to spare either
Johnny or Brian the ordeal. Maybe they'll learn something from this yet. Frankly, they're lucky they haven't
been sent on to the Juvenile Detention Center. That
would have been my next step.''

Merritt was silent as he moved forward to the last
cell, unlocked the door. Johnny and Brian were sharing
a lone metal bunk. Both boys looked pale and drawn
and were silent. When they saw Merritt relief quickly
flooded their tense features, to be replaced by wary sus-
picion almost immediately. Behind her the cell door
shut. For the moment at least, teacher and students
were alone. Merritt stifled the urge to take both impetuous rebels in her arms and smother them with a
fierce maternal hug. Sighing, she leaned against the
wall, one ankle crossing her other booted foot. After a
quick assessing glance from her, both boys guiltily refused to meet her probing gaze.

''What are you doing here?'' Brian asked finally,
scuffing his shoe against the floor.

''I might ask both of you the same question.'' Merritt folded her hands across her chest. ''Where were
you today? We missed you at school.''

''If you knew where we were, then you probably already know the answer to that, too.'' John leaned back

against the bunk, one knee raised, his arms twined around the bent limb.

Merritt wasn't fooled by the nonchalant tone. He was scared as hell. Both were. Their hands were shaking. "Why'd you skip school, John?" she asked quietly. "Brian?" She turned to his blushing companion.

Brian shrugged and cast John a wary sidelong glance. Neither responded. "Are we in trouble?" Brian asked finally. John gave a good appearance of pretending not to care.

"Suspension seems likely." Merritt sighed.

Silence fell among them. As the seconds ticked by the boys' fear became more and more evident. "Are you going to get us out of here?" Brian asked.

"John's uncle is talking to the desk sergeant now."

John rolled his eyes, muttered something disparaging beneath his breath. "Now we'll never be let go," he complained, reclenching the hands twined around his knee. Merritt's brow raised, and he met her reprimand rebelliously. "Uncle Tom could have gotten us out of here. He could have pulled some strings. Talked to one of his buddies—"

Tom appeared in the door, his rugged face taut with anger. Apparently, he'd caught the tail end of his nephew's statement. "You're right, kiddo, on all counts. If it were up to me alone, you'd be here for another week at the very least. After what you pulled—"

"You're not my dad!" John shouted, eyes flashing as he got to his feet. "And I'm sick and tired of you trying to tell me what to do when my mom isn't around!" Artie Kochek stepped in behind Tom. At the sight of the blue uniform and flashing silver badge, the boy backed down.

Brian swallowed and looked grim, suddenly not all that anxious to be caught up in the middle of what was turning out to be a full-fledged Porter family war. "Did you call my folks?'' Brian asked finally, his voice shaking slightly.

"Your mother's out there now," Kochek supplied.

"Good luck," John grumbled beneath his breath, slapping the open palm of his partner-in-crime. "You're gonna need it if we know your mother. Hysterical time."

"You said it." Brian gathered his macho bravado.

"If I were you," Tom advised, taking a threatening step forward, "I'd watch those mouths."

Swallowing, Brian departed. John started to retort, then apparently thought better of it. "I'm not leaving here with anyone but my mom or my dad," he stated finally. "So you can just forget about taking me home, either of you."

"Fine with me." Tom whirled toward the door, dragging Merritt along in his wake before she had the chance to reply. "Maybe the extra time alone will do you some good. Up until now, you certainly haven't been using your brain."

"Tom, maybe we should—"

"The wait will do him good," Tom decided, pausing to shut and lock the door behind him. Through the glass, Merritt saw Johnny bury his head disconsolately in his hands.

"Tom, he's crying," she implored, her heart going out to the rebellious child.

"Let him." His uncle's pronouncement was grim. "Ten to one it will be the most honest thing he's done yet today."

Tom drove Merritt home in silence. Exhausted, she shut her eyes and rested her face against the winter-cool glass. Together, not touching, they walked the distance to her door. "You're angry with me, aren't you?" Tom whispered finally in the darkness of the front porch.

Merritt recoiled instantaneously from the warm,

tender touch of his hand. Why couldn't he have shown some of that compassion toward the boy? Merritt knew he loved his nephew. That had been evident from the first. "You shouldn't have left John there at the station alone. You said yourself it will be hours before Ellen can pick him up."

"Precisely why he should stay there," Tom said coolly. "It will give him time alone. And we won't have to worry about him going out and doing yet another impetuous thing."

Merritt remained unconvinced. Tom's hand dropped. He shoved both hands in his pockets, looked past Merritt toward the lights glowing on the street. "Beyond which, John did have a point. I should stop pinch-hitting for Ellen and Ted. I'm not John's father."

"What else could you have done?" Merritt said gently, seeing for the first time what a difficult position Tom had been put in. "Ellen wasn't home this afternoon. Ted Porter's still in Columbus trying that case—"

"It's a two-hour drive for Ted to get home. And maybe John's right. Maybe it is time Ellen made some adjustments in her schedule, regardless of the effect it has on her career."

Merritt studied the tension in his jaw. With every second that passed he seemed to be putting another emotional mile between them. She wanted to reach out and pull him toward her, lace her fingers through his, wrap him in a passionate embrace and return the kiss she knew just moments before he had been prepared to give. But when she reached out to tentatively touch his hand, he withdrew.

"You think I'm some sort of a monster, don't you?"

"I—"

"I care about John," Tom said finally. Thrusting his hands in his pockets, he strolled to the other end of the porch. "But this is one family problem they're just going to have to resolve. We have no part in it, Merritt. Either of us. I don't want you bailing John out again." He descended the steps without so much as a good-bye kiss or touch of his hand. Merritt stared after him, wondering if she would ever see him again.

As Merritt had predicted, John and Brian were both expelled from school for the duration of the week. This time their make-up work would be penalized with a twenty-five percent reduction of every grade. Merritt also received a stern slap on the hands.

"This isn't the first complaint we've had about your lax administration, Ms. Reed," the principal advised. "Mrs. Anderson contends if you'd notified her earlier of Brian's truancy, he wouldn't have been picked up for shoplifting."

That's right, Merritt thought angrily, *shift the blame.* "Brian Anderson was marked absent. With the flu epidemic circulating, there was no reason to suspect he was gone for any other reason."

"I know that," Mr. Tierney advised patiently. "And technically, you're above reproach. I think, however, that you should be aware Mrs. Anderson is not willing to let it go at that. She wants you removed from your post and is prepared to lobby through the school board to achieve it." He paused, running a hand tensely across the back of his neck. A packet of antacids was just inches from his hand. "So watch your step. I can defend you against this issue and possibly the frank discussion of family life as it pertains to your students and children of divorce, but that's about it."

Yards of solid blue and sheer white covered Merritt Reed's living room. The coffee table had been pushed aside, a portable sewing machine set up in its stead. The doorbell rang just as she was finishing a lengthy machine-hemmed edge. "Coming!" Merritt shouted.

Dusting off her warm-up suit, she carefully edged her way to the door. Leaded glass revealed the shadow of a man on her porch. "Tom," Merritt whispered, opening the door.

"Mind if I come in?"

Merritt unlocked the screen, holding it open as he passed and caught the frame. "I wanted to apologize for the other night," he began. "Family problems or no, I shouldn't have taken out my frustrations on you."

Merritt nodded, her glance straying consciously down to her sweat-socked feet. Nervously she smoothed the wispy strands of hair haphazardly framing her face.

"You don't have to do that." He caught the back of her hand, bestowed it with a tender kiss. "You're beautiful just as you are." As if to emphasize the sincerity of the comment, he reeled her in obligingly. Several lengthy kisses later, the last of Merritt's reserve melted away. Eventually, Tom looked past Merritt toward the chaos decorating her living room. "What's all this? Or should I ask?"

"Not only can you ask, you can help," Merritt replied tartly. "They're your drapes for your Spring Valley home. Want to lend a hand?"

"Sure," Tom agreed cautiously. He squinted suspiciously at the gleaming electric sewing machine. "That is if you think I'm able."

"You can pin and measure and leave the stitching to me," Merritt decided dryly, taking him by the hand. Relief relaxed his frame as Tom casually shed his coat and tossed it over the back of a dining room chair. "Point the way, boss."

They worked in silence for a while, Tom first pinning up a two-inch hem Merritt had previously measured and marked lightly with dressmaker's chalk. Shoeless, sitting cross-legged on the floor with a mouthful of pins, and drapery fabric on his lap, he had never looked more at ease or attractive. Merritt felt a rush of longing. She wanted him physically. She also wanted his company, the simple pleasure of working on a project side by side, sharing one another's problems, surviving the good times as well as the bad.

"How are things at school?" Tom asked finally.

Briefly Merritt confided her warning from the school principal. "John and Brian will be back on Friday. There's a field trip scheduled for that day, though, so maybe it won't be so awkward." Maybe by the following Monday it all would have been forgotten.

"I don't know. I hate to say this, but I think you're being too optimistic." Frowning worriedly, Tom rose and strode lithely over to give her another drape to run through the machine. "John's still giving Ellen a pretty hard time. He asked to go live with his dad. Ted doesn't want him. He said point-blank he just didn't have the time or the energy to mess with everything going on at his firm, the divorce, a new wife, and the problems of an eleven-year-old boy. Plus the fact he'll be in Columbus for at least the next few weeks, so school-wise it would be out of the question. Unfortunately, John heard the whole exchange—he was listening on the phone extension in Ellen's room. Evidently, there was a pretty nasty row. Ted drove up to see Johnny yesterday, spent the evening with him and tried to explain, but John wasn't buying any of it. Ellen looks worse than ever."

"Oh, Tom, I'm sorry." Tears of compassion moistened Merritt's eyes.

Tom sighed heavily. He walked back to finish pinning up the last piece to be hemmed. "All things considered, that kid has had one rough time. Of course, John hasn't gone out of his way to make things easy on himself, but I guess it's no wonder he's misbehaving."

Conversation turned to the work at hand as they finished stitching the drapes. Routinely, Tom folded them into neat squares upon the sofa. "When I asked you to go to Spring Valley with me over the holidays, I didn't mean for you to work yourself into the ground supplying window coverings for my weekend home."

Merritt strolled closer. She shrugged carelessly, the indolent gesture belying the complacency in her eyes. "It was my pleasure, believe me. Besides, I wouldn't have had anything else to do tonight except watch television or read."

"Solitary endeavors." Tom stretched long legs. "I am very familiar with those."

"Care for some hot spiced cider?" Merritt asked. She was suddenly very glad he had dropped by. She hadn't realized how much she'd needed to see him or how happy he could make her feel.

"Sounds good." Tom followed her out to the kitchen. Arms folded casually across his chest, he leaned against the counter, watching her heat cider and add spices and cinnamon sticks. "I've missed you," he said softly. "It's only been a day and a half since we've seen each other and it feels like six weeks."

"I know." Merritt handed him the mug. Their hands brushed and she thrilled at his touch.

"I didn't want to marry again, Merritt. I didn't want to even get involved on a regular basis."

"And now?" For a moment she wasn't sure what he was trying to tell her. Panic made her heart race. But her tone and demeanor were coolly composed.

"My perspectives are changing," he said softly. "I want you with me all the time. I want to make love to you more than I thought I would ever want any woman." The relaxed stance, the casual words, his assumption in simply dropping by all added to the sensation their budding relationship was being taken for granted. He didn't want to court her or know her more intimately. He wanted to sleep with her. And abruptly, it wasn't enough.

Merritt turned and glided wordlessly into the living

room, fighting for composure, though her first instinct was simply to throw him out. Tom followed, settling his long frame on the other end of the overstuffed sofa. He watched her carefully. "You're still angry with me because of our disagreement the other night," he assumed.

That much was true. Tom could have been more sympathetic to his nephew's plight. "I'm wondering where our relationship is going to lead," Merritt admitted, sipping the cider.

He stared at her quietly, stunned. "You're asking me for some sort of commitment or promise? Marriage?" Obviously, nothing could have been further from his mind.

Was she? "You'll forgive me if I'm not more experienced in the etiquette of a love affair," she said icily. "I haven't had much experience along those lines, so I don't know how to proceed. I'm also not very good at taking romantic involvements one day at a time." She paused, voice softening at the utter bewilderment lining his face. "I have to know where I stand with you, Tom." The more she talked, the less she felt she knew. He was holding something back, whether it was a part of himself or a fear she didn't know.

"I've told you I love you. I'll be with you whenever I can. My work doesn't leave room for much else. And knowing the way you feel about cops in general..."

Merritt stared steadily at the floor. "Everything that's happened the past few days has made me come to a few realizations of my own, Tom." She glanced up imploringly. "I want a family someday, Tom. Children of my own."

He didn't deny wanting the same, but his words were purposefully cruel. "Tell me the truth, Merritt. Would you really want to have a child by someone who might walk out the door to go to work someday and never come back?" They both knew it could happen.

"That could happen to anyone," she countered, trying desperately to convince herself as well as him.

"In my case, the odds are double."

Silence fell between them. Tears burned behind dark lashes, threatening to spill over onto Merritt's pale, drawn cheeks. She set her cider aside with a deliberate thud, hoping Tom would pick up on the signal and simply leave. Instead, he reached over and lowered the lamp next to him. His cider took up a place on the coffee table next to hers. Before she could take a breath, he was sliding forward across the sofa. Her hands were ensconced in the compelling warmth of his. "I'll go if you want me to," he said, very low. "But you have to know it's not what I'd prefer to do."

Merritt's heart thudded faster. "At this point, I'm not sure what I want." Which was all the more reason he should go. "And until I am, Tom, I'd rather not see you again."

"I don't believe that," he said softly, waiting.

Merritt's pulse raced faster. "It's true." Her chin lifted defiantly. Tom knew very well what the noble thing to do would be. Desire won, hands down. "Then let me help you change your mind." His lips moved across hers tentatively, searching out the sweet liquid warmth of her own. Merritt's head dipped to the side evasively. She wanted him. She didn't want to be hurt.

"I care about you." Her whisper trembled with the husky vibrato of tears.

Pliantly his hand moved beneath her chin, tilting her gaze up to his. He searched her face seriously for long moments. Merritt didn't know what he hoped to find. "Then don't send me away," he whispered, lips pressing against her jaw, the curve of her cheek. His fingers wove through the tangled strands of her hair. "Not tonight. Not ever."

His kiss lingered on her lips. Merritt's hands laced around his neck and her fingers melded in the soft layers of his hair. She drank in the unique scents of him as ardor took command swiftly, dictating her every movement, her every breath. He responded with a ruthless, steady dominance that made it impossible for her to think. She could only experience the changing moods and pressures of his kiss, the thoroughness of his embrace.

The soothing weight of Tom's body slid her backward onto the stacked pillows of the sofa. "Whatever happens," he whispered, sliding open the front zipper of her warm-up to reveal naked breasts, "neither of us will be able to walk away unscathed." He would always remember her, and Merritt knew, she could never forget him.

"I don't want to leave you unscathed," Merritt whispered. She wanted to scale the heights of ecstasy with him, never to come back down, experience again and again the driving pressure of his mouth. "I want to spend the entire night in your arms," she confided, wishing the dawn would never come.

His hands slid beneath the knit jacket to lightly caress the silken skin of her bare back from shoulder blade to waist. His lips teased the upper curves of her breasts, then slid temptingly across the lower arches. Using both hands he slid the warm-up pants and her panties from her thighs.

Merritt divested him of his shirt, then the belt came undone, next his trousers were thrown to the floor. Tenderly she explored the hair-roughened muscular legs. She liked the tautness of his thighs, the flat plane of his abdomen, the breadth of his chest above his ribs.

Their gazes met. Merritt surrendered to the fierce desire in his. The touch of his exploring hands was infinitely, deceptively patient as he lowered her slowly back onto the cushions, the curve of her body accommodating the demanding heated silhouette of his. He moved against her, tongue insinuating its way into her mouth, exploring the honeyed crevices, never ceasing until he had extracted the most potent ardor she was capable of giving, until she was returning kiss for kiss, initiating an aggression of her own, making him groan, shift, clasp her to him in an unshakable embrace.

And then abruptly he was moving down, his lips caressing the flat plane of her abdomen, the curve of her lissome thigh, the lines of her calf, the back of her knee, the arch of her foot. Merritt cried out, and then once again as his tongue moved tantalizingly upward, within. He settled in the softness of her thighs, his bold caress sending her into a heated cataclysm of sensation. Merritt rose partway on her elbows. Her hands moved beseechingly under his shoulders, lifting him closer. He moved swiftly then, crushing her with his weight. Her senses swirled as they clung together, joined, moved to more breathtaking heights.

They clung together for long moments afterward. Finally, Tom reached above her head to turn out the last dim living room light. Entwined together in the darkness, the last thing Merritt recalled before she drifted off was the steady comforting beat of his heart against her breasts, the fragrant mingling of his breath exhaling in cadence to her own.

Merritt woke an hour later. Tom was dressing silently in the dark. An afghan covered her naked state. She didn't say anything at first, simply rose on her elbows, watched, one hand tangling through the unruly length of her hair as he prepared to sneak out of her house like the proverbial thief in the night.

He swiveled around when he saw she was awake. A frown tugged at the corners of his generous mouth. "I'm sorry," he said softly, walking over to perch on the side of the sofa. "I didn't mean to wake you." The apology was rough with fatigue, as if he hated to have to speak to her at all.

"Going home?" Merritt tried without success to mask the hurt in her voice.

"Work." Tom laced his fingers through her hair, traced tenderly the angle of her jaw, the shell of her ear. "We've had this stakeout going for weeks now and—"

"I don't want to hear it." Merritt turned her gaze away. She sat up straighter, gathering the afghan around her like a cloak of pride. "I don't want to hear anything about your police work, not ever." If possible, she wanted to forget the fact Tom Hennessey was a cop. It was the only way she would ever survive.

The hand cupping her face did not drop or lessen its grip. Gradually the pressure increased until Merritt had no choice but to turn her face back to his infuriatingly calm surveyal. "If you're thinking I should have told you earlier, you're right," he pronounced matter-of-factly. "However, I didn't want to fight." Reluctantly he got up to retrieve his shirt. "And if I had mentioned earlier that I would have to leave, you can bet we would have had a dilly."

"If you had mentioned it, I never would have let you stay." Defensively Merritt swung her legs around to the floor. She tucked the knitted fabric discreetly under each side of her arms.

"Reason number two." Tom methodically buttoned his shirt, slipped on his shoes. Merritt watched dismally as he swiftly reclaimed his coat. Worse than the sadness, she realized belatedly, was the fright. The fear she might never see him again, at least not alive. The terror of what would happen to *her* if that did occur.

Tom stretched a compelling hand to hers, pulled her heedlessly to her feet against him. Her hands slid unbidden into the lining of his coat, to better caress his shirt-clad chest. Emotions warred within her, adding to the passionate confusion she felt. For once, Merritt desperately hoped he would not kiss her.

"Don't let me leave on an angry note," Tom

whispered, mouth once again passionately and tenderly claiming her own. When the kiss ended, Merritt was so dizzy with desire she could hardly stand. It was no huge comfort to see ardor stamped all over his lean physique. What kind of death wish did she have? Tom was still a cop, their affair still doomed from the start and irrevocably, Merritt thought, probably to the finish as well. "I'll call you," Tom promised, slipping out of her embrace and heading toward the door.

Merritt wanted to say "Don't bother." Predictably, the words never came.

Chapter Seven

Thursday brought no word from Tom except a hurried phone call between work sessions at the police station. Friday brought the much-touted class trip to the Museum of Natural History near Eden Park and the return of the two expelled students to class. Merritt welcomed both boys as if nothing out of the ordinary had ever occurred. Their classmates were not as easily distracted. Comments ranged from the provoking to the commiserating.

John and Brian stuck close together during the bus ride through the holiday decorated downtown area. Not surprisingly, much of their thinly veiled truculence was directed at Merritt. She was, after all, the handiest authority figure there, and with the exception of parent chaperon and homeroom mother, Mrs. Stratton, the only other adult.

The class waited excitedly on the sidewalk in front of the museum. "All right, everyone, stay close," Merritt advised. "We only have an hour and a half to tour the major exhibits before we adjourn for lunch."

Disgruntled murmurs rippled the pre-adolescent crowd. Girls fidgeted with purses and cameras and boys practiced stepping on the heels of the person in front of them.

It was somewhere between a full-scale replica of a cavern with a waterfall and the upright carnivorous Allosau-

rus that Merritt first noticed Brian and John lagging behind. "Boys, let's keep up now," she admonished. "We
don't want anyone getting separated from the group."

"Yes, ma'am," Brian Anderson retorted, a rebellious smirk twisting his lips. Johnny Porter said nothing. The way he looked at her, then allowed his gaze to
slide defensively away, made Merritt recall the ugly encounter he'd had with Tom at the police station earlier
in the week. This once, she wished she had no personal
involvement with any of his family. It would have
made things so much easier.

"I'm hungry." Bobby Martin's complaint broke her
reverie.

"My feet hurt," said Patty Dunlap.

"If you'd wear tennis shoes instead of those ridiculous Wedgies..." Kristin Stratton remonstrated.

"Who asked you? Besides," Patty shot back with a
dramatic swirl of her waist-length red hair that left all
the girls envious and the boys agape, "I think the high
heels make me look older."

The last statement was met with a host of guffaws
and more wisecracks from the boys. A few of the girls
muttered frank remarks ungenerously beneath their
breath. Merritt held up a silencing palm. "Lunch is in
Eden Park. There will be hot chocolate and marshmal-
lows for all. So let's get going. On the bus now."

A head count and roll call five minutes later proved
the group intact. The bus driver escorted a rowdy
eleven-year-old crowd to the chill of the park beyond.
As Merritt had expected, the sack lunch and hot drink
regime was enthusiastically welcomed by the free-
wheeling class. Forty-five minutes later the task of
rounding up the sprites began. "Three missing by my
calculations." Kristin Stratton's mother frowned.

Merritt looked behind her. Troy Simmons was strolling out of the park restroom, idly glancing up at the web
of bare tree branches and winter-gray sky.

"Make that two." Merritt checked around quickly. "No doubt Brian and Johnny are still in the restroom, too."

"No, they're not, at least not in the men's room," Troy commented complacently as he joined the group. "*I* was the last one out."

Warning bells sounded in Merritt's head, but five years of teaching kept her calm. "Check again, Troy. Maybe you just overlooked them."

"I didn't."

"Check."

Troy stomped off, only to be back a minute and a half later, still shaking his head. "Told you. No one in there. And I checked *everywhere*," he elaborated before Merritt could grill him about the respective stalls.

She turned to the class, irritation slicing through her voice. "Okay, class. Anyone know where the two boys might have gone?" Her question was met with perplexed shrugs. "Anyone see them wander off in any specific direction?" she asked. Again, the response was uniformly negative.

She and Mrs. Stratton exchanged a worried glance. "Keep asking the children about the boys," Merritt advised quietly. "Try and determine the last time they were seen by everyone. At this point, any clue at all will help." Walking briskly toward the restrooms, Merritt shouted for the errant boys. She was met only with silence. Not trusting their absence to be as genuine as it looked, she went back to the men's room, and after nervously knocking, searched the premises herself. It was, as Troy had asserted, empty. The ladies' room was equally deserted, and aside from the shelter of trees and picnic tables, there was no other place within walking vicinity to hide.

Eventually, Merritt returned to the bus. If the children were playing a trick, as she half-feared they were, there would be the devil to pay later. If they weren't...

Merritt dismissed the thought abruptly. She would find the boys. Misunderstanding or no, deliberate or otherwise, they would find their way back to the group soon.

Inside the bus, the children were sitting quietly in their seats. Merritt handed Mrs. Stratton her clipboard. "Call roll and keep everyone here," she said quietly. "I'm going to have another quick look around. They can't have gone very far," she reassured, as much for her own sake as Mrs. Stratton's. "They probably just got turned around and went in the wrong direction." Maybe they'd even taken off to try and find a water fountain. The possibilities were endless and all equally benign.

Methodically she jogged from one section of the central quadrant to the other, half expecting the two frolicsome boys to peer around the base of an oak any second. They didn't. Neither did they show up at any of the other logical restrooms, phone booths, or covered shelters. Glancing at her watch, Merritt finally returned to the bus. "This park covers a hundred eighty-six acres," she panted breathlessly at last. "There's no way I'm going to be able to traipse through it alone and on foot with any hope of catching up to the renegades." Merritt looked at Mrs. Stratton. "If you wouldn't mind taking sole responsibility for the group, I'd like you to escort the children back to school and see they return to their regular classroom. Barring any other major catastrophes or delays, they should all be able to make their usual buses home. I'll notify the school, stay until the boys are found, and escort them home."

Mrs. Stratton looked worried, the school bus driver plainly bored. "How will *you* get home?"

Merritt grimaced tightly. "I'll worry about that *after* I've collared them."

A check with the park superintendent and his employees proved just as fruitless as Merritt's earlier search. Tom Hennessey arrived shortly after four. "I got here as soon as I could." Despite the ruddiness highlighting his face, he looked gray with worry. "What happened?"

Merritt resisted the urge to throw herself into his arms, and instead remained a discreetly aloof distance, hands shoved in the pockets of her camel winter coat. A crocheted ivory muffler hung casually around her neck beneath the upturned collar. "John and Brian disappeared during lunch. We were touring the museum, stopped here for a minipicnic so the children could let off steam. When we went to collect the children, they were nowhere to be found."

"Wasn't anyone watching them?"

"We had thirty children running wild after a morning of total, whispered control and near-perfect manners. I was assisted by only one other adult, Kristin Stratton's mother, since for the most part our driver preferred to remain on the bus. Of course we were watching them!" Merritt's temper momentarily got the better of her.

Tom sighed, his gaze only slightly less chastising. "Any clue as to where they might have gone?" The words were an angry staccato.

Merritt frowned. "None."

"I might have expected something like this would happen!" Brian Anderson's mother flew into the park office like a runaway mare. Her champagne-frosted hair was perfectly coiffed despite her hysteria, her outfit a coordinating mint-green skirt and sweater set, in cashmere. Her heels made an angry pounding across the polished linoleum floor as she threw herself directly into the circle of worried searchers. "God knows you're incompetent, Ms. Reed—"

"Now hold on just a minute here," the park superintendent interjected.

"I'll hold on when you've found my son! Well?"

Helen Anderson approached Merritt, both hands on her hips. "What have you encouraged him to do now?"

"I beg your pardon?"

Tom stepped front and center to the group. Reaching into his pocket, he flashed the Cincinnati police department badge, routinely recited rank and name. "Let's just concentrate on finding the two boys, ma'am. There will be plenty of time for discussion later."

Helen caught the warning note in the detective's tone. "Fine." She nodded succinctly at last. "I assume you've taken charge here?"

"Yes, ma'am. It appears your son Brian and his friend John Porter have run away. At the very least deliberately wandered off."

Helen Anderson sent a withering glare toward Merritt. Wrinkles added a hard, uncompromising edge to her eyes, her mouth.

"Do you know if Brian had any money with him?" Tom interrogated quietly. "Is there anyplace in particular he might have gone?"

The angry mother's gaze was still fixed on Merritt's ashen face. She replied offhandedly, "Brian would never have done anything like this on his own. If it was a deliberate attempt to run away, then it had to have been John Porter's idea."

Tom's jaw went rigid, but he said nothing as he scribbled a notation on his pad. "Does Brian have any friends in the area? Any relative to whom he might turn?"

Mrs. Anderson shook her head. As the anger wore off, the reality of the situation began to sink in. "Then they really are lost?" Her voice was suddenly very small.

Tom nodded. "Ms. Reed questioned the children before they left the park. We sent an officer over to talk with them before they were dismissed from school. No one can account for where the boys might have gone.

A cursory search of the area revealed no evidence of struggle. As of yet, they haven't arrived at any of the park shelters or information stations for help. So all we can assume is that either they were abducted—and there's nothing to suggest that in fact did happen," he stressed with deliberate calm, "or the boys have run away. Going by their intractable behavior the past week or so, it seems a logical conclusion. Now"—he sighed wearily—"about the money..."

"Brian had at least twenty dollars in his piggy bank, maybe more. Allowance money he had saved." Mrs. Anderson sat down weakly. Merritt walked over to the machine, returning with a cup of hot coffee she pressed into Helen's shaking hands. Woodenly Helen Anderson continued, "I checked the house before I left. It was all gone. That, and another ten from my purse."

The park staff and police force searched the area thoroughly as darkness fell over the River City. Tom seemed reassured to find no evidence of any kind. "Runaways," he pronounced grimly over his fourth cup of coffee. A tersely muttered summation of his nephew's behavior followed, ending just as his sister Ellen came in through the door. "Tom." Tears filled her eyes as the frail woman threw herself headlong into her older brother's arms.

Reflexively Tom tautened his affectionate grasp. "We'll find him, Ellen. He can't have gone far."

"I ran home before coming over." Ellen choked back her tears. "There's no sign he's been there since we left this morning. Oh, Tom, what are we going to do?"

"Keep looking." The detective's advice was grim. "Do you have any idea how much money he might have collected?"

"No, though there was nothing left in his room just

now. His billfold was gone. Ted's been giving him extra money, sometimes doubling his allowance.''

"A guess?" Tom continued to prod.

"Somewhere between fifty and a hundred dollars. I don't know. He was saving for a new telescope all summer. I think he was getting close to the amount he needed."

All were silent. An enraged Helen Anderson joined the group. The looks exchanged between the two mothers were full of rigid animosity. Tom's sigh was audible. Merritt felt her spine stiffen with dismay. She simply wanted both her students back, not World War III.

Helen Anderson was the first one to speak. Her words were every bit as vile as Merritt had expected. "This wouldn't have happened if you'd been home with your child in the first place, Ellen."

Ellen's blond brows raised. "Jealous, Helen? Isn't there enough in the Decency in Textbooks Committee to keep you busy anymore? Now that you've thrown Thomas Hardy, Aldous Huxley, and Flannery O'Connor off the list, what more is there to do?"

"As a divorced single parent, I'd hardly expect you to know what constitutes moral or immoral fiction," Helen sniffed.

Ellen's glare was extremely level, and surprisingly poised. "You would be surprised what I know, Helen. But then that's hardly the issue at hand, is it? The morals of your husband or my ex?"

Helen paled to the shade of the stucco walls. Unexpectedly, Artie Kochek walked in to give a status on the city-wide search. Everyone else in the group simultaneously breathed a sigh of relief. "We've got descriptions out at every bus terminal in the area, as well as the airport and the train stations."

Tom nodded. "Maybe something will turn up." It was clear, though, he wasn't convinced and as the night wore on indefinitely, Merritt, Ellen, and Helen began to have their doubts. "Why don't you go home?" Tom urged his sister quietly at last. "Maybe Johnny's turned up by now. If not, you really should be there in case he does try to call and let you know where he is."

Merritt volunteered to go with Tom's sister. As they left the park station Tom was still deep in conversation with Helen. Merritt didn't envy him the night ahead. "What was all that about with Helen Anderson?" Merritt asked, once they were back in Hyde Park. Wearily she fixed them both a cup of tea.

Ellen buried her face in her hands, confessing tiredly, "Oh, Merritt, it's a long story. Helen befriended me when Ted and I first moved to Hyde Park. Johnny and Brian were just babies. We shared the same pediatrician, the same social cliques, the same country club. Helen had this vision of us working together through the various civic organizations to turn this town on its ear, really establish ourselves as the movers and shakers of our decade. Her husband didn't have the same political connections Ted did through his law office, but he made other friends through his coaching of the university basketball team. Anyway, it didn't take long before we saw our thinking was very divergent. While Helen was trying to get books off the library shelves, I was trying to get them on. I supported profeminist material of all sorts. Helen hated everything, including the unabridged version of the *Webster's Dictionary*. Eventually we went our different ways entirely. I didn't see much of her again until the past two years when John and Brian were put in the same class at school. On their own, they became great friends, championed each other. Funny how those things work out, isn't it?"

"You think Helen resents that friendship because of what happened to yours?" Merritt stirred lemon into her drink.

"I think she resents me," Ellen said quietly. "What I've accomplished in terms of my career, the fact I've gone ahead and made a life for myself separate from that of my former husband and my child's. Helen has a lot of energy, a lot of drive. I don't think she's getting the recognition she needs from her work as charity fund-raiser and community activist. And that frustrates her into taking the attack."

"And that remark about what you knew in reference to her private life?" Merritt queried.

Ellen blushed, looking away embarrassedly. "*That* I shouldn't have said no matter how I was baited. Her husband has an eye for the coeds," Ellen admitted with the remorse of a woman who had been there. "For Helen's sake, I hope that's all it is. Not that she'd ever divorce Ron. No, she'd stay on and maintain the marriage no matter what it cost her, just as a way of saving face. Another one of our differences, I suppose."

An hour drifted into two. Ellen jumped every time the phone rang. It was only Tom or Artie or the park superintendent checking in to see if they had any news.

"Sometimes I think Johnny's current problems are all my fault," Ellen confided dully at last. "If I'd been the perfect wife, content to stay at home and do the ironing or the laundry or whatever—"

"You can't be something you're not," Merritt advised. "You couldn't have made John or your husband happy if you were everything but personally and intellectually content. And besides, what happened today has very little to do with your career. John has been upset and angry, true. He's also entering puberty. Who's to say this wouldn't have happened in response to peer pressure? John might have rebelled against curfew if you and Ted hadn't divorced. Brian's parents are together. His mother is primarily a homemaker. And yet he's in on this, too. You're going to have to stop blaming yourself and look forward to possible solutions."

Ellen brushed back a tear. "I guess you're right. Sometimes I think if I had just known twelve years ago what I know now I wouldn't have married someone who would protect me but someone who would accept me. Tom and I grew up in one of the worst neighborhoods of the city. Our father died when he was in his twenties, leaving my mother to singlehandedly raise us both. I never forgot how hard it was for her, working as a teller by day, taking in ironing by night, just to make ends meet. Tom always protected me, both from the neighborhood kids and every kind of snub or hurt. Materially, we didn't have much, and you know how cruel kids can be. I guess it was only natural that when I grew up I would look for someone equally strong. And since mother couldn't afford to send us both to college, it left me to get married.

"For a while it did work. I had Johnny, a new home, a husband who was well-respected in both the business and social community. And I had a chance to go to college, continue on with my education one or two classes at a time."

"How did your husband feel about that?"

"He never really supported me intellectually or emotionally while I was at UC. But it was okay, even socially desirable, for an attorney to have a college-educated wife. It was only after I graduated and wanted to get a job the trouble began. Maybe I knew then I had made a mistake. Maybe the drive to succeed or carve some kind of real financial and emotional security for myself apart from all the rest—and any other single person or factor—overrode all the rest. I only know I wanted to work. And at a time when it wasn't popular for a woman with a kindergarten-age child to make that kind of total sacrifice.

"You can't succeed in business without a full-time

commitment to your work, or in your case students."
She smiled at Merritt tentatively, running an anxious
hand through her hair. "Suddenly there wasn't enough
time for symphony and the Junior League and Helen
Anderson's fund-raising ideas, spur-of-the-moment
dinner parties for twenty. I tried hiring a housekeeper."
Ellen shrugged. "But nothing she did was ever to my
ex-husband's satisfaction. Eventually, Ted found a
more sympathetic shoulder to cry on. We parted."
Ellen sat, introspectively thinking of all that had happened, the uncertainty both still knew over the where-
abouts of the boys. Fresh tears rolled down her face.
Her mouth clenched with frustrated grief. "Damn it,
why would John do this to me?"

"Attention?" Merritt predicted.

"I give him every second I can spare."

Merritt shrugged, trying to look at the dilemma as
positively as possible for all their sakes. "Maybe he just
wants to make a point. Maybe he was bored. Heaven
knows Brian Anderson has never been averse to taking
any kind of dare. Maybe it was just some sort of prank
that backfired on them."

A knock sounded softly at the door. Ellen got up to
get it. Her diminutive form hunched slightly as she admitted Tom Hennessey. Quietly Tom answered the un-
spoken question hanging in the air. "Nothing yet."

Looking utterly defeated, Ellen buried her face in
her hands. Tom's arms went around his sister. They
stood for several seconds. Eventually, the younger sibling released her despairing hold. "Are you going to be
all right?" Tom jostled her shoulders slightly, forcing
Ellen's chin up to his.

Ellen nodded, her throat constricting visibly with the
effort it took not to cry. "At least he's with one of his
friends."

"Ten to one, they're holed up somewhere for the
night. We've checked all the hospitals. The streets are

pretty quiet. With the APB issued, they'd be spotted in a minute if they showed up at any public place."

Ellen sniffed, backhandedly wiping her watery eyes. "The advantages of having a cop in the family."

Tom turned to Merritt. His eyes raked her searingly. But she could read nothing familiar or affectionate in the rugged man's face. A chill slid down her spine. What if Brian and John weren't found? "Have you checked your place?" he asked abruptly.

Merritt shook her head, frozen by the distant nature of his gaze. "Frankly, after they slipped out on me earlier, it never crossed my mind they would try."

Tom shrugged. "Who knows, maybe they'll get the guilts and want to apologize." He held out her coat, then turned back to his sister. "You'll be all right alone until I can get back?"

Ellen gathered her composure. "Of course. I really should check with Ted again, anyway, see if he's heard anything there."

Tom nodded. They let themselves out and walked to the car. At 2:00 A.M. the streets were bare of traffic. "You blame me, don't you?" Merritt asked.

"I wish Ellen didn't have to go through this," Tom said tightly, hands gripping the wheel.

What about me? Merritt thought numbly, turning her gaze forward once more. He had comforted everyone else, worried about everyone else. With effort she concentrated on the blur of streetlights, the dark shadows of houses and trees. *Does he care about me at all?* she wondered.

Eventually, Merritt slanted him another glance. His jaw was still set determinedly, his mind and attention miles away. His thoughts were with his family, Merritt realized. Truthfully, what was she to him? Mistress? Lover? Even *girlfriend* seemed too strong a word for the fragile thread of their relationship. Had she made a mistake, giving herself to him too soon? Had she been

too abandoned, too passionate? Then again, how could
loving him ever be a mistake?

The car glided smoothly to a halt next to the curb in
front of Merritt's house. Without waiting, she slid open
the door. He circled the car just in time to wrap an as-
sisting hand around her elbow and slam the door behind her. "I would have opened it, too, had you given
me the chance," he remonstrated temperately. Tom
led the way to her door.

A quick, thorough tour of the outside and interior of
the house determined neither boy had ventured to
Merritt's residence. Merritt paused wearily in front of
the phone. "For once I wish I had invested in an
answering machine of some sort," she observed.

A sigh rippled Tom's frame. Without asking, Merritt
knew what was in his thoughts. He had to get back to
his sister. Every moment with *her* was a wasted one, as
far as he was concerned. Blinking back tears, she
turned away. She blamed weariness rather than injured
feelings and the uncertain future of their short-lived
romance on the emotional display.

She walked back through the darkened front hall, to
the door, where she paused with her hand on the knob,
waiting impatiently for Tom to follow her lead. "Let
me know if you hear anything. It doesn't matter what
the time." Realistically, she'd given up on the rest of
the night, as had apparently he.

Merritt pulled open the door. The flat of his palm
pressed inches above hers shut it just as swiftly. Merritt
swallowed. She'd been afraid he wouldn't just let it go.
Her gaze was directed at the slope of his neck, the open
vee of his shirt, just below his chin. "Tom—" Her
voice quavered with defiant resolve.

The reserve broke. His passions came pouring out,
showering Merritt with feelings and blame she'd been
terrified to explore. "Yes, I'm angry with you, damn
it!" he swore. "I'd be angry with any teacher or baby-

sitter or friend who would be fool enough to lose my sister's son! But that doesn't change the way I feel about you, the fact that I'd much rather be in your bed with you right now than out scouring this town for an eleven-year-old adolescent who, lately anyhow, doesn't deserve even the sneakers on his feet!" His breath drew out raggedly. Both hands circling her arms, Tom dragged her the six inches to his chest. One hand wound through her hair, pressing her face against the tweed of his blazer, the other gently encircling her waist. Merritt's tears flowed freely.

"I'm soaking the fabric," she choked.

"It seems to be the night for tears and remonstrations," he soothed, something viable quavering in his voice. "Go ahead."

They stayed like that for several seconds more. Eventually, his hands found their way to her face, framing her salt-drenched cheeks with both palms, he lowered his mouth to hers. The kiss was more tender and searching than anything they had yet shared. Merritt felt a wave of relief, followed swiftly by joy, and then desire. With a surge, she pressed her body more fully into the encompassing warmth of his, reveling in the scent of his cologne, the tang of his sweat, even the faint stubble of his chin. Merritt loved the man, flaws, temper, compassion, and all. It didn't matter how long the tempestuous affair between them lasted, she realized. She wanted to hang on to whatever she could get. She wanted to preserve the warmth and gentleness he brought to her soul for all time.

"I have to go." Tom reluctantly dragged his lips from hers. A frank expletive hissed between his teeth as he mentally and passionately reviewed all they would miss.

"The boys," Merritt whispered, reminded of the crisis prevailing.

"We'll find them," Tom assured with a great deal

more confidence than either could possibly feel. "Let's just pray it's soon, for all our sakes." A fleeting kiss was pressed along her temple, then he departed without another word or glance. Merritt watched the street, her face pressed against the glass long after the taillights had disappeared from sight. A stray tear darted singly down her cheek.

Tom showed up again Saturday morning. Together, he and Merritt canvased every pizza and chili parlor in the vicinity as well as the bus stations, airport, and museum, to no avail. Sunday brought more tension, no leads. Ted Porter arrived from Columbus with his fiancée. The three adults manned Ellen's home and phone, their concern for Johnny and Brian obliterating all else.

Rest was elusive and by Monday morning, Merritt was exhausted. Her class, of course, was all too aware of what had happened. Rather than avoid the subject, Merritt decided to tackle it head-on and ask for suggestions or thoughts on where the boys might have gone if indeed they had been running away as primarily supposed by police and parents alike. Unfortunately, they drew no possibilities except those already exhausted by the Cincinnati Police Department and the group of concerned adults. Only Kristin Stratton was silent, head bowed, her face slightly suffused with heat.

"Kristin, are you feeling all right?" Merritt detained her as the others filed off to Physical Education.

"Yes, ma'am." But Kristin flushed even more.

Merritt delayed her with a gentle touch to the slender shoulder. "Kristin, look at me. I know how close you are to both John and Brian. Has this upset you, our talking about it this morning? Because if it has—"

"I didn't mean to do anything wrong, Ms. Reed. I

swear!" she blurted out through a torrent of gasps and tears. "It was just a trick. The boys thought it up. But then the police got involved and—" Kristin hiccuped.

Merritt shoved the door shut with one hand, directed the sobbing girl to a chair with the other. "All right, Kristin. Just calm down and tell me what happened from the beginning."

Kristin swallowed hard, taking a great gulp of oxygen into her lungs. "At first they were only going to pretend to be lost. They said they were going to run away and showed me the money, but I didn't believe them. But then the bus left without them. And Brian said, 'Why not really give the old warhorses a scare.' And Johnny said it would probably serve everybody right as mean and awful as they'd been to *him*, so—"

Merritt held up a silencing palm. "How do you know all this, Kristin? Have you talked to them since Friday? Did they call you?"

Reluctantly Kristin nodded. "Sort of." Again, fear took over. She clammed up.

Merritt trod gently. "Have you *seen* them?"

"Yes," the young girl replied, very meekly.

Merritt could feel her heart pounding triple time against her ribs, her elation at their safety making it very difficult to remain calm and low-key. "Do you know where they are now?"

Kristin studied the scuffed toe of her running shoe.

"Kristin!" Merritt reproached.

A flash of defiance registered in the adolescent's eye. "They're my friends, my best friends. I promised I wouldn't tell," Kristin pronounced, tears forming again in her eyes.

"Their parents are worried sick," Merritt countered. "Kristin, please, honey, you've got to tell us whatever you know. For the boys' sakes as well as your own." Kristin vacillated, fingers shaking, then finally gave in.

The story was as simple as it was amazing. Merritt's relief was hindered only by the parental and police furor the disclosure would greet.

Tom met Merritt at the Strattons'. "What do you mean they've been camping out right here in the neighborhood? How, may I ask you? We've searched the area inside and out. Besides that, the temperature's dipped into the low twenties at night. How'd they get back to Hyde Park from downtown?"

Merritt slanted a glance at Kristin.

The frightened girl clung closer to Merritt's hand. "Hitchhiked, I guess."

Tom's brows went up. But this was no time to reproach Merritt's methods or grill Kristin further, as she was the only one with the answers. Wisely, he said nothing more. Soon they were joined by the Porters, the Andersons, the school principal, and Mr. Stratton. "Kristin, if you were involved in this at all..." her father began tightly. Mrs. Stratton simply looked miserable.

"Kristin's helping now, that's all that's important," Merritt declared. "I believe you have a wine cellar off the main basement?"

"Well, yes," Mr. Stratton stammered. "But it's kept locked at all times."

"Well, evidently the boys have also learned the fine art of picking locks because they had no difficulty getting into it once Kristin had let them inside the house that first night. Mr. Stratton, if you'll lead the way, I believe we'll find our missing boys."

The group filed down a rickety open-backed wooden stairway into a dark musty-smelling cellar. Merritt shivered as Kristin's father unlocked and shoved open the door. There, lounging on either side of a Monopoly game board, were two dirty, disheveled boys, three bags of potato chips, several half-eaten sandwiches, and bottles of Coke. They looked only relieved to find they had been caught. That relief soon turned to acute chagrin once the parents of the runaways started in.

The media had a field day with that story on the two boys in your class," Blanche observed early the next morning.

Merritt continued pinning up new intellectual puzzles on her BRAINSTORM bulletin board. "I know. Thank heavens they're safe, though. I don't ever want to be caught in the middle of a runaway situation again."

"Good thing you were, though." Blanche took a seat on the heating unit next to the windows. "What'd the boys have to say for themselves?"

"They both apologized to me privately yesterday afternoon. Neither John nor Brian ever meant to get me in any sort of hot water. Frankly, they were so absorbed in their own problems, the possibility I might be dismissed for negligence never crossed their minds." She sighed, reaching for her stapler and another intellectually challenging puzzle. "Evidently, John had hoped the prolonged search for him would reconcile his parents and call off his father's plans to eventually remarry."

Blanche's brows raised speculatively. "Did it?"

"No. The last I heard, Ted Porter's still planning to remarry early next spring, or as soon as their property settlement is hashed out, and his divorce to Ellen finalized. With the new laws, most uncontested divorces now only take thirty days. And Ellen has no intention of fighting his desire to be free. However, all this has had one positive aspect." She stapled another puzzle to the wall. "According to Tom, Ted and Ellen are on much better terms now, and they're unified as to John's discipline."

"What about Brian's parents?" Blanche sipped the coffee in her hand.

Merritt relaxed, knowing it would be another hour

before any of the children would arrive. "That's another story entirely. Both Brian's parents are extremely upset and not likely to get over it soon."

"What did the principal decide?"

"Both boys are going to be admitted back into class, without expulsion. However, they're on probation for the rest of the year, and they're barred from any other class trips or recreational activities."

"Tough luck." Blanche moved forward to help Merritt hang another puzzle.

"I know. However, all things considered, they're probably lucky to get off with that little." Merritt raked a hand through her hair, pushing it from her face. "The Cincinnati Police Department wasn't very happy, either. According to John's uncle, some of the officers felt they were made to look like fools. Amazing, isn't it, how that possibility could have escaped us all?"

"You can't find two children if they're safely hiding in a private citizen's house," Blanche philosophized.

Merritt agreed, stepping down from her chair. "Anyway, that's not my main problem. My dilemma is getting those two hotshots involved in their work again. Both are still pretty truculent."

"Would you like me to counsel them?" Blanche asked. Her friend's schedule was full, but she could always make room for one more, Merritt knew.

"I'd like to get them entrenched in schoolwork first. They feel singled out enough as it is without adding the pressure of that. John and Brian are so bright. I can't help but feel if I could just challenge them thoroughly enough, their penchant for the high jinks would stop no matter how much or why they're personally disgruntled."

Blanche remained skeptical, but long friendship and respect for one another's work and judgment prevailed. "All right, Reed. But you know where to whistle if you need help. And this time, teach, don't wait until they run off."

Chapter Eight

Tom Hennessey threaded his way through the throngs of parents, reporters, and spectators crowding the high school cafeteria. "Why didn't you tell me there was a special session of the school board meeting tonight?" he asked Merritt. The crowd had all the characteristics of a hysterical lynch mob.

Merritt backed against the far wall, quite aware of all the interested stares focused her way. "Actually, it's a hearing to determine whether or not there are adequate grounds for my dismissal," she corrected tonelessly. "Because I've got tenure here, the board is compelled to give me public opportunity to answer the charges against me before turning the matter over to superior court."

Tom studied her incredulously. "You act as if you've already been convicted. Merritt, you didn't do anything wrong. In fact, you cut short a trauma for them all by finding the boys."

"Funny, you didn't feel that way when Johnny was missing," Merritt said tightly. A defeated sigh rippled her slender form. "Besides, Helen Anderson and her husband have their hearts set on seeing me fired, despite the tenure I've accrued. If nothing else, it will clear their consciences about the turmoil last weekend, whatever responsibility they might have had in Brian's attempt to run away."

The chairman of the school board rapped his gavel

sharply against the podium. The board filed in to take
their seats. After the pledge and the prayer, the intro-
ductory statement was issued.

"Specifically, we're here to discuss the 'misplace-
ment' of two sixth-grade students during a recent
school field trip. The issue of negligence on the part of
teacher Ms. Merritt Reed has been raised. Ms. Reed,
are you here?" the chairman inquired. From the back
of the room Merritt stepped forward slightly, then
raised her hand. Heads turned. The murmurs in the
room picked up.

"Did you know they were going to do this?" Tom
whispered.

"The principal, Mr. Tierney, hinted as much," Merritt whispered back, outwardly remaining calm.

"Why didn't you get a lawyer?" he hissed, edging
protectively near.

Merritt shrugged indolently. "There wasn't time.
With all the publicity surrounding the boys' disappearance, the board has been pressured to act. Parents are
calling in from all over the city, wondering if the same
thing could happen to their children."

"But the boys deliberately ran away. It had very little
to do with you."

"Not according to Helen Anderson. And besides, at
this point, it's their word against mine. Face it, Tom,
someone is going to have to take the fall for this and it
looks like it's going to be me."

He swore his frustration. Before he could persuade
further, Mr. Tierney and Blanche walked over to join
Merritt. "Ten to one tomorrow this will all be just a bad
dream." Blanche linked hands with her friend.

Merritt appreciated the support. "Thanks."

"What about the other concerned parties?" the chair-
man continued, glancing around. "Are they here?"
Helen Anderson, her husband, and an unfamiliar man
Merritt guessed to be their attorney marched rigidly

down the aisle and seated themselves at the table facing the board.

Helen leaned forward and adjusted the microphone to her height. Clearing her throat, she began, "We're all familiar with the events of last weekend. My quarrel with Ms. Reed goes back much further." She cited Merritt's studies on contemporary family life, the cafeteria kitchen brawl between Brian and John, Merritt's error in initially reporting both Brian and John absent from school instead of truant. "It's also been brought to my attention Ms. Reed has allowed records with highly questionable lyrics to be played during her class."

"It's true the children take turns bringing in records," Merritt admitted quietly.

"Then you don't censor their selections?" Helen Anderson queried sharply.

Tom's restraint ended. He opened his mouth as if to speak, but Merritt held him back, one hand on his arm. This one she wanted to answer for herself. "The Code of Ethics adopted by the National Education Association specifically states subject matter is not to be distorted or suppressed. I adhere to those principles, whether it be in books, records, or in questions to be discussed."

The Andersons' attorney spoke up, contradicting smoothly, "The teacher's duty, Ms. Reed, as outlined by the NEA, is also to protect."

"Only from conditions that may prejudice their safety or learning," Merritt shot back calmly. "Realistically, we have got to assume that at some point children will begin to select and discriminate for themselves. One of my goals is to help them learn to do that."

"What age should this process begin?" the attorney asked with all the charm of a prosecuting district attorney.

Merritt held her own. "Hopefully from the moment the child is able to think." A murmur ran through the cafeteria this time in her favor. Bolstered, Merritt continued, "It's an ongoing process, one that optimally should be supplemented by the parents' discretion and guidance at home."

"What if the teacher involved has no discretion?" Helen Anderson queried out of turn. "You have my child seven hours out of every day, Ms. Reed. I think we as parents have the right to expect more prudence from you."

No, Merritt thought, *you just want me fired.* "I'll be glad to supply all the expedience in the world if the board and the parents can agree on a specific code of what is to be taught—a code that would encompass all religions, life-styles, and points of view." Which was exactly what Merritt was trying to teach. "My job is to expand the awareness of my students, teach them to think and observe for themselves, not rigidly categorize what was once known as status quo in a world that is constantly changing. It's the only way we can prepare our children for the future."

The board echoed their assent. "A teacher in our district cannot restrain a student from independent action in the pursuit of learning or deny him access to different points of view."

"Even if it means exposing him to the more sordid details of current society?" Helen Anderson asked.

Merritt blanched. The chairman's jaw tautened. "Ms. Anderson, make your point."

"Gladly. It appears Ms. Reed's lax judgment spills over into her private life, too." She whirled to pin both Tom Hennessey and Merritt with a meaningful glare. "Frankly, I'm not sure she can be trusted to uphold the quality education of our youngsters, nor distinguish what are morally acceptable learning materials. Her living—"

The chairman cut her off angrily. "Ms. Reed's private life is not the issue here, Mrs. Anderson."

Helen grinned victoriously. "Then let's talk again about the weekend disappearance of those two boys. Grounds for terminating a teacher's contract include inefficiency and incompetence. I charge Ms. Reed with both, and hereby petition the board for her dismissal."

Comments sizzled in the air as the assembled board perused the appropriate forms. Tom reached over and squeezed Merritt's hand tightly. "They can't do this to you," he whispered. "I won't let them."

"Neither will we," Blanche and Mr. Tierney agreed. But to Merritt the damage was done. Either way, her freedom and effectiveness as a teacher had been destroyed.

The outcome carried little surprise. "The board finds this an administrative matter. Until a decision can be reached, Ms. Reed will be allowed to continue to teach. Subject matter and discussion will be limited to textbook material, her classes monitored."

"I'll take you home," Tom decided as soon as the meeting was adjourned. He sheltered her through the crowd, past the local reporters, to the parking lot. Merritt declined his offer succinctly. "Thanks, but I'd like to walk. I have some things to sort out."

Ignoring her, Tom put a hand around her upper arm and jerked open the car door. "I'm not leaving you alone. Get in."

He didn't seem to bequeath her any choice. The car motor had no time to warm up. It pitched reluctantly, nearly stalling at every touch of the brake. Tom's driving was just as abrupt. Angrily he directed the car through the congested traffic, drove a few blocks, pulled up on a quiet residential street opposite a small, deserted city park with tennis courts, swing sets, and trees. "You wanted to walk, we'll walk."

Merritt faced him stonily. "This isn't what I had intended." Or needed.

"I know what you intended." He paused, capable fingers circling the door handle. "But you've had a rough night. And for once we're going to do it my way, regardless."

Swiftly he rounded the front of the car and held open her door. The invigorating winter air refreshed her battered sensibilities. Tom's comforting arm about her waist reassured. She leaned into his strength silently.

"I hated every minute of that meeting tonight," he admitted tersely at length. His grip roughened possessively. "I wanted to punch Helen Anderson in the face."

"Join the club." Merritt sighed. "Though in her own way I guess she's just trying to do what's best for her son."

"Like hell she is," Tom muttered contemptuously. "Helen Anderson knows what she is doing at all times. And it generally isn't in the best interests of anyone but herself, sometimes not even that." He paused, spinning her abruptly around. "There's something else I realized tonight," Tom said seriously. "I want to marry you."

The words she had longed to hear for months were obliterated by the situation, her fear Tom was doing what he felt chivalrously best. Her defenses took over. Her stubborn resolution not to cry added a defiant edge to her voice. "Funny, you've never considered matrimony a viable possibility before. I don't want your charity, Tom."

His jaw tautened defensively. "I don't offer marriage to a woman out of charity, Merritt. I'm doing this because I love you."

She didn't believe him. He saw it in the faint arch of her brows. Without warning his fingers dug into her shoulders. He shook her slightly, forcing her chin up. "Damn it, Merritt. Stop the Joan of Arc act!"

"Why? You know as well as I that my effectiveness as an educator, at least in this school district, has just been ruined, regardless of what that board eventually finds. The publicity is too damaging. Not to mention the fact I actually did lose two boys on a school-sponsored trip. My students will be constantly upset. I'll be monitored continuously, severely limited in my freedom to teach, or to just casually discuss anything on my students' minds. And, believe me, they ask a lot of off-the-wall things!" Merritt shrugged free of his grip and spun away, her hands shoved in the pockets of her coat. "I don't know. After what went on there tonight, I'm tempted to just resign for the good of the kids in my class. At least then *they* could go on."

"That's a smoke screen and you know it. You're running!" Merritt had seen him angry before. But he'd never been pushed this far, nor been as powerless to stop what he held in contempt. She fought to get a grip on her emotions, too, then lowered her voice with a sigh.

"All right, maybe I am. But what does it matter now?"

"I'm not going to let you quit." Tom's decision was swift and high-handed. "You're too valuable an educator for this district to lose."

Merritt laughed bitterly, shaking her head at the antiquated notion of power. "About that, Tom, you really don't have any say. If I want to quit my job, I will."

Tom was frustratedly silent. When he spoke again, his voice was tranquil. "All right. I agree that is your decision. But I don't think you should do anything until you've spoken with a lawyer."

"I don't have the money for something like that."

Tom relaxed slightly, as if feeling the battle were won. "Then I'll get it for you."

His efforts to simply take over in her time of crisis were amazing. "And have Helen Anderson add 'accepted financial support from a close sexually involved male friend' to my multitude of sins? No, thanks.''

"I understand fully what Helen Anderson was trying to do to you, Merritt," he said softly. "I may even understand why. What I can't comprehend is why you're suddenly so willing to let her."

Silence fell between them. His unexpected insight destroyed any quick reply Merritt might have had. Hot, bitter tears welled up behind her eyes. "So I'm not as sophisticated as I'd like to be sometimes."

Tom moved behind her, slower now, his voice calmly extracting. "It bothers you we're not married, doesn't it?"

"When it's brought to public attention like that, yes." As unfashionable as it was, she'd been embarrassed.

"You saw for yourself the school board could have cared less."

"Only because it's not a valid reason for dismissal. If that were to change..." Her voice trailed off. In reality, Merritt knew that had nothing to do with her humiliation. The reasons for that were all within her heart. *She* needed marriage. *She* needed the public declaration of love and commitment from Tom. It was as simple and as complicated as that. "I felt as if I'd been branded with a scarlet letter A."

"Maybe by yourself," Tom said gently. He turned her toward him and Merritt leaned into his warmth. "The offer of marriage is still open, Ms. Reed."

His pragmatic attitude only strengthened her negative resolve. "No, Tom. Not just to please the school board or get Helen Anderson off my back. It's not reason enough." She walked toward the park merry-go-round, her head bent against the wind. She told herself the moisture stinging her eyes was due to the biting cold.

"Then how about to please me?" Deftly Tom caught

her arm and yanked her around, reeling her in close to his warmth. Merritt resisted the sudden, searing look of passion in his eyes. "You're just doing this out of guilt," she gritted. "Because I'm feeling the social pressure."

"That's not true."

"Isn't it?" When he didn't reply, Merritt crashed through the leaves covering the ground. His footfalls echoed behind her. "Merritt, don't go. Not when you're angry and hurt."

A command would have been easy to ignore. The soft, imploring note of his low voice was something else again. Merritt paused. Tom waited, neither touching her nor speaking. Eventually, they moved so they stood toe to toe. "Merritt, I love you," he confessed.

She wanted desperately to believe that. More, she needed his embrace more potently than she ever had before. Merritt's arms lifted to the back of Tom's neck. Her mouth maneuvered closer until it fitted acquiescently beneath his. Strong arms wrapped securely around her waist, pulling her lower torso near. For the first time hesitation warred with the desire in his dark green eyes. "I don't want to take advantage of you. I've done enough for one night and I know you're upset."

Merritt gave in to her impulse and moved nearer still, reveling in the beguiling fit of her body against the warm cocoon of his. "I need you more than I need time alone." Her teeth caught his lower lip gently. The softness of her lips surrounded the captured skin. With a groan, he caught her against him even more roughly, the hard imprint of his desire searing itself into her flesh. His mouth covered hers hungrily, robbing her of the initiative, the right or will to resist.

Merritt's palms molded the broad lines of his shoulder, the slope of his neck, the loosened tie and collar of his button-down shirt. When her hands slid lower to the demanding contours of his hips and thighs, the low sound of urgency reverberating in his throat echoed the depth of the need she felt.

Reluctantly Tom drew away. He stared down at her in the darkness. "You're crying." The observation was made softly.

Merritt tried to pull away. His arms held her in place. "Take me home, Tom." Once again numbness pervaded her voice. "You were right. I do need time to sort things out." Both personally and professionally.

"All right." Tom stared down at her, an unfathomable expression on his leanly carved face. "But promise me you'll call me if you need me."

Merritt promised. They both knew she wouldn't call.

Tom leaned negligently against the stone balustrade on Merritt's front porch. It had been three days since he had seen or heard from her. The difficulty of the situation dictated he not call her at work. She wasn't answering her phone at home, or simply *wasn't* home. He fought the rise of jealousy in his gut, his jaw hardening as he shoved his hands in his pockets and looked away. He had no claim on her. She'd made that clear. Probably under the recent difficulties with the school board and his inadvertent part in them, she didn't want to see him at all. So why, then, was he there? Torture? Or just the overwhelming urge to make sure she was all right?

The sound of a car motor brought his head up. Merritt's VW halted just short of the curb. Tom felt his pulse quicken as she emerged from the car. Pausing to shut the door with one booted foot, she lingered, glancing upward at the frosty gray of the sky. Her footfalls were slow as she moved across the grass to the walk. She stopped when she saw him, her face turning even more pale. A surge of resentment went through him. Tom felt like a fool hanging around her house, just waiting for her to come home. What if she never wanted to see him again? What if this were it? "Hi."

"Hi." Merritt's voice was tremulous and uncertain. Swiftly regaining her composure, she flashed him an artificially bright smile. Her attempt to hold him at bay with false sociability irritated him even more. "Have you been waiting long?"

Three days too long, Tom thought. "No, though even if I had been, it would have been my fault, since I didn't call and, instead, just took the chance you would be coming home directly after work."

The breathless denial he wanted never came. Evidently, Tom noted with chagrin, Merritt would have preferred a more formal approach despite all they had been to one another. Merritt hesitated on the top step, heavy books and briefcase cradled in her arms.

"I am glad you came by," she said softly at last, ducking her gaze evasively. "There are some things I'd like to discuss." She glanced at the street, then reluctantly unlocked the front door and directed him inside.

Tom followed her in. Nervously Merritt slid her belongings onto the kitchen counter. Stacked neatly on a chair in the small dining room were a pair of his gloves, his razor, his toothbrush and shaving cream, the drapes she had made for his Spring Valley home—drapes they had never had the opportunity to hang. "Kicking me out?" Tom's voice was laced with deceptive humor. He could feel the raw tension snaking into every nerve, tautening the lines around his mouth.

"I thought it would be best if we didn't see each other anymore, at least for a while," Merritt said quietly. Casually she shrugged off her coat and draped it over a chair.

Tom noticed the snug fit of her lilac trousers, the softness of the cashmere sweater covering her breasts. His fingers ached to tousle the length of her dark hair, crush her against him, and kiss her fears away. Her wary glance kept him aloofly in place. "How much of this has to do with the trouble the other night?"

Merritt ran a hand wearily across the back of her neck. "It has everything to do with that."

Anger laced his voice. "Don't let them dictate the terms of your personal life, Merritt, even temporarily."

Outrage clouded her eyes. "Easy for you to say, Detective. I've worked my whole life for this job."

Tom relaxed slightly, deciding on a more casual approach. "How are things at school?"

Merritt laughed tonelessly. "Rigidly defined. And I can't afford any more trouble, believe me. Today we had Helen Anderson, her attorney, and three members of the school board monitoring our class. Yesterday, it was the school principal, Blanche Beck, a professor from the Communications Department at UC, and a free-lance writer for the *Education Press*. We had to summarize the whole family life-styles unit again." She sighed. "Thankfully, the kids were already bored with the subject matter, so very few questions were asked. And since Brian's mother was there, nothing free-wheeling was contributed, even in jest."

Tom moved swiftly across the parquet floor. His arms closed around her shoulders. She pushed him away before he even had time to fully take in her perfume. There was no way he could miss the defeated tears simmering in her eyes. "Just go," she whispered hoarsely, gesturing behind him toward the door. "And take your things with you. I don't want them around anymore."

"You don't mean that," Tom said softly.

Merritt pushed past him toward the door. Melting Greenland singlehandedly would have been easier than getting through her reserve. "We had a nice time," she ground out dispassionately. "But it's over. Please accept that and don't come here again. Because I won't see you if you do." She didn't react in the slightest as he left.

"Don't be stubborn, Merritt," Ellen Porter admonished the next day after school. "Ted and I both want to help."

"Thanks." Merritt erased the day's assignments from the board. "But even if I wanted legal backing, I don't have the money to pay even the basic charges for an attorney just starting out." Much less the fees Ted Porter's firm commanded.

Ted Porter faced her pleasantly, looking more relaxed and human than Merritt had ever seen him. "We don't expect you to pay. My firm will handle it free of charge. We'll recoup in publicity generated. Beyond that, once we get started it won't take long to clear up. They don't have a legal leg to stand on and they know it. Your record speaks for itself. The entire Alomar Street elementary staff agrees. Helen Anderson is just stirring up trouble." He and Ellen exchanged a unified glance.

Merritt walked back to needlessly restack a bundle of papers on her desk. "Thank you for your support. I wish I could share your faith. If it were up to the current administration, I probably would never have been brought up before the board for the initial hearing. But the current board operates in a highly political manner. Many of the board members are personal friends of the Anderson's. They could fire me on trumped-up charges of inefficiency, incompetence, even failure to obey reasonable rules. Right or wrong, what would it matter? The furor Helen Anderson and her book-banning cronies are stirring up would die down. The press would lose interest and the parents would forget."

"Maybe," Ted Porter theorized. "And then again maybe not. Maybe it's time the rest of us took a stand, too."

"You would do that for me?"

"And for the rest of the teaching staffs in our district. Too many of our teachers have been hired and fired at will. You're not the only one, Merritt. But you just may well be the last.''

Merritt had not known how many devoted students and parents—past, present, and future—she had garnered on her behalf until Ted Porter took over. His efforts had a snowballing effect and by the end of the week the school board had officially asked Merritt to stay on, at least through the remainder of her current contract. Not about to quit before gaining full victory, Ted Porter and his associates then tackled the more complex battles of uncensured teaching and more specific detailed guidelines for contract renewal and termination. The battle looked to be a long and arduous fight, one that might last several years, but at least Merritt's job and livelihood were secure.

The only disappointment was that Merritt did not hear from Tom Hennessey again, and she couldn't bring herself to call him. After all, she had kicked him out when the going got the least bit rough. Chances were he would never want to see her again. And Merritt couldn't blame him, as angry and disillusioned as he'd been when he left.

"Going to the basketball game tonight?" Blanche asked as they walked out to their respective cars.

"No." Merritt sighed, stretching languidly. "Frankly, all I want is a hot bath and a nice relaxed weekend alone before facing the last week of school before Christmas break."

Blanche laughed. "Still mooning over that detective friend, I see. Should have hung onto him while you had him."

"I'll try and remember that next time I get a hot date," Merritt rejoined dryly, fitting her key into the car door.

"And stay away from all things derived from the cocoa bean this weekend," Blanche added. "We don't want to have to pour you into your slacks for the annual staff eggnog and cookie party next week."

"Thanks heaps," Merritt muttered, slamming into her car. Though, come to think of it, she thought, sighing, a steaming cup of cocoa would hit the spot. "Better yet, maybe chocolate fudge bottom pie," Merritt mused, parking in front of her Hyde Park home. "Chocolate ripple ice cream," she fantasized, getting dreamily out of her car. "Chocolate éclairs..."

"Planning a menu for tonight's dinner or a celebration in honor of your recent reprieve?" A low voice drawled from the shadowy front porch.

"Tom." Merritt stopped just short of the steps.

"This is getting to be a habit with us." He rose lithely, moved forward to stand on the edge of the porch, one capable hand gripping the supporting brick beam. His eyes caressed her in a manner that was disturbingly physical and uninhibited. "Hello, Merritt. How are you?"

"Fine." Caution tempered her words. Because she seemed frozen in flight, he descended the steps lithely. The palm of his hand traced the curvature of her cheek, lingered beneath the silk of her hair against the increasing pulse at her temple. Involuntarily, Merritt leaned into the familiar warmth, wishing with all her heart he would take her more fully into his arms.

Instead, he leaned back with a casual smile. The caressing grip dropped. "Can I give you a hand?"

"Sure." Merritt gave him her bundle of papers and grade book and texts, then fumbled for her key as they mounted the steps of her house side by side. "I've missed you," he whispered, tantalizingly low, as she slid the key into the lock.

Her eyes held his. Tears of gladness gleamed within their depths. She let him see them unashamedly before blinking them away, forcing another tremulous smile. "If I'd have realized how much I was going to miss you, I never would have kicked you out. I'm sorry."

"Don't be." The back of his hand brushed tenderly across her cheek. "We can all use a little time to ourselves now and then. I brought you something." His head tilted in the direction of the opposite end of the porch.

Merritt's gaze followed his. "A Christmas tree!" Abruptly Merritt became aware of the scent of freshly cut Scotch pine lingering in the air. "Oh, Tom—"

"I've driven by your house a few times in the past weeks," he admitted, jamming his hands in his pockets after they had entered the house and dispensed with the belongings in their arms. "I noticed you hadn't decorated. I hope you don't mind."

"It's lovely, both the tree and the thought—"

Merritt's words were cut off by his stealthy approach. His mouth covered hers swiftly, decisively, leaving no time for either contemplation or denial. Only the sensation of his lips upon hers was real, the taste and texture of his tongue entering her mouth, the scent of his after-shave, the possessive feel of his hands. Merritt wrapped herself closer in his embrace, willingly returning kiss for kiss, caress for caress. It was some time before they broke away, and then only because of the cold drafts of air still sliding into the house.

"That was some welcome," Tom assessed with a wink. Effortlessly he carried the six-foot tree into the house. "Where do you want it?"

The heat of pure pleasure suffused Merritt's face. She had missed him. Until that moment, she hadn't been aware of just how intensely. The desire to drag him off to bed was still potently, embarrassingly strong. But she supposed if he could wait, she could, too. That was, if he still wanted her.

"Living room," Merritt directed. Rubbing her palms together, she followed Tom. "I've got decorations and a stand somewhere downstairs in the basement."

"Well, then, you'd better move it, lady." He affected his best John Wayne drawl. "Because I ain't going to stand here holding this tree all day."

When Merritt returned, he had taken off his coat, moved the rosewood secretary away from the window facing the street. Together, they fitted the base of the tree into the metal holder. While Merritt went to fetch some water and a decorative cloth for the base, Tom swept the stray needles off the rug. Merritt began unsorting a string of hopelessly tangled lights. "Got any coffee or is hot cocoa the only thing on the menu tonight?" he quipped facetiously.

Merritt leaned back against the sofa, studying his ski sweater, the beautiful fit of his cream corduroy slacks. "I've got both." She started to put down the lights.

"Stay put," Tom commanded with the ease of a man who had never really been away. "I'll get the coffee. I know where everything is. I assume you want some, too. Or would you really prefer cocoa?"

"Coffee will be fine, thanks."

Merritt located a stack of Christmas records, put them on the stereo. Tom returned with the coffee and together they fastened on the lights. "This is nice," Merritt said shyly. She wanted to hold him prisoner there the rest of her life, everything was so perfect, so romantically right.

"I can think of better," Tom said softly. His gaze traversed her slowly from head to toe. But he didn't elaborate on the pass with any physical or seductive moves. It was as if, Merritt thought, he was doing his best to be distant and perfectly controlled.

"Are you hungry?" Merritt asked when they had finished trimming the tree.

"Always." His gaze held hers. The green eyes darkened. His breaths became deeper, slightly less frequent. They were two feet apart. Electricity flowed as if they'd been locked together in the most intimate of embraces. Reluctantly Tom tore his eyes from her,

looking around idly until he had located the jacket he'd
worn. For one horrifyingly disappointing second, Merritt thought he was going to leave.

A sigh echoed through his sinewy frame. The taut
shoulders raised, then lowered. And finally, his gaze
came back to hers. His chin lifted in silent challenge,
lowered with the last ragged release of his breath. "If I
were smart I would get out of here now," he said.

"Yes," Merritt agreed, her heart pounding.

"I'm not."

"I want you, too. More than I've ever wanted anyone in my life." Merritt's hands were trembling. Why
was he making this so difficult? she wondered despairingly. Could it be he was as frightened and unnerved as
she?

"I wanted to give you more time," Tom admitted as
he closed the distance between them languorously,
folded her into the taut warm cradle of his sinewy arms.
Tears streamed unchecked down Merritt's face. "Right
now all I want is you." The drum of his heart intensified hers.

"Well, that you've got." Her voice was muffled in
the soft warm fabric of his sweater.

Love was never mentioned as they walked arm in
arm up the stairs to her bedroom. The thread of their
relationship was so tenuous, she feared by pushing him
for the words she needed she would destroy his new-
found commitment. And the feelings they shared were
too precious, too fleeting to risk.

The bedroom was shrouded in darkness. As Merritt
moved to draw the drapes Tom came up behind her,
encircling her waist with his forearms. He leveled her
back against him. The hand on her waist drifted lower,
across her abdomen, teasing, tantalizing, testing as his
teeth found her earlobe and worried it gently. Pleasure
flooded her, along with joy. Her breasts strained against
the confinement of her bra, aching for his touch. His

whisper-soft explorations were contained between her abdomen and thigh. "Tom—" His name was wrenched breathlessly from her lips.

"Let me touch you, Merritt."

"You're driving me crazy."

"And you've no idea of all the incredible things you've done to me." He sighed, his thighs nudging hers with a deliberate provocativeness that made her heart race. "I've been angrier, giddier, even more depressed in two short months—"

"You didn't mention happy," she observed, her hand latching on to his exploring one.

"I didn't think I had to," he murmured passionately. "I thought that much at least was understood." Wordlessly he turned her to him. He surveyed her ardently, longingly. Passion sliced through her in waves, destroying the last shreds of doubt.

"Take off your panty hose, Merritt," he said softly.

She flushed, stunned by the request. "But—"

"Just do as I say. Please. I want you so badly. Trying to untangle you from them, well, my skill might just elope with the rest of my control."

Her throat dry, she complied, kicking off her shoes to unroll the sheer fabric down past her toes. The thought she had wreaked havoc on his senses delighted and amazed her simultaneously. More powerfully, it aroused.

"Everything all right?" He grinned.

"Yes—" Her reply was ragged and hoarse and she couldn't quite meet his eyes.

"Then come here and unbutton my shirt."

She understood then what he wanted. "I've never been an aggressive woman—sexually," she warned, blushing her unease. And yet part of her wanted him to find her as irresistibly desirable as she found him.

"Then it's about time you learned, don't you think?"

Trembling, she unbuttoned his shirt, and on impulse followed with her mouth every inch of skin her fingers traversed. "Oh, God, that feels good." He sighed. "Yes...take your time...I don't want you to do anything you don't want to do, though," he cautioned, his hands loosely cupping her hips as she nuzzled the slope of his collarbone, the brush of new beard on his chin.

With the activity, the rest of her inhibitions had fled. Emboldened by his response, she withdrew his hands from around her and slid lower still. "How about this?" she murmured softly. She dipped her tongue into his navel, slipped her fingers beneath the waistband of his pants and rubbed them against his skin. "Do you like this?"

"Yes." His answer was half surrender, half delight.

"Then I want to do it," she affirmed haltingly between kisses, "so much." She wanted to give him the pleasure he gave her.

His fingers bit into her arms as he pulled her up against his taut length. "You're playing with fire when you tease me like that, woman," he warned, a humorous glint in his eyes.

"I know," she whispered back boldly, taunting lightly.

His laugh was cut off by the meshing of their mouths. He kissed her as if that would seal their commitment to one another, as if that would somehow make her his, forever. She responded in kind, telling him all the emotions and love she felt, the awe that they were even together at all, considering the fateful forces against them.

"Merritt—" Shifting restlessly against her, he slowly drew her skirt above her waist. The bareness of her thighs chafed against his trousers, creating an exciting awareness within her. His palms slid beneath the elastic of her panties, molding her softness against him. "You see how much I need you," he murmured, nibbling on her mouth with a deliberate sensuality that was shattering. "You see what you do to me."

Slowly Tom began undressing her, a dark intensity blazing in his eyes. He set Merritt's body afire with need until she was hardly able to keep still. Merritt collected herself long enough to kneel before him and, with equally slavelike devotion, remove the rest of his clothes. Aggressively, wantonly, she learned the inner planes of his thighs, the flex of his muscles as his own control lessened dangerously, the silhouette of his desire.

One hand tangling in her hair, Tom sank to the bed. Observing her with half-shuttered eyes, he watched as her hands and mouth moved lower still. Merritt knew pleasure that came from giving, until at last he grasped her upper arms and pulled her back up onto the bed beside him.

"Now it's my turn to love you," he said softly. He traced the contours of her flesh in a dazzling trek, evoking a wave of sensations, a rush of love. Merritt arched and writhed with the intensity of the desire, the low, insistent ache within both body and soul. She needed to possess him as much as he needed to become a part of her.

"This is the way it should be," Tom whispered, aligning her frame with his own. "Always, now and forever."

Merritt's gasp of pleasure echoed in the silence of the room and then there was only his face, his breathing and hers, the tempo, the pleasure, the joining that for the moment and eternity seemed made in heaven.

Merritt lay, her head against Tom's chest, her shoulders tucked beneath the soothing caress of his arm. His breathing was even and deep as he slid peacefully into sleep. Merritt was too vibrantly awake to rest. Her emotions soared because of the intimacy they had just shared. This was life and love as it was meant to be experienced, Merritt mused, mesmerized by the intensity of her feelings. She wanted to cling to the moment forever. She wanted, foolishly and uncharacteristically, to cling to him.

Eventually, though, fear she would wake him in her restlessness sent Merritt sliding away from the bed. In the darkness of her bedroom she reached for her robe, wrapped it around her and belted it securely around the waist. Barefoot, she padded downstairs to the living room, and the Christmas tree Tom had bestowed.

Ornaments of all shapes and sizes and colors gleamed from every branch. Colored lights flickered. Silvery tinsel garlands adorned the pine-scented silhouette. Only one thing was missing, Merritt realized. The star for the top. Rummaging through the boxes of decorations still scattered about, she located the additional decorative garland meant for the fireplace mantel, the green wreath adorned with red velvet and pine cones for her front door.

The star was in a tissue-stuffed shoebox at the very bottom of the last carton. Next to it was something else Merritt had forgotten, something ten times more precious. Tears gathered in Merritt's eyes as she cradled the small sterling silver angel in her hand. It was from her first Christmas with Eric. She could still remember the moment he had given it to her on Christmas Eve.

"This has been the best year of my life," Eric had confided over mugs of rich brandy-laced eggnog. They'd been so young then, so idealistic, so sure nothing would ever harm or hinder either of them, Merritt recollected fondly, drifting. She'd been his angel, the woman of his dreams. And Eric had been her first real love, the flamboyant, often riotously funny youth she had expected to share her entire life with.

Merritt's hand lovingly traced the engraved ornament. "Oh, Eric," she whispered softly, still lost in the quiet reverie of the past. "There was a time when I didn't think I would be able to go on without you. A time when I felt nothing would ever come close to what we had shared. Then, for a long time, I hoped someone would come along and be exactly like you. I guess I wanted someone to take your place. Now I know that will never happen." Because of Tom she was learning to live and love again. She no longer looked back with yearning, because she knew in her heart it would never be the same as it had been then. It couldn't be. Merritt was a different person, an independent woman used to being on her own. And Tom was a man, fully responsible with a clear-cut sense of where he was going and what he wanted out of life.

"Merritt?" Tom's voice sounded softly behind her.

Merritt turned to see him standing sleepily in the open door, shirt and trousers on, his sweater caught casually in the palm of one hand. She rose, poignant memories forgotten. Her bare feet moved soundlessly across the floor. She pressed a tender kiss on the masculine jaw, was immediately—and fiercely—encircled by the breath-robbing grasp of both strong arms. And then almost as quickly released. "Did I wake you?" Merritt searched his eyes for a reason as to the cool withdrawal.

Relaxing slightly, Tom shook his head, then turned away to slip on his sweater. "No."

"I came down with the intention of fixing us something to eat." Merritt smiled, encouraged by the subdued neutrality of his tone. "I got sidetracked by the decorating still to be done. I can fix us something now if you like." How unexpectedly domestic this all was, she thought happily, how cozy.

"Thanks, but—"

"You're not staying?" Merritt's face fell.

He grimaced slightly, glancing away. "I can't."

He didn't elaborate. Clutching the belt of her robe,

Merritt turned away, distancing herself from the intimacy they had shared in order to cope. "I guess I'm going to have to get used to this." She laughed lightly.

His eyebrows lifted inquiringly, and Merritt explained with a forced smile, "Your work schedule. The crazy hours. When Eric was with the force he just worked one shift or the other. It wasn't as erratic as your hours seem to be."

Tom studied her a moment longer, his green eyes darkening with an emotion Merritt didn't want to define. She knew immediately it had been a mistake to bring up Eric's name. Her nervousness, the memories just jarred by the discovery of the engraved silver angel, were no excuse. She knew what type of reaction that would prompt from Tom or any man. Darn it, what was the matter with her?

Tom raked a hand through his hair. "I, uh, guess I should have said something about it earlier." Swiftly he reached for his coat. Again, he explained nothing more.

"I'll see you tomorrow?" Merritt asked, walking him to the door. She could only hope her pretense of sophistication covered her hurt.

"I don't know." Tom's jaw jutted out rigidly. One hand hooked restlessly around his waist. His other reached for the doorknob.

Merritt's hand closed over his forearm, delaying his exit. She couldn't bear the suppressed emotion warring behind his jade eyes. He was holding something on a very tight leash. "Tom, please. Is it something I've done? Said? Tell me."

For a moment it seemed he would explain. Merritt's heart constricted expectantly in her chest. "I've got to go," Tom said brusquely. He dismissed her with a quick impersonal kiss, then was gone, footsteps echoing on the walk.

It wasn't until almost an hour later Merritt noticed

the security badge lying halfway beneath the sofa cushions. She cradled the computer-coded identification folder casually. Surely if Tom were going in to work he would need it. The problem was, he probably didn't know where he had left it. She hesitated only briefly, then walked to the phone and dialed the station where he worked. After a five-minute wait, his pal Artie Kochek finally came onto the line. "Merritt, how are you doing?"

"Fine, Artie. Listen, is Tom around?"

"No, can't say I've seen him." Artie's tone was clipped and cautious.

"Do you know if he's working tonight?" Bravely Merritt ignored the warning bells sounding in her head.

There was a lengthy pause. "Uh, can't say as I know that, either," Artie replied. "Do you want me to find out?"

"Umm, no." A thin film of perspiration covered Merritt's hand. The possibility Tom had lied to or purposely misled her seemed clear. To avoid an all-night encounter? she wondered. Or because once physically sated there was no more need for him to hang around? With effort she pushed the disparaging thoughts from her mind.

"Merritt? You still there?" Artie sounded concerned.

"Yeah, uh, listen, the reason I called is that Tom left something of his here, a badge of some sort. It looks rather official. Would you just leave him a note? Tell him I found it?"

"Sure." Artie paused again and then offered solicitously, "You know I can try and find him if you like. Locate him at home or ... wherever."

"No," Merritt's protest was quick and dreadfully embarrassed. Beneath her chagrin a finely tempered umbrage was beginning to boil. "I'm sure a note on his desk will do just fine."

Chapter Nine

"I'm going to get that man out of my system if it's the last thing I do," Merritt swore determinedly. Tom Hennessey had been nothing but trouble since the first day they'd met, wrecking the calm complacency of her life, making her want more, making her want him!

"What's next? Skinny-dipping in Fountain Square?" Blanche Beck faced her best friend cantankerously. Snow flakes fluttered erratically from the pewter-gray mist above. Roller-skating in Eden Park in the dead of winter was not her idea of seventh heaven, no matter how much they needed to brush up on their skills for the school fund-raiser next month.

Undisturbed, Merritt leaned forward to give her shoestrings one final knot. "I read this book detailing how to speedily get over defunct relationships. You don't listen to sad or romantic music. You don't over-eat or drink. You get rid of everything they own. And above all, keep busy. Exercising is mandatory."

Arms flailing, Blanche tested out her skates, skating raggedly from one side of the blacktopped path to the other. "Why not jog, then?" she puffed, clinging desperately to the trunk of a nearby tree.

"Because jogging makes my sides hurt," Merritt said wryly, pushing away from the bench. "I wanted to do something fun for a change. I wanted to do something wild and unpredictable." She wanted to stop feeling so *old*, as if life were passing her by at an unprecedented, unstoppable rate.

"You *want* Tom Hennessey."

Merritt's jaw jutted out rebelliously. "I thought we agreed not to talk about that."

"You agreed. I didn't promise you anything."

Merritt thought of the rocky road fudge she'd had for breakfast. "Come on, skate. Or this time next week I won't be able to budge."

Determined to break free of her depressed mood, Merritt speed skated ahead, did a showy figure eight, and then spun around, her hands on top of her head. Just as her mood picked up, her complexion paled. "Oh, no..."

Blanche whirled in the direction of her friend's panicky stare. "Well, how about that. Looks like Tom Hennessey made it after all," she mused, delighted.

"You told him?" Merritt extracted disbelievingly, both hands planted squarely on her hips.

Blanche owned up to it with a careless shrug. "Friend, I can't keep baby-sitting you forever. These old bones of mine won't hold out!"

Merritt glared straight ahead, pretending not to see the determined, angry strides of Tom's powerful thighs, the tension-clenched fists, the steady perusal that was anything but casual. "From the straight line of his mouth and the maniacal gleam in his eyes, I'd say the old buzzard feels about as kindly toward me as I do toward him," Merritt muttered beneath her breath, already contemplating strategies of battle. "Darn it, Blanche, how could you do this to me?"

'You'll thank me later, believe me." Blanche straightened the hem of her coat. "Now be cool. If it really is over, you can look him straight in the eyes and say so, no matter where or under what conditions you happen to meet or who arranged it. You're both adults."

"And if not?" Merritt grimaced, taking another deep breath.

"Then that ought to tell you something, too. Ta-ta." Heightening the volume of the transistor radio clipped to her belt, Blanche prepared to depart and skated between the two ex-lovers.

Merritt whirled, not waiting to watch the exchange between conspirators. The scenery passed at a rate ten times beyond her physical expertise, but Merritt was more afraid to slow down. Footsteps sounded on the pavement behind her. Her heartbeat increased. A minute later Tom Hennessey was jogging at her side. He moved in front of her. When she would have gone on, he grasped both arms, halting them both. Merritt's lungs were burning with the exertion as her skate wheels slid across icy black pavement. She lurched into him, the brunt of her weight nearly knocking them both to the ground. And still he held her there securely, possessively.

"Mind telling me where you've been the past ten days?" The rejoinder was curt.

"None of your business." Merritt jerked away.

Tom stared at her, breath rising and falling in his powerful chest. The two-piece gray-and-blue warm-up he was wearing was thin. Despite the slight wind and twenty-nine degree temperature, he was broiling. Merritt had haunted and exasperated him for days. Now that he was actually there, he didn't know where to start. He did know he wanted to shake her. Beyond that, kiss her until she swooned. Somehow, get things back the way they were before she'd shied away again. With effort he held on to the last of his calm. "Obviously, we have a few things to clear up. Let's go somewhere we can talk."

"No, thanks." Merritt pivoted. For a few brief adrenaline-filled moments all the expertise she had possessed as a child came back. The sidewalk moved by at a breathtaking rate. She could hear his metered steps behind her, the soft, fierce swearing, and wasn't the least bit intimidated by his swift progress. "Serves him right for deceiving me," she said. The next thing Merritt knew the toe stopper on her right skate was caught in a stray spreading root of a tree. She tumbled head-first into the landscaped area at the junction of two paths. Tears stung Merritt's eyes as her hands scraped the bark of a tree and she landed seatfirst in a cluster of shrubs. The laughter behind her only added to her humiliation. Muttering an oath, Merritt tried to get up.

"I ought to just leave you there," Tom muttered tightly, approaching. Anger fought with amusement on his face.

Merritt glared at him wordlessly. Briars poked through her clothing to her skin. Between the hopelessly snared leg warmers and her roller skates, she didn't think she could get up without further injury or insult. The bushes were already horribly crushed.

"Please do," she agreed icily, waiting. Tears pricked behind her lowered lashes.

Tom flexed his shoulder muscles, gave his head an exasperated shake. "You do have a way of making the most ordinary things extraordinary, Merritt Reed." Extending a hand, he attempted to pull her free. The leg warmers and briars remained caught. Swearing between his teeth, he began freeing them one by one. When she protested her ability, one arm slid behind her waist to hold her prone. "Do me a favor this once and be still." His hands were cut and bleeding by the time he was done.

"Thanks." Her apology was muffled. Embarrassment tinged her face with bright color.

"My pleasure. Now, do you want to tell me what this is all about?"

Merritt swayed forward on her skates, ignoring the plea in his eyes. The man was a cad, she reminded herself firmly. How many times did she have to have her heart broken to find that out once and for all? He had loved her and left her with barely a civil word. She couldn't and wouldn't go through that again. "If you'll excuse me, Detective, I have a few more calories to burn." She turned, determined to glide past.

He caught her arm and yanked her back into the crush of his arms. The bright glitter in his eyes stole the breath from her lungs. Wordlessly he waited. "I don't have the faintest idea what you want from me," Merritt swore.

Air hissed between clenched teeth, but he remained perfectly still. "Don't you."

With effort she swallowed. "No."

"Then try explaining that last impetuous action of yours, the one I assumed was meant to end things between us permanently."

"Oh." Merritt laughed nervously. "That one."

"Yes, that one." Reaching into his pocket, he extracted his photo identification badge. "Maybe this will help refresh your memory." The badge was dangled deliberately under her nose.

Stormily Merritt's glance flicked over the glossy surface. "I'm glad to see you got it back."

"Are you? I wonder." His voice was just as sarcastic.

"Believe me." Merritt smiled tightly. "I didn't want to keep mementos of our affair."

"You could have given it back to me personally." Unbidden, passion crept into his regard. Merritt's senses reeled. Defiance covered her desire.

"Why prolong the agony now that the ecstasy has passed?"

His ardor fled. Tom looked away a long moment. Merritt had the intuitive feeling he was counting backward from two billion in an effort to hold on to his fraying temper. He didn't seem to be having much success. "You're aware, of course, I had to go through an Internal Affairs investigation to recoup my badge?"

Merritt blanched inwardly. "That, I didn't intend," she said, hanging on to her composure by a thread. "But if you're expecting an apology—"

"The boys in the department were quite amused." Tom seemed quite anxious to tell her about it.

Merritt shrugged indifferently. "If that's all—"

"It's not." She knew by his quick indrawn breath she'd infuriated him to the heights. "I want to know what prompted this. I want to know what you're so all-fired upset about!"

Merritt shot back just as swiftly, "You lied to me!"

"When?"

"Implying you had to go back to work that last night, when all along you were just in a hurry to get out of there, away from me, away from any reminders of what we had just shared!" Merritt bit into her lip. She turned to flee, knowing she'd just said too much. Tom's hands clamped down over her shoulders resolutely. She was propelled back to the closest park bench, directed squarely to a seat in the middle. Without uttering a word, Tom knelt grimly in front of her, already unlacing her skates.

"What are you doing?" Her tone was icy as Merritt attempted to pull away from his deft fingers.

The edges of his white teeth clenched one over the other as he worked. "I'm getting ready to take you home!"

Merritt tried unsuccessfully to extricate her leg. "I am quite capable of doing this myself." Her mittened hands closed tightly over the slats in the bench. She used the wood for leverage, this time actually shaking free of his grasp.

In one lightning-swift action, Tom was on his feet, leaning over her, a palm flat against the seat on either side of her. He lowered his face to within inches of hers, his entire body rigid with repressed aggression. "Then think of it this way, Merritt. It will give me something to do with my hands, because the way I am feeling right now, I could cheerfully strangle you.''

At his rough tone, Merritt's breath had suspended in her chest. She stared hypnotized into the impassioned glitter of his eyes. Never in the whole time she had known him had he been so angry, not even when his nephew was in jail. She swallowed, wondering at the affect she was having on him. Could it be she had misunderstood?

With a dramatic economy of motion, Tom reached for the Nikes strung over her shoulder. She flinched slightly. He glared, waiting. Wisely Merritt decided not to delve verbally into her options, at least not until she had her shoes on and was capable of making an escape.

She bent to lace one shoe while he tied the other. Tom caught her faintly accusing gaze. His mouth tautened. "I never intentionally lied to or misled you," he thundered between gritted teeth, as if unable to contain his hurt and disappointment with her actions any longer. "I just needed time to think."

"Well, so did I," Merritt insisted stubbornly. Tears clouded her eyes, but she blinked them determinedly back. "And now that I've had it I want this affair to end." She wanted the hurting to stop.

Finished, Tom stood. He towered over her like an angry giant, both hands splayed resolutely across his hips. "Like hell," he growled. "If you did you wouldn't have been so afraid to face me. You wouldn't have palmed off my badge on the front desk sergeant of the wrong precinct just to reduce the possibility of your chances of running into me or any of our friends!"

Merritt admitted softly, "I thought it would be easier if we didn't run into each other again."

"Avoiding the issue is never easier, Merritt," he remonstrated in a gentle voice that caressed her like a kiss. When she didn't reply his irritation returned tenfold. "Are you ready to go?"

She didn't seem to have much choice as he tugged her along the path toward the parking lot. He held open the passenger door, tossing the skates into the back. It was several minutes before Merritt realized they were not headed in the direction of Hyde Park. She swiveled to face him. "I thought you'd like to see where I live my days in the city," he said roughly, both hands still encircling the wheel.

More likely he wanted "home-court" advantage, Merritt thought.

The car was directed to a halt in a quiet, slightly rundown residential area. Tom led her up a rickety staircase to an apartment above the garage. Inside, it was little more cheerful. The only furniture was a hideaway bed of aging tan fabric, an end table and lamp, a small dinette with one chair. "As you can see"—Tom pointed out the small refrigerator, rusted-out stove, and sink—"I didn't get much from the divorce settlement. This is what my life was like before I met you, Merritt. I slept here, changed clothes, and showered. The rest of my time was spent either working—as much overtime as I could get, coincidentally a situation which hasn't been as easy to reverse, due to the shorthandedness of our staff—or working on my place up in Spring Valley. As for a personal life, I had none." He walked over to pull open the drapes. The illumination didn't add much to the sparse decor.

"You didn't even put up a Christmas tree of your own," Merritt murmured, thinking of how much trouble he'd gone through to get a beautiful, freshly cut one for her.

"Foolishly, I guess I expected to spend the holidays with you. I thought that was what you wanted too, Merritt. Tell me, how was it possible for me to go so far wrong? I thought we had something together, Merritt, something good, something worth continuing, something lasting."

Merritt swallowed convulsively in the silence that fell. "Why didn't you ever say anything?"

He swore softly, raking a hand through the tousled waves of his hair. "I asked you to marry me. Wasn't that enough?"

"Not when it's done out of pity and guilt, no."

He gritted his teeth again, taking another step forward. "Lady, I'm not that much of a fool. I've been married once. I wouldn't voluntarily step up to the chopping block again. Not unless I were absolutely sure it would work."

"And you were?"

"I left you Friday night because I'd walked downstairs to find you in the middle of a very private one-way conversation with your deceased husband. Yeah, I saw the whole bit, from your discovering the angel to the caressing way you held it in your hands, and then slowly put it on the tree. I felt like an intruder. I felt ... I didn't know what I felt. I just knew I had to get out of there, had to have time to think and sort out my feelings."

"So you let me think you were going in to work."

"It seemed easier than trying to explain. I didn't want to say anything that would hurt you, Merritt. I didn't want to risk what we had, not until I knew what the future held, how I felt. So I went up to Spring Valley. I hung the drapes you made. I walked around the farmhouse, thinking of how much of a difference you'd made just being there that one weekend. I thought about how it felt holding you in my arms. I thought about your temper and your recklessness and your stupid foolish pride. And I decided I didn't care how much you had loved your first husband. I didn't care what memories or artifacts you held on to. I didn't care if they were in every room and cluttered cabinet or drawer of the house, as long as you were there for and with me every night. I figured finally that loving you was going to be enough. It had to be, even if that was all it ever amounted to, me taking second place to a ghost. Because living without you wasn't living at all." He stepped forward, taking her gently into his arms, the warmth of his breath stirring her hair and her senses.

Eventually, though, he moved away, intent on letting Merritt hear it all undistracted by his touch. He roved the room restlessly, voice low, eyes never leaving her face, though he stopped often to idly finger the collection of dusty papers and glasses littering the small apartment. "I came back hoping to find you and propose again, Merritt. There was a For Sale sign in your front yard and an Internal Affairs investigation going on at the precinct in my behalf." He paused, watching her blush. "Oh, it was real amusing, Merritt, with questions like: 'Who was the mystery woman who had sole possession of my badge? Why had she turned it in anonymously and at the wrong station house yet? What had I been doing with or for her when I lost it?' The questions were endless, Merritt, and all hilariously put. I wanted to find you. I wanted to wring your neck!"

Merritt swallowed, stepping back. Her fingers gripped the table behind her in order to steady her badly shaking legs. "Good thing I laid low for a few days, hmm?"

"Probably," he agreed.

Silence fell between them. He stared at her without expression. Merritt knew then he would never forgive her. And after the humiliation she had put him through, she could hardly blame him. "What now?" she asked tremulously.

"I don't know. That all depends on you." Tom approached slowly. The palms of his hands caressed the slope of her shoulders, the slender thread of her neck.

"I do care about you, Tom," Merritt whispered, tilting her head back so her face would meet the soothing ministrations of his hands. She swayed toward him willingly, her body arching into his as her arms wreathed his neck.

"Enough to marry me?"

The wall of previously identified difficulties came tumbling down between them. Merritt wanted him with all her heart. But she was still afraid.

"It's Eric again, isn't it?" Tom presumed in a voice no longer steady.

Merritt glanced down at the unevenly looped, worn ivory carpeting covering the floor. "I'm always going to feel something for Eric," she admitted honestly, pausing to take a very ragged breath. "I loved him deeply, Tom. He was my first love, and for a long time the only man I thought I would ever care for." She turned, her eyes beseeching him to understand. "What you and I have shared is so different, so special. Eric and I were married in college, for all intents children just playing house. Police work for Eric was just a temporary job until he figured out what he really wanted to do with his life. There wasn't a future for us, there wasn't a past. We had only the present. When I look at you, I think about children and commitments and plans that would last a lifetime. The difference is I know what I'm getting into this time because I have been married before. And I want it, more than you could ever know."

Merritt took a deep hiccuping breath, tears misting her eyes. "The only reason I ever refused your proposal was because I thought you were just asking out of pity. I thought you felt sorry—or maybe partially responsible—for my potential school board dismissal. I couldn't allow you to marry me for anything less than real love." She'd thought if he truly loved her, he would ask again, at a more appropriate time, when he wasn't being bulldozed into anything by negative public opinion. She swallowed, recalling how they'd parted.

"But then, when you left that last night, without any real explanation, and later, I found out you were evading...I—"

Tom crossed the distance between them in one swift stride. His arms enfolded her fiercely. "Oh, Merritt, I love you so much, don't ever doubt that." He kissed her hungrily, exploring the dark, sweet mysteries of her mouth, his hands roving intimately from shoulder to thigh. Merritt stepped closer into his burning embrace, her palms splaying demandingly into the taut muscles of his hips. She had missed him so badly. It seemed eons since they had touched. His breath quickened and warmed with each subsequent caress, and still he kissed her, as if their lives depended upon the touching of their lips, the physical communication of their hearts and souls. "Marry me," he whispered when at last they could breathe again.

"Try and stop me," Merritt promised. Together, they tossed the sofa cushions to the floor. Tom pulled out the mattress then tumbled her back onto the softly mussed sheets. She trembled at the hunger on his face as he slid a tantalizingly soft finger across the upper curve of each full breast. She felt the electric contact all the way through her sweater and it was all she could do to stifle the low moan of ardent desperation in her throat.

"If you only knew how many nights I had dreamed of having you here in my bed," he said hoarsely.

She wound her arms around his neck, kissing him thoroughly, tenderly. "I've wanted to be with you," she confessed on a soft ragged note before his mouth once again covered hers.

"Then show me how much you want me," Tom demanded softly, harshly. "Show me how much you love me."

She knew then that he was as afraid of losing her as

she was of losing him. The knowledge both excited and
enthralled. With an abandon Merritt barely knew she
harbored, she placed the flat of his palms across her
chest, feeling her breasts tauten to rosebud softness
against his hands. Her eyes meshed with his, unafraid,
unashamed, and her responsiveness tore a harsh groan
of pleasure from his throat. His answering weight
forced her farther back onto the bed. They tumbled
together like two teenagers, wrestling, loving, undressing each other bit by tantalizing bit.

"You're so beautiful," Tom whispered. "Sometimes
I have trouble believing you really are mine."

"It's true."

"You're doing a wonderful job convincing me."

"And you're everything I could ever want in a man
or a friend or a lover—a husband." Beneath his touch
she trembled with passionate excitement. "And I want
you."

His lips drifted down across the nape of her neck to
her shoulder. His fingertips trailed lightly over her
breasts, circling the taut crests again and again, moving
with shimmering awareness over her abdomen and
lower. He explored lightly, deliberately, as if intending
to heighten their lovemaking to shuddering, explosive
depths. Merritt moaned, her thighs parting reflexively.
He moved restively against her, in her, his hand cupping her close, his breath hot against her neck.

Blinding, tormenting sensations overwhelmed her.
She arched against him, drawing deep, drawing closer,
aware of the iron band of his arm beneath her ribs. And
still he moved slowly, deliberately, prolonging each
sensual stroke until she shuddered, gasping with the
depth of his possession. He seemed part not only of her
body but of her heart, her soul, and the pleasure they
could give.

"Tom—"

Withdrawing swiftly, he gazed reverently down at her, his love for her reflected in the tenderness of his expression.

His knee nudged hers and she shifted to welcome him again. Once possessed, her body climbed quickly, building to the fiery point of explosion. He held her tightly against him, more vulnerable in his need than she ever would have imagined. And then all was lost in the final wild burst of pleasure.

Shuddering, clinging, they were still. "I love you," Merritt admitted softly, before drifting off to sleep.

"And I love you." He added softly, sighing, "More than you will ever know."

The marriage preparations went more swiftly than Merritt had anticipated. A justice of the peace agreed to perform the ceremony at City Hall. Blanche and Artie were to witness the small private ceremony.

"You don't have to sell your house," Tom pointed out after the last candlelight dinner they would share before becoming man and wife. Although the wedding was still several days away, Tom had pulled night duty for the rest of the week.

Merritt snuggled next to him on the broad sofa. The Christmas tree lights twinkled merrily. A fire glowed warmly in the grate. "I know. But realistically, it was a decision I had made even before you proposed."

"Why?"

Merritt lifted her shoulders evasively. "I don't know. I guess I felt the time was finally right. I wanted to put all of my first marriage completely behind me, including, I guess, the place where Eric and I had lived."

Frowning briefly, Tom poured her some more coffee from the insulated carafe on the table. "I won't deny three months ago I would have given my badge to hear you say that."

Merritt nodded, running her fingertips lightly and possessively over his thigh. "I know. Others have been encouraging me to do the same for months now."

"Seeing your face when the realtor stopped by earlier to show those prospective buyers through changed my mind."

Merritt tried to shrug off the awkward experience. "So I didn't like what they had to say about the 'abysmally dull' color of my bedroom carpeting. I guess that's par for the course, though I must say there's nothing wrong with the white enamel fixtures in either the bathrooms or the kitchen. Granted, they're old-fashioned and a little more difficult to clean, but that takes nothing away from their charm."

"Are you selling this house or defending it to its death? Sorry. But prospective buyers are entitled to their opinion, Merritt. Particularly if they do put a bid on this house. If you want to sell it, you're also going to have to stop pointing out all the flaws."

"I felt I owed it to myself to be honest," Merritt grumbled disparagingly, disengaging her hand from the gentle warmth of his and reaching for her coffee. "How would I feel, knowing they'd unwittingly bought a lemon?"

"Detailed descriptions of the time the garbage disposal backed up three years ago are not necessary." Sandy eyebrows knitting together, he continued to remonstrate tenderly.

"Look, can we change the subject?" Venting a sigh of exasperation, Merritt set down her coffee. But when, hands shoved in the back pockets of her corduroy jeans, she tried to rise, he pulled her back down onto the sofa beside him, one hand hooked implacably about her waist.

"You won't get a better interest rate than you now have or be able to find as convenient a location, no matter where else you're able to buy," Tom pointed out calmly. "And frankly, I can't see you living in my efficiency apartment."

"And the Spring Valley farm is too far away to commute to," Merritt agreed miserably.

"On our salaries, you're right." They sat in silence, contemplating options.

"I guess a larger apartment might be feasible," Merritt decided. She couldn't buy a second house until her current one was sold.

"You don't really want to move." Tom turned toward her.

"I do," Merritt protested.

Tom set aside his coffee, then draped one arm along the back of the couch and stared up at the ceiling. "What kind of marriage are we going to have, Merritt? Because I'm telling you right now, if it's going to be self-sacrificial, I don't want any part of it."

"I don't know what you mean." Merritt's jaw clenched. Her eyes stubbornly evaded his searching stare.

"I want a partnership, Merritt. An equal opportunity union. I'll do part of the housework if you bring in part of the bacon. We'll both help cut the grass and take out the garbage. I don't want you selling the house you've spent years making uniquely your own just to please me, regardless of who shared it with you before. I don't want to have to give up the work I love for a more lucrative position as security officer at some private firm. And I don't want to be forced to work nine-to-five, just so we'll live status quo."

"But somewhere down the line we will have to compromise," Merritt cautioned.

"Only on things that don't take anything away from us as individuals," Tom specified. "Things like leaving the toothpaste cap on or off. How often the garbage goes out. Who writes out the bills and who goes to the post office to buy stamps and mail them. I love you, Merritt, just the way you are.''

"And I love you. It's a deal." They sealed it with a kiss, her lips sweetly moistening his.

"Let's go upstairs," Tom suggested softly. His hand traced the lush fullness of her breast.

"I'll turn out the lights," Merritt offered, anxious to get him into the warmth and comfort of her bed.

"We'll do the dinner dishes later, or in the morning," Tom imparted.

Merritt laughed. "Is that a compromise, mutual decision, or macho command?" she teased. The buzzing of the phone interrupted. "And who gets to answer that? Or should we make a chart? I take the first, third, and fifth rings, and you—"

Tom silenced her with a rough, passionate kiss on the lips. Simultaneously he reached for the nearby receiver, his arm drawing her closer yet. He halted the kiss reluctantly as the receiver reached his ear, a possessive arm still wrapped around Merritt's waist. "Reed residence." He favored her with a mercilessly intimate look as he listened. After a second his expression turned grave. "Yeah, sure, I'll be right there," Tom agreed before he hung up.

"That was Artie Kochek. He's down at that Italian restaurant three blocks from here, Gianni's. Seems they've been robbed. The precinct's shorthanded. Unless they get someone else down there to help dust for fingerprints and get descriptions from the customers, Artie's going to be there all night. Apparently, they've got several good witnesses. Besides coming in too late to get the bulk of the cash before it had been sent to the bank, the felon didn't even have sense enough to wear a mask."

Merritt tried not to think about the danger as Tom shrugged into a jacket. "How's Gianni doing? Was anyone hurt?"

"No injuries, according to Art. Don't worry," he emphasized, leaning toward her for a tender parting kiss. "I'll be back sooner than you think." He flashed her a winning smile and was gone.

Merritt used the ensuing minutes to finish up the dishes in the kitchen. When an hour had passed and she still had no word from Tom, she mopped the kitchen floor. The living room got dusted, the entire house vacuumed, and still no word. Merritt thought briefly of calling the precinct, then turned on the television. Neither the late-night movie, Home Box Office, or Johnny Carson could hold her attention. A late night news bulletin did.

"We interrupt this program to bring you a special report. Hostages are being held in a Hyde Park restaurant. . . . Shots have been fired. At this time, communication with the people inside is limited. We do not know, repeat, do not know if anyone has been hurt . . ."

Merritt's hands turned to ice. Her heartbeat intensified in volume until she could hear it pounding inside her head. Visions of Eric came spiraling back: the last night she'd seen him alive, that awful time in the city morgue, and the funeral services that had been even worse. It was happening all over again. She was in love with a policeman and he was going to be killed . . . .

The next few minutes passed in a blur. Merritt put on her coat. Somehow she managed to locate her house keys and remember to lock the door. Her car got no farther than the next street. Police had partitioned off a two-block area around the restaurant. Flashing red lights blinked above the static of police radios. "Ma'am, this area is closed to the public," an officer leaned down to speak into her open car window.

"You don't understand." Merritt's teeth were chattering with reaction. Her throat was constricting horribly, and tears slid torrentially down her face. "I've got to get in there. My fiancé is in there."

"I don't care who he is, ma'am. No unauthorized personnel are allowed in this area. Now move your car, please. You're blocking the paramedics trying to get in." The words were a staccato of authority. Realizing eventually the hopelessness of her attempt to intervene, Merritt did as told. The radio in her car confirmed that residents from nearby houses were being evacuated as well. No one seemed to know precisely what had happened. Only that the people inside definitely had guns. And at least one cop was being held hostage.

Dawn found Merritt back at her home, still ensconced beside the dying embers of the fire. Local television stations had long since gone off the air. Radio news staffs were equally skeleton, and featured no additional information. It didn't surprise Merritt. Crime was something one accepted in the current day and age. You hoped and prayed it would never touch you or anyone you loved. When it did, you stood powerlessly by. She thought of Tom, his dedication toward fighting both the violence and the apathy. Had she ever known anyone more noble, tied to his sense of right and wrong? Had she ever resented it more?

Her front door clicked open. Tom stood perfectly still, his gaze riveted on her curled-up form as he removed his key from the lock. His jaw was stubbled with beard. The whites of his eyes were rimmed with the red of fatigue. "You've been crying." It was a harsh accusation, though in retrospect, Merritt realized, he didn't seem that surprised.

Merritt wiped the back of her hand across both cheeks, saying nothing. Relief had turned swiftly to anger. If he had known she might be worried, why hadn't he phoned? "Is it over?"

"You know about it, then." His head went up slightly as if he were girding himself for battle, but his eyes remained expressionless. Merritt hated his composure even more than she hated the logistics of a cop's life.

"Only what was on the radio, that there were some shots fired, people held hostage at Gianni's."

Tom nodded, not elaborating. Merritt knew the news was bad by the taut, uncompromising line of his jaw. Her hands gripped the fabric of her corduroys until the knuckles turned white. Still watching her, Tom sank into the nearest chair with a weariness that was all the more unsettling. He stretched his long legs out in front of him, resting the palms of his hands on the creases of his trousers. "Artie Kochek's been shot." He looked away for a long moment, fighting for control. "He's in surgery now."

Merritt felt tears burn her eyes anew. They rolled unchecked down her face as she thought of the man who was Tom's best friend. "Is he going to make it?"

"They don't know."

"What happened?" Her knees were shaking, her voice trembling as badly as her legs. Tom made no move to comfort her, rather got up to prowl the room restlessly, anger and resentment etched clearly on his face. "The initial investigation was routine. Artie talked to patrons and Gianni while I dusted for prints. We sectioned off the area in front of the place, closed it for the night. Everyone left. I went down to headquarters to file my reports. Artie was going to see what he could do about securing the locks that had been broken in the back. Gianni and his wife went along, nervously chatting about employing a security guard in the future.

"Before Artie could manage to bolt the door, the suspect was back, armed with an automatic. He was spaced out on speed, scared because he'd botched the earlier attempt so badly, and he knew he could be identified. Art could have drawn his gun and fired, in the hopes he was faster than the suspect—who already had his gun primed. Fearing a bloodbath, he tried to talk

the suspect into surrendering. The man refused ada-
mantly and there was a scuffle. The suspect's gun went
off a few times, bullets lodging in the floors and walls.
In the confusion, the gunman managed to grab Gianni's wife. He said he would kill her.

"Artie could have gotten the suspect, but according
to Gianni, he would have done it at a risk to Gianni's
wife. So Art waited it out and tried to reason with the
guy, talk him into giving himself up. In the meantime,
the shots had attracted the attention of a neighbor and
more squad cars had arrived. They trotted in the staff
psychologist and the deputy commander and God
knows how many news crews and squad cars and paramedics. The suspect tried to ransom his way out. Gianni's wife went into premature labor. Gianni panicked
and rushed the suspect without warning. Artie moved
to shield the woman and pull her out of the way and got
caught in the line of fire."

"The suspect?"

"Sitting it out in the county jail, unscathed."

"Gianni's wife?"

"Hospitalized."

"Her baby? Is she going to lose it?"

Tom shrugged helplessly. "They don't know."

Anger surged through Merritt. Anger that the world
was sometimes violent. Anger that Tom felt he had to be
personally involved in fighting that same characteristic.

"Well?" Tom whirled back around to face her. The
girded strength of his legs told her he had accurately
read her thoughts. His arms crossed defensively over
his broad chest. Contempt stabbed at her from his jade
eyes. "Aren't you going to say it?"

Abruptly Merritt decided not to fence. She owed him
her honesty. "I lost one husband to the Cincinnati police force, damn it!"

"I wasn't even there at the time of the shooting," he
pointed out.

"But you wish you had been."

His jaw clenched. "Maybe I could have helped."

"Not maybe," Merritt corrected, surprised at the ice in her voice. "You're certain you could have prevented the shooting. Isn't that so?"

Tom didn't answer, but affirmation was written all over his face. "You'll never give it up, will you?" Merritt raged very low. Hysteria welled in her throat. "No matter how often your life is in danger or how often you or one of your buddies gets shot or killed—"

"Someone has to do it, Merritt. We've been over this before. And it's not a subject open to discussion."

She was filled with a defensive anger of her own. "All right, then, let me ask you this. What happens if it turns out I can't take it again? Because I'm not sure I want to go through anything like what I did tonight. What happens if I ask you to choose between your job and me?" She hadn't realized until that moment just how very tough it was going to be. She hadn't known she would be facing a gut-wrenching fear everytime their phone rang or he walked out the door to report for his job. Detective rank or no, there was always going to be someone else out there with a gun, someone on the other side of the law, someone who knew her husband was a cop, and therefore a lethal threat to them.

"Don't say anything more," Tom cautioned flatly. His tone said the night alone had been more than he could take without additional nagging from her.

Merritt was silent, watching.

"I've got to go," he said finally, heading back toward the door. Numbly she watched him go, knowing this was one time she couldn't walk with him and wish him well and kiss him good-bye, not if he was going back to work.

Concern for their mutual friend finally yanked her from her reverie. "If you're going to the hospital, I'd like to go with you."

"No." The refusal was definite, and very remote. "I'll call you."

But he didn't call, not that day or the next. Merritt finally went over to the hospital where Artie Kochek had been admitted. Tom was pacing the corridors outside the injured cop's room. He paused when he saw her, yet he didn't speak or attempt to put her at ease in any way. Merritt knew then how badly she had let him down by even suggesting he quit the force. She was powerless to help her feelings. She wanted Tom Hennessey alive, not dead behind the smoking barrel of some criminal's gun. "How is he?" Her voice was hushed as she approached.

"I think he'll pull through. It'll be awhile though, before he's back on the streets. The surgeon said maybe two months before he's even able to return to work."

Merritt took a deep breath. "How is Artie taking it?"

Tom shrugged his shoulders, then lounged against the wall as he studied the dregs in the bottom of his Styrofoam coffee cup. "At the moment, he's pretty damn high. I doubt he'll feel that way when they reduce the morphine or whatever they've got him on."

Merritt nodded. "Can I see him?"

Tom glanced both ways down the hall, studied the two employees hovering over the nursing station phones. "Technically, no. However, I've never known Artie not to be cheered up by a good-looking woman, so—"

Covertly Tom opened the swinging hospital room door and they slipped inside. Artie was sleeping soundly. Intravenous tubing was taped into the veins on the back of his hand. His features were ashen, skin looking almost gray against the pale blond hair. He stirred at the sounds of movement in the room.

Tom treaded steadily toward the bed. "It's only me and Merritt."

"Merritt." Artie favored her with a lopsided grin. "I knew Tom would bring me something good."

Tom laughed, abruptly looking as if he hadn't a care in the world. "Not that good. She's a visitor, not a gift."

Artie sighed, lifting a leaden hand. "Possessive already, and not even married."

"Don't worry, sport. You haven't missed anything yet," Tom joked very low. "We're not exchanging so much as a ring until you're out of this place, and able to do the honors of best man like you promised."

"But—" Artie sputtered, blinking himself into further wakefulness.

Merritt picked up on Tom's cue. "Tom's right, Artie. Our wedding wouldn't be the same without you." She glanced back at Tom and their gazes collided. She knew then that the ceremony was off indefinitely and he just hadn't had the guts or the time to make a clean break. "We'll wait until you're out of here and able to handle the heavy responsibility of keeping track of the ring. Until then," Merritt continued, before Artie could speak, "I promise to keep him in line."

Artie laughed. "Poor Hennessey. Domesticated already." Unexpectedly a nurse came barreling in the door. She glared at Tom. "I thought I instructed you to let Mr. Kochek sleep."

Tom raised both hands in surrender. "We're going."

The nurse held the door. Artie held tight to one of Merritt's hands, preventing her immediate departure. "Seriously, don't wait," he implored. "The man loves you and you love him. Go for it. Who knows what tomorrow's going to bring?"

"Ahem!" The nurse loudly cleared her throat.

"Take care." Merritt planted a kiss on Artie's brow. "And I'll see you soon."

"See, Hennessey?" Artie crowed between coughs. "I'm stealing your woman already!"

"Fat chance!" Tom remarked as he laced his arm possessively around Merritt's waist, directing her from the room. He lifted his hand in a lazy wave. "See you later, buddy. And don't give those nurses too much h—"

Artie mumbled something appropriate as the nurse moved forward to alternately scold and take his pulse. The door shut quietly behind them. Merritt and Tom faced each other, alone in the hall, abruptly ill at ease again. He shoved his hands in his pockets. "I've got to go back in to work. Can I drop you somewhere on my way?" He used the indifferent voice of a stranger.

She shook her head. She didn't want their relationship to be over. She didn't want to be just a memory to this man. "Can I see you again?" The words were impulsive, undeterred by the hurt simmering deep inside her.

"I don't think that would be wise." He studied the wall behind her with great concentration.

"Just to talk." Her hand lifted involuntarily and her fingers brushed his sleeve imploringly. The chill look he gave her made her drop her grip tensely. She knew then how much she'd hurt him, too. If there was anything she could do to change it, somehow go back, she would. But she knew that was impossible.

"We've said everything we had to say, Merritt, there's nothing else to discuss." His tone was flat, final.

Tears blurred her eyes, but stubbornly she tried to make him see the enormity of what he was doing, what they would both be losing. She'd lost her first husband. She didn't want to lose Tom. "I love you," she whispered, her voice trembling.

His jaw tautened. He pivoted to fix her with an accusing, challenging stare. "Apparently not enough to accept what I do."

"I don't want to see you get hurt, true. Does that

make me a heartless monster?" He made no reply. She moved closer, her eyes shimmering with unshed tears, her voice thick with suppressed emotion. "Couldn't we at least salvage something?" If only their love affair or friendship. "Couldn't we talk about trying to remain close?"

He stepped aside brusquely. "I can't handle not being totally supported by the woman I love." Taking her by the elbow, he led her to a more sheltered spot by the coffee machine. "Damn it, Merritt, you know how I feel about you! But you also know how I feel about quitting the force."

"I'm sorry I said that. If I could take back those words—"

"What would be the point? You meant them. Even if you hadn't said them, I still would have known how you felt. I can't go to work day in and day out, knowing I don't have your backing. It's too distracting. It's too self-destructive, for us both."

"I can't help how I feel. I wish I could."

He observed her quietly, some of the tension leaving his frame. "I know you can't. I wish circumstances were different, too, maybe more than you know. But what kind of marriage would we have if I ignored how you felt in this matter, or you tried to disguise your own fears? You'd end up resenting me and I you. Where before there was truth, there would be lies or evasions. How could we go on that way, Merritt? How would either of us survive emotionally under those conditions?"

"Tom, please—"

"All the rationalizing in the world won't change the facts, Merritt," he said bluntly. "Face it, our affair is over."

No! She wouldn't let it be. She didn't want it to be. "There's got to be some way to compromise—"

"I told you before, Merritt," Tom informed bitterly.

"I tried that in my last marriage. I won't go through it again."

"I still want to see you," Merritt insisted as they walked, not touching, to the elevators, Tom taking the lead.

He shook his head. "And prolong the hurt? No, Merritt. I think it's best we just cool it for a while. If things change—" He broke off in midsentence, shaking his head. "Now who's fooling himself?"

Who indeed? she wondered. Her throat constricted. It infuriated her to know he wasn't willing to even try, at the very least continue their love affair. She also knew he was right. In the long run, maybe this was for the best, at least from a practical, reasonable view. "I really thought it would work," she said miserably as the doors glided open in front of them.

Tom followed her into the elevator, hands pressed into the pockets of his tan corduroy pants. "I know. So did I." He took a deep breath, and for a brief moment, Merritt thought he was just as affected and tormented as she. But the moment passed. Casually he pressed the lobby button. "I guess it just goes to show what real fools we mortals can be."

Chapter Ten

Merritt's sixth-grade classroom windows were open, letting in warm sleep-inducing drifts of May air. The scent of lilacs mingled with poster paint and glue. Her class was hard at work on a blackboard-length collage of memorabilia that would in the end represent every nation in the western hemisphere. Blanche Beck strolled in to admire the imaginative handiwork. "Hey there, Reed, how's it going?"

"Busier than in the guidance counseling office, evidently."

"Actually, I'm just here to check out a rumor." Blanche shoved her hands in the pockets of her cotton print wraparound skirt. "There's a report you've been offered a position at Riverview Academy? Is that true?"

Merritt dragged her friend to the back of the room, out of earshot of the kids. "Yes."

"Going to go?" Blanche asked without skipping a beat.

Merritt shrugged. "I don't know. The superintendent called me yesterday to renew my contract here. I told him I'd have to think about it."

"How long have you got?"

"Till the end of next week."

"You wouldn't seriously think of leaving us?"

Merritt's brows arched. "You've got to admit, my

record for a class being monitored beats every other staff member's hands down. I'm not sure I like all that attention.'' She wasn't sure it was good for her students.

"You also upgraded the textbook allowance for us all. That's no easy feat."

Merritt agreed. "I have to admit I was looking forward to using that new series of books." One that was famed for their nonstereotypical views.

Merritt watched the children programming the personal computer. Facts about individual countries were flashed one by one on the video screen. "Who programmed all that data in?" Blanche asked.

Merritt slanted her an amused glance. "Would you believe John Porter and Brian Anderson? They've been staying after school nearly every day to look up and add something more."

"Another educational conquest in your favor," Blanche remarked. Merritt shook her head, blushing humbly, but she couldn't negate the warm flush of pride she felt. Both boys were doing better now, and she liked to think, privately at least, it was due in part to her diligence and dedication.

"How's John's father by the way?" Blanche asked moments later as they strolled down the hall to the teachers' lounge for a quick two-minute break.

"He remarried a few weeks ago, as planned." Merritt slid the appropriate amount of change into the dish next to the refrigerator. "And as you can see, John has apparently adjusted. His mother is looking well and more relaxed. And though she evidently still has to work long hours, he doesn't seem to mind as much. In fact, John was quite proud of Ellen the days she came to school and explained to our class how to program one of the six computers her firm had loaned to the school."

Blanche helped herself to a Coke. "Brian's doing well, I presume."

Merritt nodded. "Hasn't been down to see Mr. Tierney for over a month now." She laughed. "Seriously, though, his mother hasn't changed, though Brian does seem to take her vigilantism with a more sophisticated detachment these days. Another sign of growing up, I guess."

Together, the two women strolled back to stand just outside Merritt's classroom door. "I also heard you had a bid on your house." Blanche studied her friend.

Merritt paused to direct a brief instruction to her class, then turned back to Blanche. "My, you have been busy, haven't you? Yes, I had a bid on my house, but I haven't decided whether to accept it or not yet. I took it off the market when Tom and I broke up, but one of the neighborhood realtors recalled it had been for sale around Christmas. He thought it would be perfect for his clients. They're moving in from out of state and need a place soon, one that's small enough and in good repair and located in Hyde Park, close to the husband's place of employment. At first, I wasn't going to show the house, but then I thought, what the hay, and did it anyway." All it held for her anymore were the memories of two men. "Whether I accept the bid depends on that job at Riverview."

Blanche nodded, obviously hoping Merritt wouldn't elect to leave. "I still think you're a fool to sell with the interest rates as high as they are these days."

Merritt shrugged. "Join the club. However, the couple that did make the offer seem very nice. They're very young, just starting out. They remind me a lot of Eric and myself when we first started out."

Blanche smiled understandingly. "You're finally over his death, aren't you?"

Merritt nodded, for once able to remember without tears clouding her vision. "Tom helped."

"Heard from him?" Blanche inquired.

Merritt's whole body stiffened. "No, and I don't expect to, either." She moved across the hall, leaned against the locker, watchful eyes still trained on her class. "It was just one of those affairs that was meant to end."

"You still love him, don't you?"

About that, Merritt saw no reason to pretend. "Yes, I still love him," she answered in a voice that was soft and ragged with suppressed emotion. "I love him with all my heart." But she hadn't been there when Tom needed her. She hadn't supported his work. And that was the one criterion he couldn't live without.

"Thought of calling him?"

Yes, she thought, many times. But deep inside she was afraid of what would happen if she did, afraid he wouldn't forgive her, or worse had found someone else who would love him and accept him in a way that she hadn't.

Merritt shook her head. "We hurt each other enough. There's no need to replay a scenario that in the end could only wound both of us more." But was she being honest? she wondered. Or just more of a coward than she had previously been?

Merritt stopped in at Gianni's after work. "Haven't seen you around much, Merritt," Gianni chided, coming forward to seat her.

"I'm sorry. I've been busy with all the year-end paperwork at school." She relaxed in a chair next to a window. "It's hard to believe my precious sixth-graders will all be heading off to junior high school next year."

Gianni handed her a menu, sighing. "Time marches on, doesn't it?"

"It certainly does."

Because the restaurant was devoid of either the lunch or evening rush, Gianni took a seat across from her. His eyes glinted as he revealed meaningfully, "Your friend Tom Hennessey has been busy, too."

Her heart seemed to stop. "You've seen him?"

Gianni nodded. "He comes in about once a month. He always makes it a point to ask about you, too."

She flushed, wondering why she'd never seen him. "I'm sure Tom's just mentioning me to be polite." Her tone was much cooler than her tumultuous emotions.

"I don't think so," Gianni said. His wife, Debbie, walked over to join them. Since the robbery, she had grown almost as painfully thin as Gianni. There were harsh brown circles of fatigue or perhaps depression beneath and around her eyes. "How are you, Merritt?" she asked softly, pushing her hair away from her shoulders.

"I'm fine. And you?"

"To be honest, still recovering." She exhaled shakily and pulled up a chair. Debbie glanced at Gianni, and he reached over and squeezed her hand. "We're learning to take life one day at a time, appreciate every precious moment that we have together."

Merritt knew they'd wanted to sell the restaurant at first, had even gone so far as to consider listing it with a realtor. But practicality along with their love of Cincinnati and Hyde Park had finally won out. Gianni's was now busier than ever. The felon who had shot Artie had been convicted and was serving time in a state correctional institution. But for Gianni and Debbie, the trauma lingered. They'd lost their firstborn child to hyaline lung disease, a complication of newborn babies born prematurely, shortly after his birth.

Debbie looked down at her hands. "Gianni and I had always planned a family, but it was several years before I was able to get pregnant. We don't know if I'll ever be able to conceive again."

"Oh, Debbie, I'm so sorry," Merritt said.

"I know and thank you. But it's taught us something, too, Merritt. It's taught us never to take anything or anyone for granted. We were careless about security

before. We now have an armed security man here
every day, every hour, every minute that we're open.
We've installed an electronic alarm system, and coop-
erated with the police in getting a Neighborhood Watch
program initiated here. We're still trying to have a
child, of course. But we've also had to face the possibility that we may never have a child of our own. The
odds are stacked against us. But we're still trying, Merritt. And we've put our names on an adoption waiting
list in the meantime. One way or another Gianni and I
are going to have a family. We're going to have a future
despite our past tragedy. What about you? You can't let
your husband's death stop you from marrying Tom."

"I'm afraid I don't have any choice about that," she
said grimly. But Merritt had to admit, the more time
passed, the more she wondered if she had made the
right decision in breaking off their relationship, in not
going after Tom more aggressively. Maybe, if she'd just
tried a little harder to understand him, they could have
worked their problems out.

"Merritt, Gianni wasn't exaggerating. Tom is in here
at least once a month now. He has been since the two
of you split up. He always asks about you and wants to
know how you're doing."

Her heart was soaring, but she forced herself to remain calm, and keep her demeanor at least outwardly
unimpressed. "So?"

"I haven't mentioned it before because I didn't want
to offend you, but damn it, Merritt, the man cares
about you! And I know you still love him. It was written all over your face the moment Gianni spoke his
name. Go to him, Merritt. Find some way for the two
of you to work out your differences. Life's too short for
you not to." Her hand covered her husband's. "We
know how tough it is to lose someone you love, no
matter how short a period you had that person with
you," Debbie said softly. "There's nothing more im-

portant than being with the people you love as much as possible, at whatever personal sacrifice necessary. Because if you aren't, before you know it the chance is gone and you can never regain it again."

Merritt spent the rest of the night and all the next day thinking about what Gianni and his wife had said. Maybe she was being a fool. Maybe Tom did still care. At any rate, could she go on much longer without finding out for herself? Merritt didn't think so. Because after all was said and done, she still loved Tom. The months spent without him had been the most personally miserable of her life. True, she hadn't had to worry about him walking out the door and never coming back. But she hadn't had anything to lose, either. In truth, she hadn't had much of a life at all.

By five that evening, she was parked outside his apartment. Having decided to take the initiative, she was a nervous wreck. It was seven thirty before his car appeared. He didn't seem to see her car on the other side of the street as he got slowly out of his. Merritt jumped out and smoothed her skirt and her hair before she lost her nerve. "Tom!" Her voice carried more than she had expected. The heat of an immediate blush filled her face. She felt so darn foolish. But for once need surpassed everything else.

Tom turned at the sound of her voice. He stood, sport coat slung over his shoulder, tie loosened partway to his chest. "Merritt, what are you doing here?" He looked momentarily dazed, as if awakening from a glorious dream.

Her heart drummed painfully against her ribs. She hadn't realized until that moment just how much she'd missed him and it was all she could do to keep from running to him and flinging her arms about his neck and pulling him to her for a swift hard kiss and bone-crushing hug.

Briefly he let his eyes roam appreciatively over her slender form as she crossed the street. He frowned. "Is something wrong? One of the kids missing at school?"

Her spirits deflated as she regarded him uncertainly, unsure as to how he really felt now that she was here, and he'd got over his shock. "No." She floundered awkwardly in the dusky light, all too aware they were standing in the path of traffic. "I just—"

A car rounded the corner half a block away. Abruptly Tom took hold of her elbow and led her swiftly toward the apartment. He glanced at the stairs leading up over the garage, then away, as if that were the last place he would ever want her to be. Desperately afraid he would send her away before she had a chance to tell him how she felt, Merritt said softly, "I want to talk to you, Tom."

For the first time he looked openly reluctant. A sigh rippled his sinewy frame. "All right, we'll talk. But not here."

Disappointment rushed through her with tidal wave force. He didn't want to be alone with her. Had she hurt him that much? Was he still angry? Or was there now someone else, someone who would object?

"If it's a personal matter, though—" Tom relented with reluctant hospitality. All this time he thought he'd forgotten her, thought he'd put Merritt Reed out of his life, his heart, his mind. Seeing her standing there in front of him, so vulnerable, so pleading, so emotional, taught him he hadn't. If anything, he was even more in love with her than he'd ever been. Could that be the reason why she was there? he thought, hardly able to believe there might even be a slight chance of his assumption being true.

"It *is* personal," Merritt said quietly. Her chin jutted out stubbornly as she tilted her face back beneath his. Part of her wanted to run. Part of her was determined to stay. She had started this, waited like an absolute fool for over two hours for him to come home. The least she could do was finish it, no matter how it turned out. If he didn't love her anymore, then at least she would know. Then maybe she could go on with her life.

"Have you been waiting long?" Tom asked calmly, leading her impersonally toward the stairs.

"No," Merritt lied. Suddenly she didn't want him to know how desperate she was. She didn't want to lose her pride as well as her heart. And the possibility for surrendering both completely did exist. If he touched her just once, or drew her into his arms...

He was silent, fitting his key into the lock. The door swung open. Merritt gaped at the changes his place had undergone: the interior had been completely redone.

"I thought it was about time I fixed up more than my Spring Valley home," Tom explained. "I've also had a lot of time on my hands since we broke up. I've moonlighted at some of the restaurants, department stores, and banks around town, acting as security expert and consultant. The extra pay has come in handy, as you can see."

"The apartment's lovely," she said quietly.

"Thanks."

She nodded in acknowledgment, her voice seeming to have got stuck in her throat. She'd expected to find Tom suffering in the same way as she. To see he was doing so well took the wind from her lungs. He had changed. "If you're expecting company—" she hedged uncertainly. Did he want her to stay?

"I'm not expecting anyone." Tom watched her steadily, giving nothing away. After a moment he looped his jacket over the coatrack near the door, then strode purposefully toward the small kitchenette. "Can I get you a drink?" he asked smoothly. She was beautiful, he thought, and so fragile.

"Yes," Merritt said, then flushing, "No—I'll have a soda, please." She watched as he fixed them both an icy Coke, admiring the capable movements of his hands, remembering without wanting to the same way those fingers had felt as they tenderly caressed her naked skin.

Tom walked over to hand her a glass. His hands brushed hers deliberately. He made no attempt to draw away. "Why are you really here?" he prodded, very low.

She couldn't put her feelings into words. When she didn't answer straight away, he cupped a hand beneath her chin gently and tilted her face up to his. His dark gaze roamed her face intently, as if committing every feature to memory. "We've established nothing is wrong. You brought nothing with you to return. So why are you here? Do I still have something that belongs to you—something from when we were going together?"

Yes, she thought, sighing, *you still have the sole claim to my heart and my soul.* In fact, had never relinquished it as far as she was concerned. "No, I have everything—all of my clothes and records and so forth at home." There had been a time, she thought dimly, when her belongings had been equally at home in his closet as in hers, and vice versa. But that had ended shortly after the engagement had been broken. She'd returned home one day to find a sealed box of her belongings positioned discreetly on her front porch. Later, she'd done the same for him, making sure they didn't have to meet again face to face. At the time it had seemed the best solution, but now she wasn't so certain. If they had met then, confronted one another and their feelings, would there be the same distance and unease between them now?

"How have you been?" Tom asked quietly. His hand dropped from her chin, pushed back a strand of her hair, before dropping to his side.

Merritt turned away, swallowing, feeling suddenly as if she were going to burst into tears. "Fine. No," she decided without warning, whirling to face him more honestly. "I haven't been fine. I've been lonelier than I've ever been in my life."

He nodded, swallowing, then took a sip of his Coke. "Me, too. Have you been dating anyone?"

Her heart was pounding so loudly she felt it might be audible in the silence of the room. "No."

He exhaled raggedly, his glance meeting hers directly. "Neither have I."

Tears of relief glistened in her eyes. He smiled slowly, then his grin broadened and he smiled some more. "So, what are we doing standing three feet apart? Come here and hold me."

He held out his arms and she glided into them. "I presume this means you still have some feelings for me," he whispered, holding her close.

"I still love you with all my heart." He smelled of familiar cologne and she reveled in both the fragrance and the poignant memories it evoked.

"I love you, too." He hugged her harder, wondering that she should be there at all, after the time that had elapsed. But she was real, he thought, and she was warm, and she was . . . willing. With slow deliberation he pulled back and stared down into her face. Her breath caught slightly. He saw more tears, and then her eyelids slowly shuttered, her head dipping back, her mouth falling open in mute, pleading invitation. He didn't need a second chance. Swiftly his mouth lowered to hers. Tenderness marked every move of his lips. She responded in kind, gently at first, uncertainly, until without thought they were little more than a passionate tangle of arms and mouths and pliant wills. Eventually, knowing he had to, Tom released her. If and when he made love to her again, he wanted it to be right. He wanted their problems to have been settled first. "As much as I want you," he said, "we still have to talk."

"I know."

He led her toward the couch, pulling her down beside him. "I'm still a cop, Merritt." His hand caressing her sundress-bared shoulder, he admitted, "I've missed you like hell the past few months, Merritt, but I never stopped loving you or wanting you to marry me. I still want that. But by the same token, I can't put you through the tensions life with me will bring unless it is what you want one hundred percent."

"I do want you, Tom." She framed his face with her palms.

He withdrew her hands, pausing only to press a brief kiss against the knuckles of her right hand. "I can't offer you anything but one day, one moment at a time, Merritt," he cautioned gravely. "Whether we have children or not, that will never change. I'm still committed to police work."

"I know that's a part of you, now," she confessed raggedly, tears streaming down her face. "I wouldn't ask you to give it up. In fact"—she took a deep breath, admitting tremulously—"I think in retrospect it's one of the qualities I love about you most, your devotion to helping other people, your dedication to keeping the city a safe place to live and work."

"And love," he added, pulling her onto his lap. He buried his face in the gently curling tendrils of her hair. "If you only knew how many nights I dreamed of having you here again with me."

"Is that why you worked so hard fixing up the apartment?" she asked, a teasing glint in her eyes.

He laughed softly. "I hoped you'd be back, I admit it." His expression grew more serious.

"I'm glad to be here, too."

"Will you marry me?"

Her heart did somersaults in her chest, but her voice was calm and without reservation. "Yes."

"You're sure?"

Merritt leaned her face against the slightly scratchy

surface of his jaw. She even loved his five o'clock shadow, she realized with a satisfied sigh. "The past few months I've only been half alive. I realized that being protected from possible tragedy was no protection at all. It was a prison, one of my own making. I want to share my life with you, Tom, regardless of how much time we do or don't have. There are no guarantees in this life."

"I couldn't have said that more eloquently myself," Tom agreed. "You realize, of course, we're going to have to go back to City Hall and apply for a marriage license all over again, though."

"That's fine with me," Merritt decided. "Do you think Artie will still stand up for us?"

"You bet! The man's been harassing me about my decision not to marry you constantly the last few months. He claims I've been impossible to work with ever since."

She laughed. "Is that true?"

"You know Artie. He does tend to exaggerate, especially when he knows he can get my dander up. But yes, I have been miserable without you and I guess it showed."

"How is Artie doing?"

"He's back on patrol, as lively and reprehensible privately as ever." His hand traced her hip in an absent caress. "What about Blanche? Do you think she'll be our matron of honor?"

"I'm sure she'll agree." Merritt grinned happily. "She's been hounding me for weeks, too. She thinks we never should have broken up.

"She's right."

"We're back together now, and that's all that counts." Merritt kissed him lightly. His arms swept around her, and he crushed her to his chest. They held each other for long moments, replete.

"Tom?"

"What?"

"Where are we going to live?"

"I don't know. It's up to you." She told him about her job offer, and after listening to the details, he said he thought she should take it.

"It would mean a lot of changes for me. I'd have to live in another section of the city."

"I don't mind giving up my apartment," he offered.

"And I've already had a bid on my house." She told him about that, too.

He reached for her and aligned her against him. A palm flat against his chest, she could feel the steady thrumming of his heart and the sensation filled her with peace. She needed to be with him. "I'd still like to keep the farm in Spring Valley," he murmured thoughtfully at length.

"I'd like you to keep it, too." She smiled. "It would be a good place to take children."

His eyes widened. "From school, you mean."

"Our own. You do want a family?" she asked.

"Yes."

"Well, I want one, too." She drew lazy circles across his chest, down his arm. His gaze locked with hers. She saw the beginnings of desire, and felt the tenderness of his embrace. "Life seems so perfect," she whispered. She traced the outline of his lips with her fingertip. He captured the appendage between his teeth, and gently, arousingly, nibbled it.

"Now that you're here with me, it *is* perfect. Which is why we shouldn't waste any more time than necessary in getting married. I want you with me, Merritt, today, tomorrow, forever."

"I want that, too," she whispered.

He shifted her over onto the cushions beside him, then stood, pulling her to her feet. His eyes worshipped her unabashedly. "Got any plans for tonight?" he asked huskily.

"Just you."

"How do you feel about driving across the river to Kentucky?" He grinned speculatively, but his gaze said he was quite serious. "There's a wedding chapel about an hour's drive from here. Nothing too elaborate, you understand, but they've got the wedding ceremony down pat. We could stop and buy flowers and gold bands on the way."

"Are you asking me to elope?" Her heart was pounding in her chest.

He nodded, watching her. "Then the answer is yes." Merritt laughed softly, seeing his delight. "When do we leave?"

"How about right now? If we're going to make it to the justice of the peace tonight, we had better be going," Tom said. Together, they left his apartment. Tom paused midway down the steps. The sun was setting in a blue-gray sky, and they lingered, enjoying the soft allure of the spring evening. "I'll make you happy, I promise," he said softly.

"Sweetheart," Merritt said, linking her hand with his securely, "you already have."

HARLEQUIN *Love Affair*

Now on sale

DAYDREAMS   *Rebecca Flanders*

Reality was always disappointing and Stacey had no desire to spoil the image of the Jon Callan of her daydreams. Stacey protested vigorously as she was ushered backstage to Callan's dressing room. When she stood before Callan himself, Stacey felt embarrassed and nervously wished she had never attended his Boston performance.

Jon had never really known a fan before; his schedule didn't permit it. The quiet woman in the simple linen suit was alien to the glittering, hectic world he lived in. She wasn't what he expected . . . but he sensed she was what he needed.

MEASURE OF LOVE   *Zelma Orr*

Nothing in her experience had prepared nurse Samantha Bridges for the situation at Bumping River. The cramped cabin possessed Stone Age facilities, and Sam's two charges were beyond belief: the ugliest dog she had ever laid eyes on and an unconscious logger of giant size. Surveying the scene, Sam knew her life had hit an all-time low, for if the dog didn't attack her, the unsanitary conditions would kill them all. . . .

But the situation would soon go from bad to worse: Nicholas Jordan was about to regain consciousness.

PROMISE ME TODAY   *Cathy Gillen Thacker*

Detective Tom Hennessey cared. He cared enough to confront teacher Merritt Reed about his nephew's grades. He cared enough to notice the little things about Merritt that signalled a half-buried sorrow. Tom cared enough to try and heal Merritt's wounds—even if the process was painful for them both.

Tom Hennessey cared enough to risk his life daily for the citizens of Cincinnati. And that was just the problem, for Merritt had learned that you could trust a cop with your life—but not with your heart!

Next month's titles

MIX AND MATCH   *Beverly Sommers*

Scott Campbell may have looked like a surfer, Ariel thought, but he could never have been a good one. Scott seemed to be as blind as a bat. Why else would he bypass the bikinied denizens of Seal Beach, California, to make a play for a woman who was almost middle-aged? A woman whose teenage daughter cast disapproving glares at him and whose younger daughter skulked around him menacingly, distressingly attired in combat fatigues.

True Ariel respected Scott's advice—he had improved both her painting and her business. But anything more than a friendly relationship was unseemly. Preposterous. And so appealing. . . .

THE DREAM NEVER DIES   *Jacqueline Diamond*

Consultant Jill Brandon walked into the offices of the Buena Park newspaper and received two rude shocks. One was Kent Lawrence, the paper's managing editor. As Jill tried to revamp the daily, Kent dogged her footsteps, hurling the same bitter accusations she had heard from him years before. Kent Lawrence had not forgotten her one rash act as a young reporter, an act that had launched her career and ruined their relationship. Nor had he forgiven her for it.

That was the first shock—that Kent still despised her. But the second shock was much worse. After all the years, Jill still loved him.

MISPLACED DESTINY   *Sharon McCaffree*

Carla didn't recognise him at first—after fifteen years, Brigg Carlyle had changed. But the atmosphere at the Shelbyville reunion catapulted Carla into the past, and she found herself responding to Brigg as though he were still her best friend's obnoxious older brother.

Brigg didn't like that. And after the reunion, in Chicago, Brigg made Carla realize that the fireworks that still erupted between them were now the result of adult emotions, not youthful high spirits. Brigg loved her. He had always loved her. But Brigg was no longer the familiar boy of Carla's past—he was a man, and a stranger.

These two absorbing titles
will be published in August
by

HARLEQUIN
SuperRomance

MORE THAN YESTERDAY by Angela Alexie
Child psychologist Lezlie Garrett had made it a
point never to become emotionally involved with
her patients. But when she saw the pain in Merri
Bradinton's eyes, Lezlie knew instinctively that
sharing the secret of her own broken heart might be
the only way to help the little girl.

Helping Merri's compelling Uncle Drew put *his* life
back together after a tragic twist of fate had made
him the child's guardian, however, was another
matter entirely.

THE GENUINE ARTICLE by Pamela M. Kleeb
Tessa always felt like Alice tumbling down the
rabbit hole whenever she encountered Jean-Paul
Heidemann, the austere new president of a Swiss
bank.

Despite Jean-Paul's insistent advances, she was determined to conduct herself professionally in the
restoration of the bank's art treasures. She was
hardly prepared for discoveries so shocking she
hesitated to bring them to light.

As pawns in an ugly scheme of art fraud, both
lovers had truths to reveal. But rather than face
painful consequences, each gambled that silence
would ensure the joy they found in each other's
arms.